About the Author

Sharon Booth writes ab
love, magic, and mystery. Her characters may be
flawed, but whether they're casting a spell, solving a
mystery, or dealing with the ups and downs of family
life or romance, they do it with kindness and humour.
Sharon is a member of the Society of Authors and the
Romantic Novelists' Association, and an
Authorpreneur member of the Alliance of
Independent Authors. She has been a KDP All-Star
Author on several occasions.

She likes reading, researching her family tree, and
watching Doctor Who, and Cary Grant movies. She
loves horses and hares and enjoys nothing more than
strolling around harbours and old buildings. Take her
to a castle, an abbey, or a stately home and she'll be
happy for hours. She admits to being shamefully
prone to crushes on fictional heroes.

Her stories of love, community, family, and friendship
are set in pretty villages and quirky market towns, by
the sea or in the countryside, and a happy ending is
guaranteed.

If you love heroes and heroines who do the best they
can no matter what sort of challenges they face,
beautiful locations, and warm, feelgood stories, you'll
love Sharon's books.

Books by Sharon Booth

There Must Be an Angel
A Kiss from a Rose
Once Upon a Long Ago
The Whole of the Moon

Summer Secrets at Wildflower Farm
Summer Wedding at Wildflower Farm

Resisting Mr Rochester
Saving Mr Scrooge

Baxter's Christmas Wish
The Other Side of Christmas
Christmas with Cary

New Doctor at Chestnut House
Christmas at the Country Practice
Fresh Starts at Folly Farm
A Merry Bramblewick Christmas
Summer at the Country Practice
Christmas at Cuckoo Nest Cottage

Belle, Book and Candle
My Favourite Witch
To Catch a Witch
Will of the Witch

How the Other Half Lives: Part One: At Home
How the Other Half Lives: Part Two: On Holiday
How the Other Half Lives: Part Three: At Christmas

Winter Wishes at The White Hart Inn

Summer at the Country Practice

Bramblewick 5

SHARON BOOTH

Copyright © 2019 Sharon Booth.

Paperback published 2022
Cover design by Green Ginger Publishing

The moral rights of the author have been asserted.
All rights reserved. No part of this publication may be reproduced, stored in any retrieval system, or transmitted in any form, or by any means electronic, mechanical, photocopying, recording or otherwise, without the prior written permission of the publishers.

This book is a work of fiction. Names, characters, businesses, organisations, places and events other than those clearly in the public domain, are either the product of the author's imagination or are used fictitiously. Any resemblances to actual persons, living or dead, is entirely coincidental.

ISBN: 9798366639552

For Julia Richardson and Jayne Beck, with grateful thanks for all your generous help and advice.

I couldn't have written this without you.

xxxx

List of Characters

Abbie Sawdon
GP at Bramblewick Surgery. Mother of three. Lives at **The Gables**.

Jackson Wade
Teacher at Bramblewick Primary School. Best friend of Ash. Lives in **Helmston**.

Anna Blake
Head receptionist at Bramblewick Surgery, currently on maternity leave. Mother of Eloise, stepmother of Gracie, wife of Connor Blake.

Connor Blake
GP at Bramblewick surgery. The Blakes live at **Chestnut House**, former home of Dr Gray, Anna's late father.
See *New Doctor at Chestnut House*

Nell MacDonald
Proprietor of the village café and bakery, Spill the Beans. New mum to baby Aiden.

Riley MacDonald
GP at Bramblewick surgery. Husband of Nell and dad of Aiden. The MacDonalds live at **The Ducklings**.
See *Christmas at the Country Practice*

Rachel Johnson
Practice nurse at Bramblewick Surgery. Mother of Sam. Daughter of Janie.

Xander North
Real name Alexander South. Famous actor now concentrating on local theatre and running **Folly Farm** as an animal sanctuary with his fiancée Rachel

and her family.
See *Fresh Starts at Folly Farm*

Isobel Clark
Known to everyone as Izzy. Teacher at Bramblewick Primary School. Best friend of Anna Blake.
Ash Uttridge
Teacher at Bramblewick Primary School. Partner of Izzy. The couple live in **Rose Cottage**.
See *A Merry Bramblewick Christmas*

Chapter 1

Jackson steepled his fingers under his chin as he stared intently at the eight-year-old boy standing in front of his desk.

'So, you're seriously going with that, Bertie?'

The boy blinked and blew his blond fringe away from his eyes. 'Yes, sir.'

'Really? That's the story you're sticking with?'

Bertie shrugged. 'It's true, sir, honestly.'

Jackson sighed. 'I see. A goat ate your homework?'

Bertie looked annoyed. 'If Sam was here he'd tell you it was true. It's his goat.'

There was some giggling from the rest of the class and Jackson gave them all a weary look.

'Yes all right, that's enough. Sadly, Bertie, Sam's not here today, as you well know, so I suppose I'll just have to take your word for it won't I?'

Bertie nodded, looking relieved. 'I s'pose so. Can I sit down now?'

'Please do, and in future may I suggest you keep all homework well away from goats or anything else likely to eat it?'

'Like my little sister?'

Jackson raised an eyebrow. 'Pardon?'

Bertie's grin lit up his face. 'My little sister. She's always eating stuff she shouldn't. She ate dog food out of the bowl last week. Mum says she's a right little pest.'

Jackson wasn't sure if the child was winding him up or not. 'Your sister eats dog food? How old is she?'

'She's two, nearly three.'

'Right.' Should he be worried? Was this a normal occurrence in the Sawdon household? 'Well as I said, make sure you keep your homework away from anything, or *anyone*, that might eat it in future, okay?'

'I will, sir.'

'Go back to your seat then.'

Sometimes, Jackson mused, as he watched the little boy hurry back to his desk, teaching provided an insight into the most dysfunctional lives. Some children seemed to have frighteningly disorderly families. What sort of irresponsible parents did Bertie Sawdon have?

But didn't Bertie's father live in New York? The children must miss him of course, although he believed the parents were divorced anyway.

He frowned. He was almost sure the mother was the new village GP. Well, some doctor she was, letting her toddler eat dog food. Ugh! Jackson's stomach turned at the thought of it.

Bertie had only been at the school for a few weeks. The family had just moved to The Gables, a large, detached house with a slate roof and overgrown garden that sat at the very edge of Bramblewick.

He had a flashback to Bertie's first day. He'd arrived without his packed lunch, having forgotten it in the rush. His mother had been clearly harassed, her face red with exertion and her hair all over the place. He recalled she kept throwing anxious looks out of the classroom window and insisting that she had to go because she had to drop her daughter off somewhere. She'd thrust some money at him to pay for Bertie's school lunch, given her son a big hug and a kiss and told him to be a good boy, then had all but run out of the classroom in her haste to get away. Frankly, he hadn't been too impressed.

It wasn't, perhaps, surprising that Bertie had failed to turn in his homework a few times now. He'd have to put another note in the boy's home school diary. Diaries were given to every child at the beginning of each school year as a method of exchanging information between parent and teacher. Any message from either party was supposed to be signed by the other as confirmation that they'd seen it. Dr Sawdon hadn't signed Bertie's diary this week, he remembered. Maybe she hadn't noticed that he'd even had homework? He'd have to watch that.

He glanced at the big clock on the wall behind him and his stomach lurched with dread. Not long to go now. Seriously, why had he let himself be talked into this? It wasn't his sort of thing at all, and he couldn't imagine how Ash had managed to persuade him. Since his friend and colleague had moved in with another teacher who was—as he frequently and rather nauseatingly stated—the love of his life, he'd been determined to set Jackson up with someone.

'You shouldn't be alone, mate. You've been single for far too long, and Izzy says this woman's lovely.

You'll like her, I'm sure you will.'

A blind date of all things! Well, he'd go along with it, buy the woman a nice meal and a couple of drinks, be polite and friendly, and that would be that. He would leave without taking her number or making any pretence of following up the date. He only hoped she would accept the situation and that she wasn't harbouring hopes of true love.

He sighed and opened the exercise book on his desk, then groaned inwardly. This was Olivia Westcott's attempt at her homework? It would probably have been better for her if a goat had eaten this too.

***

Abbie glanced at her watch and pulled a face. The school bus would have already dropped her eldest daughter off by now. If she didn't hurry up Isla would make it home before she did. Again.

'Thanks ever so much for having her, Janie,' she said, smiling despite having to deal with the wriggling child in her arms. By sheer willpower she was still managing to hold on to her bag, which was full-to-bursting with all the paraphernalia that went with a two-year-old, while also grappling with Bertie, who was doing his best to make a break for it. 'Especially with Sam not being well. I hope she behaved.'

'She was as good as gold,' Janie promised her. 'Luckily she's a big animal lover so there's always plenty to keep her occupied here. She's been having a lovely time with the guinea pigs, haven't you, Poppy?'

The little girl let out a wail and lunged forward, clearly not wanting to leave Folly Farm behind just yet. Abbie groaned inwardly but forced another smile.

'Well anyway, I must be going, or poor Isla will be standing on the doorstep wondering where I am.'

Janie nodded. 'I don't know, love, you're always rushing here, there, and everywhere. You need to get some sort of order in your life, for all your sakes.'

Abbie tried not to feel offended. 'It's not easy, juggling three children with a career, but we manage, don't we, kids?'

Bertie folded his arms, looking cross, and Poppy hurled herself so far forward, in a bid for freedom and guinea pigs, that Abbie almost dropped her.

'Well, er, anyway, we're having fun. And things will calm down once we've got settled in properly at The Gables,' Abbie said, not sure if she was trying to convince Janie or herself.

Janie didn't look too convinced anyway. 'Hmm. There's a lot of work to do on the house, though isn't there?'

'It's not too bad,' Abbie assured her, crossing her fingers inside Bertie's shirt collar, which she was clinging onto for grim death to stop him careering off into the farmhouse. 'It's liveable right now, and we can do more to it as the weeks progress. We should be able to get on during the summer holidays.'

Janie briefly opened her mouth, as if she'd considered arguing the point but had changed her mind. Abbie could guess what she'd wanted to say. If anything the summer holidays were going to bring more difficulties, not fewer. With no school there would be greater problems with childcare. She could hardly ask Janie to babysit all three children, and Isla, just short of her thirteenth birthday, was too young to care for her siblings whatever she said to the contrary. It was just another headache she'd have to deal with. Still, she'd been through worse.

'Must dash,' she said, determined to stop Janie from keeping her any longer. She was grateful to her friend Rachel's mum for stepping in and offering to care for Poppy, of course she was, but she could do without the judgmental looks and worried asides that kept coming at her from Janie's direction. They would get there in the end if people just let them be. 'Come on, Bertie. Get in the car or Isla will be locked out at home.'

'Can't I stay here and have tea with Sam?'

Abbie was mortified. 'You don't invite yourself to people's houses for tea, Bertie! You know that.'

Sam tugged at his grandmother's arm. 'Can he stay for tea, Nanna?'

Janie gave him a sharp look. 'Hmm. You seem to have made a remarkable recovery, young man.' She turned to Abbie. 'He can stay if he wants to. Rachel could drop him off at yours since she's babysitting for you anyway.'

'No, honestly,' Abbie said. It would be a help if she were being honest with herself, but she felt she imposed enough on Rachel and Janie as it was. 'Sorry, Bertie,' she added as he let out a dismayed wail, 'but that's the end of it.'

'If you're sure?' Janie said.

'Bertie wanted to see how Duke was doing,' Sam said sulkily.

Abbie gave him a rueful smile. 'Another time, Sam. Maybe you could come to us for tea one night?'

Janie looked doubtful. 'I think you've got enough on your plate for now don't you?' she said gently.

Abbie prickled. She knew Janie meant well but...

'Bertie! Car. Now.' She practically dragged him to the car and pushed him inside, cursing as he climbed out again through the other door while she fastened Poppy into her seat.

'Get back here now, young man, or you'll be in trouble!'

'Just saying goodbye to Folly,' Bertie protested, running over to pat Sam's blue roan cocker spaniel. 'Isn't she cute, Mum? Can we have a cocker spaniel?'

Abbie rolled her eyes. 'We have two dogs already. Don't you think that's enough?'

Janie laughed. 'In my experience it's never enough when it comes to dogs. Go on, Bertie, get back in the car. Your poor mum needs to get home. Big night tonight, eh, Abbie?'

Abbie blushed. She'd been trying to forget all about it but she might have known Janie wouldn't let her off the hook that easily.

'Rachel will be at yours around seven,' Janie continued, oblivious to her discomfort. 'Are you looking forward to it?'

'Looking forward to what?' Bertie queried.

'Nothing for you to worry about.' Abbie gave Janie

a meaningful look and bundled her son into the back of the car.

Muttering, he allowed himself to be strapped into his car seat but pulled a face and refused to help Abbie as she fumbled with the fastenings.

Tucking her hair behind her ears and feeling weak with relief, Abbie climbed into her own seat and took a deep breath.

'Thanks again. Tell Rachel I'll see her at seven,' she called through the open window, as she manoeuvred the car out of the farmyard and began the journey to The Gables.

She wiped the sweat from her brow, her spirits sinking as she passed crowds of school children heading away from the bus stop. God, she hoped Isla hadn't already made it home. They lived at the other end of the village, right on the outskirts, but it was possible. All she needed was to give her eldest child another excuse to throw a strop. Twelve-year-olds were as much trouble as two-year-olds in many ways. And as for an eight-year-old...

She gritted her teeth as she saw, upon arriving home, that Isla was already sitting on the doorstep, clearly livid.

'Sorry, sorry!' Abbie jumped out of the car and rushed over to unlock the door. 'You've not been here long have you?'

'Long enough. What was it this time?'

Abbie shrugged. 'You know Janie. Likes a chat.' She gave her daughter a hug but was pushed away immediately.

'I was worried. I'm always worried when you're late. I start to panic about—'

'As you can see all is well,' Abbie interrupted her. 'Just lost track of time, that's all.'

'This wouldn't happen if you'd let me have a mobile phone,' Isla said sulkily.

Abbie couldn't see what difference it would have made. 'You'd still have been on the bus at the same time.'

'But you'd have known I was home and would have hurried up,' Isla retorted.

Abbie didn't like to admit that she'd already suspected Isla would be home and it hadn't helped at all.

'You're too young for a mobile phone,' she said for the thousandth time, as she unstrapped Poppy and picked up the changing bag.

Bertie rushed past her and into the house, his arms outstretched as he pretended to be an aeroplane. Two excited dogs immediately shot out into the garden and Bertie ran out after them, swooping and soaring around them as they barked and jumped up at him.

'Stop acting like a child,' Isla muttered.

'He *is* a child,' Abbie said. 'As are you.'

'I'll be a teenager in a week or two,' Isla said. 'And then what will your excuse be for making me a laughing-stock with all my mates?'

'If they're your mates they won't laugh at you,' Abbie said reasonably. 'If they do, who needs them?'

'You don't understand anything,' Isla said.

Abbie was about to reply that she understood all too

well, but she heard the wobble in her daughter's voice and recognised the warning signs. Sure enough, when she looked closely she saw the gleam of unshed tears in Isla's eyes and experienced the familiar sinking feeling as guilt overwhelmed her again.

'Maybe you can have a phone next year,' she soothed, inwardly shuddering at the prospect. The thought of her beautiful child being subjected to the vile cesspit that was social media made her feel quite ill. She'd put restrictions on Isla's laptop so she could only visit sites that were suitable for homework purposes but wasn't convinced she could monitor a phone so easily.

Isla glared at her. 'Another year? They probably won't even have mobile phones by then. We'll probably all be chipped or something.'

'Well, if that's the case it's not worth wasting money on one is it?' Abbie said, trying to sound cheery.

'Oh god, you're impossible!'

Abbie narrowed her eyes. 'I think we've had enough of this subject for now, don't you? Get yourself indoors. I've got to get your tea ready before I go out.'

Isla tutted and hurried into the house, not even bothering to take off her coat as she headed straight upstairs to her bedroom.

Abbie sighed, ushered Bertie and the dogs back indoors, shut the door behind her and carried Poppy into the kitchen. 'Right, kids,' she said, doing her best to sound cheerful. 'Tea. What are you having?'

Even as she said it she remembered to her horror that she'd forgotten to go to the supermarket. She'd meant to collect Isla from the bus stop and take all three children to the big one near Whitby, but it had completely gone out of her mind. Now what?

Hoping against hope that she'd overlooked something in the freezer she rummaged around its icy compartments, but her search yielded only two frozen Yorkshire puddings, half a bag of sprouts, and some sweetcorn. Great.

'Let's see what we have in the cupboards,' she said brightly. Bertie tutted and headed into the living room with the dogs to watch the television. Poppy sat on the floor and started to cry. Abbie scooped her up and showed her the inside of the cupboard, which seemed to distract her enough to shut her up for the time being.

'Okay, kids,' Abbie called from the hallway, hoping that both Isla and Bertie could hear her, 'on the menu tonight we have egg on toast, beans on toast, spaghetti hoops on toast, egg and beans on toast, or egg and spaghetti on toast. Or any of the above combinations without toast. Which would you prefer?'

Isla appeared at the top of the stairs. 'You're kidding, right?'

'Nope. Oh, you could have chicken soup if you prefer. By the way there's no butter, but there's sauce with the beans and spaghetti hoops, and the egg will be runny so...' Her voice trailed off as she saw the look of disgust on her daughter's face.

'I'll have egg and beans on toast,' Bertie called, evidently not as fussy as his sister.

'There's some canned fruit and a tin of custard powder so you can have pudding,' Abbie said, vaguely wondering how old the tins were, since they'd lingered in the cupboard in the old house for ages. Why had she even brought them with her to Bramblewick? 'Oh, except the milk's gone off, so maybe not the custard.' *I must remember to put those tins in the dustbin.* 'There are some chocolate biscuits in the bread bin,' she added hopefully.

'And bread in the biscuit tin I suppose?' Isla said.

Abbie didn't like to remind her that the biscuit tin had somehow mysteriously vanished during the house move from their rented cottage near Kearton Bay to The Gables a few weeks ago, along with several other items. She had an awful feeling she'd written "Charity Shop" on the wrong box.

'I'm doing my best, Isla,' she said with a sigh. 'Poppy's really heavy so can you hurry up and decide what you want?'

'I don't want anything,' Isla replied, flouncing back to her room. 'It's all rubbish.'

'Fine,' Abbie called. 'Spaghetti hoops it is then.'

'Yeah, feed us the slop,' Isla called, 'while you stuff your face at some fancy restaurant tonight no doubt.'

Abbie wished she'd never confided in her eldest daughter. She should have known that it would be hurled back at her as ammunition. Her stomach turned over in dread. She couldn't imagine eating a thing and, besides, they weren't going to a fancy restaurant thank goodness.

Oh, why had she ever let Izzy talk her into this? Who was this mysterious man that she'd been set up with for a blind date? She must have been mad to agree to it. The last thing she needed was a man in her life. She had more than enough to deal with already, as she would make very clear to whoever he was before he got any ideas.

Poppy tugged on her hair. 'Tea,' she reminded her firmly.

Abbie smiled. 'Sorry, Pops. Come on then. Let's get you all fed before Rachel gets here.'

Chapter 2

They'd arranged to meet at The Bay Horse in the village. Somewhere nice and neutral, as Izzy and Ash had said.

Jackson arrived early and headed straight to the bar. He needed a drink to steady his nerves but, since he was driving, he didn't have that option. He ordered a Coke and stood sipping it gloomily, his heart thudding in his chest. His palms were sweating, and he held the cold glass between them, trying to cool off. It wasn't an attractive look was it? He could hardly shake her hand with sweaty palms.

Shake her hand? Was that what he should do? Or should he kiss her on the cheek? Give her a light hug? Was that inappropriate? He'd never been on a blind date before and had no idea what to do.

Run for the hills, he thought desperately. *Get out of here as fast as you can.* Instead, he smiled at Sandra, the landlady, as she wiped the bar in front of him.

His throat felt tight as he croaked, 'There's a table booked in the name of Ash Uttridge.'

She nodded. 'That's right. I'll get Ernie to show you.' She gave him a knowing look. 'Ash booked it a few days ago. Corner table by the window, he said. Nice and cosy like.'

Jackson cursed silently. Great. She knew everything and no doubt found the whole thing highly amusing. He'd have hoped that his so-called mate could be a bit more discreet than that. God, he'd kill for a pint of Lusty Tup right now.

Ernie, Sandra's husband, was just as bad. He practically did the whole *nudge, nudge, wink, wink* routine as he led Jackson to the table in the far corner of the pub.

'Just the job this,' he told him. 'Proper intimate. Just the place for a bit of *getting to know you*.' He gave Jackson a wide grin and handed him two menus. 'Give us a shout when you're ready to order. I'm sure the little lady won't be long.'

'Thanks. I'm sure she won't.' Jackson sat down and stared at the menu without seeing it.

Ernie wandered off and Jackson let out a long breath and tugged at his shirt collar, feeling he was being choked by it. Never again. Never, *ever* again.

He sipped his Coke and stared miserably out of the window. Even the lovely views of the beck and the village green didn't soothe him. He was too nervous to take it all in. What would this woman be like? What if she was a horrible person? What if she hated him on sight? Heck, what if she didn't even turn up?

He considered this for a moment and decided that, just maybe, that would be the best solution all round. If she didn't come he wouldn't have to go through this awful ordeal, and he'd have the perfect excuse to refuse to ever be set up by his so-called friends again. On balance, this mystery woman's failure to turn up for the date would be the best possible outcome. He could only hope.

Ten minutes later he glanced at his watch again and scowled. She was ten minutes late now!

Ernie was clearing the table next to his.

'Taking her time isn't she?' he said cheerily. 'Woman's prerogative I suppose.'

Jackson picked up the menu and studied it carefully.

A short while later, when he'd changed his mind about the main course three times and was now studying desserts, even though he wasn't in the slightest bit hungry, Sandra sidled up to him. She gave him a sympathetic look and patted him on the shoulder.

'Would you like another drink, lovey?'

He looked at his empty glass and considered the matter.

'No, it's okay,' he said eventually. If his date didn't turn up within the next few minutes he'd be leaving anyway. 'I'll wait for her to arrive,' he added, confident that she wouldn't arrive at all. It looked as if the gods were smiling on him, and he would be able to get away with this.

Sandra sighed. 'Bless you.'

Jackson bristled. He didn't need pity. He couldn't be happier that his blind date had changed her mind. He looked over at the large clock on the wall above the fireplace and pursed his lips. Twenty minutes late. Twenty-two minutes late, to be accurate. She wasn't coming was she?

He decided to wait three more minutes, then he

could reasonably and justifiably leave.

Sandra hurried back to the bar and muttered something to Ernie. They both looked over at him. Sandra tilted her head to one side, sympathy oozing from her. Ernie gave him a wry look and pretended to adjust the beermats on the counter.

Jackson put down the menu and stared at it blindly. This was humiliation on an epic scale. He would never forgive Ash for this, and if his so-called mate ever suggested anything like it again, he would punch him square in the nose. He stood up, determined to go home. From the corner of his eye he noticed that Ernie was pointing in his direction and his heart began to thump hard. Too late.

'Oh hell, I'm so, so sorry!' There was a flurry of scarlet, a scraping of a chair and the table shuddered as someone knocked against it.

Jackson sat down with a thud and stared at her in horror.

'It's been a bit hectic at home,' she gabbled, dropping into her seat, and rummaging around in her bag, not even looking at him. She produced a glasses case and slapped it on the table. 'And Poppy just wouldn't settle, even for Rachel, and Bertie was being an absolute pain as usual, and Isla just wouldn't help, even though I begged her and—' She broke off and gazed at him, looking puzzled. 'I know you don't I?'

Jackson took a steadying breath and surveyed her. 'I believe we've met, yes.'

She was red-faced and her shoulder-length, tawny-coloured hair looked as if it hadn't been combed. He noticed the dog hairs on her coat and wondered what on earth Ash had been thinking. Or was this Izzy's idea of a joke?

She narrowed her eyes and tilted her head, thinking.

'Oh, I know!' Her expression changed and she looked rather crestfallen. 'Hell, you're Bertie's teacher aren't you? Mr, er—'

'Wade,' he supplied. 'Jackson Wade.'

'Right.' She nodded. 'That's it, yes. I'm Abbie Sawdon.'

'I know,' he said.

They stared at each other, not knowing what else to say.

'This is a bit awkward,' Abbie said eventually. 'Is it even legal?'

'Sorry?'

'Going on a date with your son's teacher. Is it even allowed?'

Jackson leaned back in his chair. 'As far as I know there's no law against it,' he assured her, wishing he could tell her it was indeed illegal and therefore they would have to call time on this disastrous date immediately.

'I suppose,' she said, 'you're only his teacher for another couple of weeks after all. After the summer holidays he's going into someone else's class.'

He didn't see why that mattered. This was strictly a one-off, so it would make no difference if he were Bertie's teacher for the next five years. He would never see Abbie Sawdon again in a social capacity, that much was certain. He was pretty sure that Ash had set this up as a prank. He wondered what he'd done to offend his friends. Ash and Izzy must have known that he and this woman had absolutely nothing in common.

'I expect you'd given up on me,' she said, pushing her bag under the table. 'I'm ever so sorry.'

'I was about to go home,' he admitted, thinking if only he'd walked out five minutes earlier. Damn!

She opened the purple plastic case in front of her and popped on her glasses. 'Well, I'm here now,' she said, taking one of the menus off the table and opening it up. 'And even though you're clearly wishing I wasn't I'm starving, so I'm going to order something to eat. If you don't want to join me please feel free to leave.'

He stared at her in astonishment. 'I never said—'

'You really didn't have to.' She put down the menu, popped her glasses on top of her head and met his gaze, her chin tilted slightly in defiance. 'Look, Mr Wade, I had no idea that it was you I was meeting tonight. If I had I'd probably have said no, just as you would. Don't try to deny it,' she added, as he opened his mouth to protest. 'It's written all over your face that I'm a huge disappointment. It's okay, I won't take it personally. I had no intention of following this up anyway. Cards on the table, I only agreed to this date to shut Izzy and her cronies up. As far as I'm concerned it's just an excuse to have a break from the kids and a nice meal in peace. If you want to go home that's fine by me. No hard feelings. I can see by your expression that you'd rather be anywhere else but here.'

Jackson squirmed. Put like that he sounded like a real rat.

'It's not that,' he said, not entirely truthfully. 'I'm just shocked that's all. When Ash set me up on this date, I had no idea that it would be with someone I already knew—albeit vaguely. It's not ideal to meet up with a parent socially but, as you say, Bertie won't be in my class for much longer.'

'And it wouldn't matter if he were,' she observed shrewdly, 'since this will never be repeated. Right?'

He adjusted his tie, feeling awkward. 'I'm sorry,' he said at last. 'This isn't about you. I'm just not very good at all this.'

'Join the club.' She gave him a wry look then grinned.

He noticed the freckles on her nose and the sparkle in her blue eyes and felt himself relax a little. Okay she wasn't his type, and they would probably never see each other again outside of school, but that was no reason not to enjoy each other's company for one evening. They could have a meal, make small talk, then say goodbye. No big deal. He needed to chill a bit. 'Do you see anything you fancy?'

Her eyes widened and he felt his face catch fire. 'I mean on the menu.'

She laughed and leaned back in her chair, unbuttoning her red coat. 'Give me a chance to look. I'll just make myself comfy.'

She shrugged off the coat and hung it over the back of her chair, then picked up the menu again.

Jackson studied the dishes on offer and after a few moments cleared his throat. 'Sorry,' he said. 'This is a bit cheap and cheerful, isn't it? I should have taken you somewhere a bit more...'

She shook her head. 'This is fine. I'm happy with traditional pub grub. Fish, chips, and peas looks good to me.'

He smiled, glad that she wasn't disappointed in that at least. 'I'll order,' he said. 'Would you like a drink?'

'Just lemonade please. I'll get this,' Abbie began but he waved his hand indignantly.

'Certainly not! This is all on me.'

'Why should you pay?' she demanded. 'You don't even know me. Well, not properly.'

'And you don't really know me either, so why should you pay?'

They stared at each other for a moment.

'Shall we go Dutch?' she suggested.

Jackson nodded reluctantly, although it went against every instinct he possessed. He firmly believed that the man should pay, and it rankled that she wouldn't let him. Then again, maybe she thought that if he paid he would expect something in return. He was all too aware that, sadly, some men still believed that.

The thought was enough to make up his mind. 'Fine,' he said, reaching for the twenty-pound note she pushed towards him. 'I'll bring you your change.'

Her eyes crinkled with amusement. 'I'm sure you will.'

Ernie and Sandra were all smiles as he approached the bar.

'Aw, she turned up,' Sandra said. 'How nice for you.'

'I was about to come over to take your order,' Ernie added. 'I told you to give me a shout.'

'It says *Please Order at the Bar* on that notice,' Jackson pointed out, nodding at the sign above the optics.

Ernie had the grace to look embarrassed. 'Yes, well, we'd make an exception for some people.'

To be nosy no doubt, Jackson thought. 'It doesn't matter anyway. One fish and chips, one mixed grill, one lemonade and another Coke please.'

Sandra rang up the order on the till. 'She's very pretty,' she whispered to him as if Abbie were hovering nearby, not sitting at the other end of the pub. 'She's a very good doctor too you know. Very popular with the patients we've spoken to. Mind you, she's got her hands full.'

Jackson nodded. 'Mm, I expect she has.'

'Busy job, three kids, and that house! I mean, have you seen the state of it? Bad enough outside, but when you think it hasn't been lived in for nigh on three years. It makes you wonder what state it's in doesn't it?'

Jackson really didn't want to think about it. No wonder she hadn't bothered to look at Bertie's home school diary. He'd love to discuss the subject of her son's failure to do his homework, but it was strictly off limits to talk about the child outside of school premises.

'Husband lives abroad I think,' Sandra continued, taking the money from his hand. 'I mean, *ex*-husband. She wouldn't be out on a date with you otherwise would she?'

Jackson shuffled, wishing she'd hurry up with the change. 'It's not a date,' he mumbled.

She raised an eyebrow. 'Not a date? What is it then?'

'Looks like a date to me,' Ernie said with a knowing

grin. 'And Ash was very specific. A nice, intimate table in the corner, where you wouldn't be disturbed. Now if that's not for a date I'd like to know what it is for.'

'Oh bless him, look at his little face,' Sandra said. 'Don't worry, love, we're only teasing. Here's your change. We'll bring the food over as soon as it's ready, and Ernie will pop your drinks over in a jiffy. You go and sit down. Keep that nice lady company.'

Jackson shoved the change in his pocket and hurried back to the table, anxious to get away from them.

Abbie smiled up at him. 'Right,' she said, holding out her hand, 'shall we start again? I'm Abbie.'

He shook it firmly. 'And I'm Jackson.'

'So, Jackson, tell me: were you bullied into coming on this date as much as I was?'

He hesitated then sighed. 'Ash wouldn't leave me alone,' he admitted. 'He seems determined to fix me up with someone. I have to say he's become quite sickeningly romantic since he moved in with Izzy.'

'I had five of them on at me,' Abbie told him. 'Can you imagine how bad that was?'

He felt a stirring of sympathy for her. Bad enough with one person nagging, but *five?* 'How come?'

'Oh, once Izzy brought it up the rest of our friends wouldn't let it go, and since I work with two of them it's been pretty much constant for the last two weeks.'

'Hell, you poor thing,' he said, meaning it.

Ernie arrived and placed their drinks on the table. 'One cola, and one lemonade for the lady. Enjoy.'

He beamed at them both then hurried back to the bar where Sandra was eyeing them with a delighted smile on her face.

'This is awful,' he muttered.

'Isn't it? People are very strange,' she said. She took a sip of her drink and sighed. 'Married people seem obsessed with making sure everyone else is securely hooked up don't they? It's like they can't bear to think of anyone living their life without the shackles of a spouse.'

'Shackles?' Jackson eyed her with interest. 'Is that how it feels?'

She nursed her glass, watching him curiously. 'Have you never been married?'

He shook his head. 'Nope.'

'How on earth did you manage that?' she said. 'You must be pushing forty.'

'Charming!' Jackson gulped his Coke and set the glass down on a beermat, not sure how to react to that comment. 'I'm thirty-eight actually.'

'See? Pushing forty.' She leaned towards him, her mouth twitching in amusement. 'Don't look so offended. I'm thirty-seven so I can't talk.'

'But you've been married,' he pointed out.

'Yeah. Look how that worked out. Brownie points for me, eh?'

'Sorry,' he said, feeling awkward.

'Oh don't be. I was joking. We were very happy for a long time and we're still good friends so I can't complain. No regrets.'

She said it softly, the expression in her eyes suddenly distant as if she was remembering. Jackson wondered if she was truly over her ex. There was something in her face that gave him cause to doubt it.

'Have you even lived with someone?' she asked suddenly.

He shook his head.

'What, not ever?' She sounded incredulous and he felt defensive.

'I just haven't met the right person I suppose.'

'You must be very picky,' she said thoughtfully.

'Is there anything wrong with that?'

Her finger circled the rim of her glass. 'I suppose not. It doesn't bode well for this date though, does it?'

He wrinkled his nose. 'Thought this wasn't really a date?'

'It's not, I'm joking again.' She looked up, smiling as Sandra arrived at the table bearing two plates of steaming hot food. 'Ooh, that looks lovely. Thanks ever so much.'

'You're welcome. Enjoy your meal,' Sandra said, looking from one to the other of them with a twinkle in her eyes.

Jackson scowled and picked up his knife and fork.

'To good food, a courteous conversation, and an early goodnight,' Abbie said, raising her glass to him.

He felt a stab of guilt and put the cutlery back on his plate, then clinked his glass against hers. 'To a pleasant evening,' he said.

He wondered if she wished, as fervently as he did, that their glasses contained something a bit more cheering than lemonade and cola.

Chapter 3

'Are you here again? Crikey, why don't you just come back to work and have done with it?'

At Holly's exclamation, Abbie glanced up from perusing the list of visits and grinned as she saw head receptionist Anna walking through the office, her six-month-old daughter in her arms. Holly, another receptionist at the Bramblewick surgery, flew to her side, cooing and purring at the baby in delight.

'Who's beautiful then? Who's a beautiful baby?'

Abbie decided she would have no chance of getting near the child just yet.

'I'll fetch Rachel. She'll want to see her,' she said, hurrying out of the office.

Rachel, the practice nurse, had just said goodbye to her last patient, and laughed when Abbie informed her that Anna was in the building.

'What again? Do you think she's missing the place or what?'

Minutes later, Anna admitted, as she sat down at her old desk and handed Eloise over to an ecstatic Holly, that she was.

'It's ever so quiet at home when Eloise is asleep, and with Gracie at school I don't know what to do with myself. I miss the gossip and the laughs. You don't mind me popping in again do you? I did wait until morning surgery was over so you wouldn't be so busy.'

'The calm before the storm,' Holly said, pulling a face.

'Where's Joan?' Anna looked around, seeking the temporary receptionist who'd been hired to cover her while she was on maternity leave.

'Gone to Spill the Beans for lunch. She doesn't like eating in an office environment, apparently.'

'What, and with our new posh kitchenette too?' Anna tutted. 'I don't know. You can't please some people.'

Rachel smiled. 'Everyone's different, Anna,' she reminded her friend. 'Now, will you please tell Holly to hand Eloise over to me and let me have a cuddle with her for a change. She hogs her every single time you bring her here.'

'But she's so gorgeous,' wailed Holly, cuddling the baby a little tighter. 'Oh, all right. Five minutes mind, then I want her back.'

Anna rolled her eyes then leaned forward eagerly. 'How did you get on, Abbie?' she enquired. 'I've been dying to hear about it all weekend.'

'Good luck with that,' Holly said. 'She won't tell us anything. We've been nagging away at her but zilch. Very frustrating.'

Abbie shook her head. 'There's nothing much to tell. We had a pleasant enough meal and said our goodbyes.'

'Seriously? That's it?' Anna's face was a picture of disappointment. 'No plans to meet again?'

Abbie gave her a wry look. 'No plans at all. Let's just say we weren't really compatible.'

She massaged her temples, feeling the first twinges of a headache coming on, then jumped, startled, as she realised Rachel was addressing her.

'Sorry. What?'

'I said do you want a cuddle?'

At Abbie's momentary bewilderment Rachel let out a peal of laughter. 'Not from me! From Eloise.'

'Oh!' Abbie burst out laughing. 'Oh, no, it's okay. You've been waiting ages for this moment, and I really must get on with the visits.'

'Well if you can hang on a moment,' Anna said, 'I've got something first. I'll just nip out to the pram and get it if you don't mind babysitting, Rachel.'

'Feel free,' Rachel said cheerfully.

Anna hurried out of the office and Abbie said, 'She's probably made a break for it. Bet she's heading off to Helmston for a day's shopping as we speak.'

'Who could blame her?' Rachel said.

'Me! Who'd leave this little poppet, even for one day?' Holly reached out to stroke the sleeping baby's pink cheek. 'Aw, she's so pretty. I want one.'

Rachel spluttered. 'You do not! Trust me, they're not always like this. Anna's struck gold with this one. She sleeps like a—well...'

'Like a baby?' Abbie suggested. 'Yes, I can't remember Isla and Bertie sleeping this much, I must admit.'

'And Poppy?' Holly queried.

Abbie shrugged. 'Probably not.'

Holly frowned. 'But surely—?'

'Here we go!' Anna hurried back into the office, carrying a plastic tray. 'Cupcakes all round, courtesy of Chloe.'

'Oh, yum,' Rachel said. 'Swap you a baby for a cupcake?' she said to Abbie, as they all peered hungrily at the tray of pretty, sparkling cupcakes, all beautifully decorated by Chloe, who worked at Spill the Beans café and bakery in the village.

Holly sighed. 'I'll hold her while you eat,' she said. 'I can't have one.'

If she'd announced she'd given up speaking English and could only converse in Latin for the rest of her life they couldn't have looked more surprised thought Abbie. Even she knew Holly had an appetite on her, and she'd worked with her for less than six months. Anna and Rachel, though, looked stunned.

'Why can't you have one? What's wrong with you?' Anna demanded.

'I'm on a diet if you must know,' Holly said, sounding reluctant to admit it.

'A diet!' Rachel gaped at her. 'You never go on diets. What's happened?'

Holly pinched at her thighs in despair. 'These happened. Look at the size of them! And this,' she added, pinching at the small roll of fat around her midriff. 'Got to lose all this. I'm not fit to be seen in public at the moment.'

'Says who?' Anna gasped. 'You look lovely, Holly, you always do. You've not been reading any stupid magazines have you?'

Holly squirmed and reached out for Eloise. 'Of course not. But I've thought for a while that I needed to lose weight, and Jonathan did happen to mention that I'd put the pounds on lately so...'

Rachel and Anna exchanged glances. 'Oh he did, did he?'

'Honestly, Rachel, not in a nasty way. Just pointing out what I already knew really. He's absolutely right. My thighs *are* chunky. I *do* have a bum the size of a paddling pool. I've got a gorgeous dress for the christening, so you three eat the cupcakes and I'll mind the baby.'

'Who mentioned cupcakes?' Dr Riley MacDonald's rich, Scottish tones cut through the conversation, distracting them momentarily from the shock of Holly being on a diet. 'Och, Anna, you here again? Do you not have a home to go to?'

Anna grinned. 'Oh shut up. I'm on my way to see Nell after this, so save a couple of cupcakes for her won't you?'

'There are plenty to go around though I hope?' Riley said.

'Plenty,' Anna assured him.

'How is Nell by the way?' Rachel enquired. 'And how's your gorgeous boy?'

Nell, Riley's wife, and the proprietor of Spill the Beans had given birth to a healthy son just three weeks previously, and both parents were besotted with him.

'They're doing well,' Riley said, beaming. 'The wee man's coming on in leaps and bounds. Nell's crazy about him. She's a born mother right enough.'

'Will she be coming to Eloise's christening?' Anna

said.

'She wouldn't miss it for the world,' he assured her. 'Social event of the year after all, what with me being godfather an' all.'

Anna laughed. 'Well obviously that's all that matters. Mind you, I wouldn't expect too much. Just a simple church service at St Benedict's and a buffet back at Chestnut House.'

'Nell's fretting already that she can't fit into her best dress,' Riley admitted. 'I offered to buy her a new one, but she said it would be a waste of money because she's planning to lose the baby weight. I don't really know what else I can suggest.'

'Leave it to Nell to work it out,' Rachel advised him. 'It's just another thing for new mothers to deal with. You're best off keeping out of it.'

'I remember when I first had Eloise,' Anna said. 'I assumed the bump would be gone the next day, but it's taken months and I'm still not back to how I was before. Maybe I never will be,' she added with a sigh.

'But what does it matter?' Riley said. 'It's all worth it isn't it?'

'Says the man,' Abbie said wryly.

'Wonder what you'd be saying if it was you dealing with all the after-effects of giving birth,' Anna added, giving poor Riley an accusing look. Her eyes narrowed as her own husband, Connor, entered the room, having finished morning surgery at last. 'Tell Riley,' she said. 'Tell him how hard it is for new mothers.'

Connor looked nervous. 'You mean—you know—hormones and stuff?'

'Hormones and stuff says the doctor,' Rachel said, laughing.

'See your medical training paid off,' Holly added.

'Bless him,' Anna said, grinning. 'He does more than his fair share. Made us a lovely tea last night while I slept on the sofa. I was too exhausted to even think about cooking, so he just got on with it. Didn't even wake me up until it was ready.'

'Whoop! Give that man a medal,' Holly said, her tone dripping in sarcasm.

Riley looked deeply worried. 'Does all this really go on for months? You've got me thinking now.'

'Months?' Connor pulled a face. 'Try years. Decades.'

'It *is* harder than you expect,' Anna admitted. 'I'll say that much.'

'But worth it,' Connor added, stroking Eloise's cheek with his little finger. 'I mean, just look at her.'

Abbie finished her cupcake and threw the paper case in the bin. 'I'd better get off on my visits,' she said. 'I start surgery earlier than you two, remember?' she added, waving the list at them. 'Don't say another word. I'm going!'

'Don't think you've got away with this,' Rachel called after her as she headed out of the office. 'We haven't forgotten. When you get back, we want to know more about your date, and we're not letting you off the hook this time!'

***

Jackson had to admit, despite his initial reservations about the place, that Rose Cottage was a stunningly pretty home and perfect for Ash and Izzy.

'I've never been a fan of older properties,' he said, making Ash splutter with laughter. 'But this one's really charming.'

'You don't say! You hid that well, mate.' Ash shook his head. 'Never been a fan of older properties. Who'd have thought it, eh?'

'Don't make fun of him,' Izzy scolded. 'He can't help being—well, Jackson.'

'Hey!' Jackson nudged her indignantly. 'You'd better have made a cracking dinner if that's the kind of insult I'm going to get served up as a side dish.'

'Salmon, new potatoes, and asparagus,' she told him.

'My favourite! How did you know?'

She grinned. 'A little bird told me,' she explained, glancing at Ash.

'I wasn't aware you even knew,' Jackson admitted. 'I wouldn't have a clue what *your* favourite meal was.'

'That's because I observe and take an interest in people, mate,' Ash said. 'Whereas you're too busy making sure they don't move anything or leave fingerprints on your furniture.'

Jackson pulled a face but could hardly deny what was, after all, true. He hated it when people visited his flat. His anxiety levels soared as he watched his carefully constructed world being tampered with and spoilt. He knew people thought he was a bit mad, but he couldn't help liking everything just so.

'Well, let's have a look at the rest of this place then,'

he said. 'I've been led to believe by Ash that it's the most beautiful house in Yorkshire, never mind Bramblewick, so I'm expecting great things.'

'I can't believe I've been living here nearly seven months and you haven't been before,' Ash said as they headed upstairs to check out the two small bedrooms and bathroom that made up the entire first floor of the cottage.

'No well, I've been busy,' Jackson said uncomfortably. He ducked his head to walk into the master bedroom and stared around him. 'Wow.'

'Wow good, or wow bad?' Ash said, sounding nervous.

'Wow good of course,' Jackson said, smiling. 'It's not exactly a big room but it's got lots of character, and it's been decorated beautifully.' He loved how neat and tidy it was. There was nothing out of place at all. All the couple's clothes had been stored within either the big pine wardrobe or the chest of drawers. No makeup or perfume littered the dressing table. The duvet wasn't wrinkled or lopsided, which was his pet hate, and there were no magazines, ornaments or books cluttering up the place. His shoulders sagged in relief and, realising how tense he'd been, he pushed away the nagging thought that kept recurring that maybe his brother was right. Maybe he should have counselling.

'Are you prepared for the shock of the box room?' Ash grinned and Jackson wrinkled his nose.

'That bad?'

'Put it this way; the only reason the main bedroom is so neat is because the overspill's next door.'

'Oh, hell.'

Ash pushed open the door of the second bedroom and Jackson winced. So this was where Izzy and Ash kept their books, their spare clothes, old ornaments and clocks, paintings they had no room to hang, photograph albums... He could barely see the single divan that took up most of one wall. Everything they owned must be piled on top of that he thought and shuddered.

'Get me out of here.'

Ash patted his shoulder. 'Let's finish with the bathroom. Soothe your nerves.'

The bathroom, he was relieved to see, was tidy and immaculately clean. He took a deep breath. 'That's much better.'

'I thought you'd see it that way,' Ash said. 'Now that you're sufficiently calm, shall we go downstairs?'

The living room was neat and tidy too, thankfully. The old beams were a problem, though. He kept having to duck, being a good four or five inches taller than Ash. It felt claustrophobic to him, and he knew he'd have difficulty living in a place like this.

'The garden's lovely,' he said, feeling he owed them a compliment for not liking the beams. He peered out of the window and nodded approvingly. 'Those roses are gorgeous. I see you've been out with the lawnmower, Ash.'

'Not him. Me,' Izzy said, entering the room. 'Had the grand tour? Huge place isn't it?' She laughed. 'Did he show you the spare bedroom?'

As Jackson grimaced, she said, 'Sorry. I told him not

to, but he thought it would be funny. Anyway, tea's ready. Come on through.'

They ate in the kitchen, which was half the size of the living room but did, at least, have room for a small table and chairs. The beams closed in on Jackson and he thought they'd be a nightmare to dust. He couldn't deny the meal was delicious though.

'Strawberries and cream from Maudie's for afters,' Izzy said cheerfully, collecting the empty plates. 'Isn't it lovely now that the weather's warmed up?'

'It will be raining as soon as the holidays start,' Ash predicted. 'You can guarantee it.'

'Best make the most of it until then,' Izzy replied. 'The garden fence needs treating again. We'll do it this weekend, while it's sunny.'

'I should have kept my mouth shut,' Ash said, but he was smiling, and Jackson realised he was smiling too. It was good to see them making a go of their relationship. They were great people. They deserved happiness.

As Izzy placed the bowls of fruit and cream on the table, Ash cleared his throat. 'I expect you're wondering why we invited you round for tea?'

Jackson paused, the spoon already halfway to his mouth. 'I hadn't been,' he said cautiously, 'but I am now. Should I be worried?'

Ash looked at Izzy and she smiled back, nodding.

'Thing is, mate, we wanted you to be the first to know. Me and Izz are getting married.'

Jackson gave a whoop and clapped him on the back. 'That's fantastic,' he said. 'Congratulations. I'm so happy for both of you.'

'Thank you.' Izzy laughed as he pulled her into a hug. 'We were hoping you'd say that.'

'Why on earth wouldn't I? I've been rooting for you two from the start.'

'We know you have, mate, which is why...' Ash swallowed and looked at him, an appeal in his eyes, 'which is why we wanted to tell you first. You see, the thing is—'

Jackson raised an eyebrow. 'The thing is, what?'

Izzy tutted. 'Oh for goodness' sake! Jackson, will you be Ash's best man?'

Jackson leaned back in his chair and stared at them. Small bubbles of delight fizzed up inside him and cascaded from him like the best vintage champagne. 'Really? Me?' He beamed at his friend in amazement. 'I'd be honoured. Really I would.'

Ash and Izzy exchanged happy glances.

'Told you he'd do it,' Izzy said. 'He was worried you'd say no.'

'Why on earth would I say no?' he demanded.

'Well, you know. A room full of people. Having to make a speech. Organising the stag night. Dancing with the maid of honour.'

Oh. He hadn't thought of all that. 'Well, I'm sure it will be fine. Who *is* your maid of honour?'

Izzy burst out laughing. 'My *matron* of honour will be Anna and don't worry, she won't have any designs on you. She's a very happily married woman.'

He grinned sheepishly.

'Sorry,' he said. 'I'm sure I can cope with it all, even

a stag night. You won't want anything too raucous will you?'

'We're not the raucous types, mate,' Ash assured him. 'And if it makes you feel any better, the wedding will be a small, quiet affair. Just our parents and a few friends from the village.'

At least that was something.

'And it will be in a proper function room,' Izzy added, 'with staff to clear up after us, so don't spend the entire afternoon going around cleaning up other people's litter. Just enjoy yourself and relax, okay?'

They knew him far too well.

Jackson nodded. 'I'll give it a go.' He smiled at them both. 'I really am delighted to be asked to be best man you know. I'll do my best for you, I promise.'

They sat in the garden for an hour after tea, soaking up the sunshine and drinking the delicious, Yorkshire Dales beer, Lusty Tup. Jackson had already decided to get a taxi home, so he wasn't worried about drinking. He wasn't really worried about anything for a short while, lying back in the sun lounger while the weakening rays of evening sunshine warmed him, and the scent of the flowers drifted to him on the light breeze.

'Abbie will be invited of course,' Izzy said suddenly, making him almost spill his beer. 'She's one of the gang now, so I couldn't possibly not invite her.'

Ash gave him a sly look. 'We've been ever so patient,' he pointed out, 'but we're not saints. Are you going to tell us about this date or not?'

Jackson groaned inwardly. He might have known

they wouldn't let him get away with it.

'I told you this morning at work,' he protested. 'We had a nice meal and said goodnight.'

'And that's it?' Izzy said, eyeing him suspiciously. 'Surely you talked? Even you can't be that antisocial.'

'What do you mean, *even* me?' Jackson demanded. 'I'll have you know we talked quite a bit. It was a pleasant evening.'

Ash and Izzy exchanged glances. '*Pleasant?*' They made the word sound quite disgusting.

'Yes, pleasant. Now can we change the subject please?'

'But aren't you going to see her again?' Ash queried, clearly disappointed.

'Of course not.' Jackson stared at him in surprise. 'Are you seriously telling me that you didn't set the whole thing up as a joke?'

Ash sat up straight—or as straight as he could manage in a sun lounger—and gave him an astonished look. 'Of course I didn't! What the heck made you think I'd do that?'

'Oh.' Jackson took a gulp of his beer. 'Well I can only assume that you don't know Abbie Sawdon very well. Or you haven't been paying to attention to *me* all these years. She couldn't be more different from me if she tried.'

'That,' said Izzy wryly, 'was rather the point.'

'What do you mean by that?'

She sighed and put down her glass of wine. 'Jackson, the last thing you need is a partner who's as neurotic as you are.'

'Neurotic? Well, thanks a lot.'

'What Izzy means,' Ash interrupted hastily, 'is that it would be incredibly stressful to have someone in your life who gets as wound up about neatness and hygiene as you do.'

'And Abbie,' added Izzy, 'is a real antidote to your, er, issues. She's very different.'

'You're not kidding,' Jackson said. 'Her coat was covered in dog hairs. It made me shudder.'

Izzy bit her lip. 'She's a lovely woman,' she told him. 'You really ought to give her a chance. I honestly believe she'd be good for you.'

'Well I hate to disappoint you, but we both agreed that Friday night was a one-off event. The truth is Abbie's no more interested in a relationship than I am. She only went on the stupid date to shut you all up. She's got enough going on in her life and doesn't need a man adding to the mix.'

'So was there no chemistry at all?' Izzy sounded genuinely disappointed.

Jackson hesitated, remembering Abbie's sparkling eyes, her peals of laughter, and their mutual opinion of their friends' attempts to set them up.

'She was nicer than I expected,' he relented at last, 'but she's not my type. I'm quite happy as I am, and I really think she feels the same. Sorry.'

Izzy sighed. 'Oh well. It was worth a try.'

Ash leaned back in his sun lounger. 'Can't win them all, Izz. Not to worry, Jackson. We tried, but we promise to leave you alone now, so let's forget all about it. Finish your Lusty Tup. There's plenty more where that came from.'

Jackson shut his eyes, relieved that the subject was closed. Tomorrow Bertie was due to hand in his English Comprehension homework. If he failed to do so yet again, he really would have to speak to Abbie in a professional capacity, and how awkward would that be? His stomach fluttered with nerves, and he took a sip of beer. Thank goodness there were only two more weeks of term and Bertie would soon be another teacher's problem. On the other hand...

He tried to quell the nagging sense of unease. No matter how he tried, he couldn't ignore the fact that Bertie seemed to be living a most disorderly life, and that sparked warning signals in his mind. As uncomfortable as it was, he was going to have to speak to Abbie about her son if things didn't improve. He mentally crossed his fingers that Tuesday would bring a page of English Comprehension and a signed homework diary.

Chapter 4

Abbie parked the car outside the school gates and walked slowly towards Bertie's classroom. She was so tired she could barely put one foot in front of the other and longed to go home and sleep. She'd already decided to take the kids to Spill the Beans for their tea. She just didn't have the energy to cook.

'Abbie?'

She jumped, then frowned as a familiar tall, dark-haired man with a neatly trimmed beard and brown eyes stepped towards her. Her stomach flipped. Probably embarrassment, seeing him again in this formal setting.

'Oh, hi, Jackson. Or should it be Mr Wade on school premises?'

'Perhaps it should be in the circumstances.'

He held out his hand and she shook it reluctantly, sensing trouble. As if she had the energy the deal with any problems now!

'Were you waiting for me?'

'I was, yes.' He cleared his throat looking a bit unsure of himself. 'I'm just a bit worried about Bertie. You do realise he hasn't been doing his homework?'

She leaned against the wall of the classroom, too

tired to stand upright suddenly, and pushed her hair back from her face. 'No, I didn't realise that. To be honest, I didn't realise he even *had* homework.'

Jackson raised an eyebrow. 'So you've not been checking his home school diary then?'

Something in his tone told her that he'd suspected as much.

She flushed and looked away, her gaze sweeping the playground, empty of all but a handful of parents making their way towards the school building. 'Er, diary? Oh, diary. Well, I've been a bit busy...'

She took off her jacket and blew out her cheeks, feeling the effects of the afternoon heat. 'What has he missed?'

'It's not much. He's too young for a lot of homework, but we do like them to do a bit of maths and English twice a week, and weekly spelling tests. He said the goat ate his maths homework the other day. Is that even possible?'

Her lips twitched in amusement, and she saw the annoyance in his dark eyes. Clearly he was taking this very seriously.

'Probably,' she admitted. 'He's often at Folly Farm with Sam—you know, Sam Johnson? I work with his mum, Rachel, and Rachel's mum looks after my youngest so we're there a lot, and he loves the animals. They do have goats so...' She shrugged. It wasn't the end of the world after all.

'Bertie was given an A4 sheet of work to do for English Comprehension. It was supposed to be handed in this morning and he failed to produce it. He only had four questions to answer so it's not as if it was a heavy workload.'

'Right. Wonder who ate that?' She gave him a weak smile and he stared back as if he couldn't believe how lightly she was taking the matter.

'His excuse was that the dog got it and covered it with mud, so you threw it away.'

She frowned then nodded. 'Oh, right. Yes, I did find a piece of paper on the floor all scrunched up and muddy. He was quite right. It wasn't readable.'

'But surely you checked—' He shook his head and glared at her as if she were the naughty pupil, not Bertie. 'It's very important that he does his homework, Dr Sawdon. I'm sure you, as a professional person, must realise how important.'

So she was Dr Sawdon again was she? Wow, she'd really impressed him on their not-really-a-date, hadn't she? She felt an overwhelming exhaustion and struggled to pull herself together. 'Sorry. What?'

As he tutted, unable to hide his impatience, she snapped, 'Look, I've just moved house, I have a full-time job to do, and three children to raise. Forgive me for thinking that a muddied sheet of English Comprehension isn't that big a deal.'

'It's the start of a slippery slope,' he said. 'I can see you're struggling but you must make sure he does the work he's supposed to do. It's not fair to him otherwise. This is his education we're talking about. I can overlook the occasional lateness, the state he often arrives in—'

'What do you mean, the state he often arrives in?' she said sharply.

He shrugged. 'I just mean, well, sometimes his hair doesn't look as if it's been brushed, and he has mud and dog hairs on his trousers—'

So she was being judged for having dogs in the house? Who the hell did he think he was? She felt her face start to burn. A prickling sensation began on the top of her head, and she tensed immediately.

'We also expect the children to read a little every night. Is Bertie doing that?'

'What? Oh for goodness' sake!' Desperation to get away from him made her tone sharper than it perhaps should have been. 'Look, Mr Wade, he's eight years old. It's bad enough that Isla has a lot of homework to do every night, but at least she's at high school. Why do we have to foist all this on young children? At eight years old, Bertie shouldn't be worrying about maths homework or English Comprehension. Let them be children. Life—' she broke off and shook her head, then rummaged in her jacket pocket for the packet of tissues she always carried. 'Life's too short, don't you think?'

'Are you all right?'

Hearing the alarm in his voice, she mopped frantically at the rivers of sweat that were running down the sides of her nose.

'I've—I've got a bit of a cold,' she said. 'My temperature's up a bit.'

'Are you sure that's all it is?' he said. 'You look—'

'I'm a doctor, Mr Wade,' she said coldly. 'I think I know what a cold looks like.'

'Yes, sorry.' He sighed. 'Look, I don't want an

argument with you. I think we should work together on this. We both want what's best for Bertie, don't we?'

'The problem is,' she said, 'that perhaps we don't agree what *is* best for him. In my opinion it's not foisting a whole lot of homework on him when he should be enjoying himself.'

He scowled. 'Dr Sawdon, I need a guarantee from you that you'll make sure Bertie reads every evening and does his homework on time. I know there isn't much of this term left, but he needs to get into the habit now. His next teacher might not be so understanding.'

She wiped her upper lip and shoved the crumpled, soggy tissue back in her jacket pocket. 'Yes, fine. I'll make sure of it.' Anything to get rid of him!

'And you'll read the home school diary every evening and sign any messages?'

She glared at him. Was he ever going to leave her alone? She heard the school bell ring at last and heaved a sigh of relief. 'Yes, fine, I'll do that.'

'Well, good. I really don't want to have to take the matter further, Dr Sawdon, so I'm glad you've seen sense.'

Take the matter further?

Abbie had spent her whole adult life working towards helping and saving people. She'd never before wanted to cause physical harm to someone, but she would have gladly slapped his smug face for him at that moment. Luckily, she didn't even have the energy to try.

'If that's everything, Mr Wade?'

He nodded. 'Yes thank you, Dr Sawdon.'

He turned and headed back into the classroom and Abbie almost fell against the wall, feeling furious and exhausted at the same time.

Bertie came rushing out, along with a whole group of children and a lot of parents, some of whom gave her the most curious looks as they passed her. She supposed they'd seen her talking to Mr Wade and knew she was in bother. He might as well have put her in detention. She certainly felt as if she'd been lectured.

'You all right, Mum?' Bertie said. 'You're ever so red again.'

'Get in the car, Bertie,' she said wearily. 'You and I have a lot to talk about.'

Chapter 5

Jackson thought about the neat, orderly little garden at Rose Cottage as he pulled up in the drive of The Gables and stared in shock at the tangle of weeds and the gigantic privet hedge in front of the house. If this was the front garden, how bad must the back garden be he wondered, climbing out of his car, and putting his sunglasses in his back pocket.

The brilliant sunshine cast the shabbiness of the detached stone house into stark relief. Paint was peeling from the front door, which looked as if it were about to fall off its hinges. Moss clung to the lower walls, and weeds sprouted up towards the windowsills. The garden gates were missing entirely. Hardly safe when Abbie had such young children. She only had to open the front door and they could be out on the road before she had time to catch them.

He shuddered, looking around him, his anxiety levels soaring. He had to concede that the lane the house stood on was exceptionally quiet, but even so. It only took one car...

He knocked quite tentatively on the front door, mindful of the fact that it could be about to fall off. There was no answer, and he heard lots of shouting and shrieks coming from the back of the house.

He peered down the drive at the side where another car was parked—a smart, silver estate. She evidently took greater care of her car than her home. Or her children. He wondered if he should knock on the side gate. He couldn't see what was going on in the back garden since that, at least, seemed secure, but he guessed the family were outside and wouldn't hear him, no matter how many times he knocked on the front door.

Hesitating, he barely registered the sound of the front door opening, and jumped as Abbie's voice said, 'Hello?'

Jackson hurried back to the doorstep and switched on a smile. 'Hello again. I'm sorry to bother you.'

Her eyes widened. 'What on earth are you doing here?'

He bristled at the tone of her voice. She clearly wasn't pleased to see him which made him wonder why he'd bothered to take time out of his day off to come here to apologise.

She clapped a hand to her forehead. 'Sorry, sorry! I didn't mean that the way it sounded. I'm just surprised to see you that's all.' She looked at him suspiciously, as if a thought had suddenly occurred to her. 'Is this about Bertie again?'

'Not directly, no,' he assured her. 'I came here to apologise. I think I was a bit rude to you the other day at school.'

'Yes,' she said curtly, 'you were.'

Remembering his comments about Bertie's

appearance and how he'd overstepped the mark, he couldn't blame her for sounding so annoyed. 'Well, it's been preying on my mind. I just wanted you to know that I'm sorry.'

Abbie's fingers curled around the edge of the door as she surveyed him for a moment, then she stepped aside, giving him a brief smile. 'Well thanks. I appreciate that. Would you like to come in?'

Jackson took a deep breath, nailed his courage to the mast and stepped inside, wondering as he did so why on earth he'd accepted her invitation. He'd said sorry and that, surely, was enough. He could be on his way home now. Whatever faced him within these walls it was his own fault.

'You'll have to excuse the mess,' she called, as she led him down a long, shabby hallway and into what he supposed was a kitchen. It was the sink and the cooker that really gave it away, although it was so far removed from his idea of the perfect kitchen that he could barely breathe. Piles of washing lay on the floor, pots were piled up on the draining board, and a laptop—which she hastily closed—sat on the scrubbed pine table.

'Coffee? Tea?'

Jackson tried not to shudder. 'No thank you, Dr Sawdon, I've just had one.'

'Oh, lord,' she said with a sigh. 'If you're going to visit me at my house the least you can do is call me Abbie.' She gave him a cheeky wink. 'You know, like on our date?'

He gaped at her, and she tutted and turned away from him, bundling towels into the washing machine.

'Am I still allowed to call you Jackson, or are we back to Mr Wade?'

'Jackson will be fine.' He wondered how he'd ended up feeling so in the wrong, when she was the irresponsible parent who didn't check her children's homework and clearly let them live in squalor.

'It's nice of you to apologise,' she said. 'You were quite mean after all. All that stuff about dog hairs and mud, and Bertie's hair not being brushed. I brush his hair every morning and night, but he's not the most restrained child. And as for the dogs—well, I can't help that they moult, nor that Bertie lets them jump up at him and leave muddy pawprints. Have you never had dogs?'

He had to confess that he hadn't, which earned him a look that was a mixture of suspicion, pity, and astonishment.

'Really? I can't imagine not having dogs. What, not ever? Even when you were a kid?'

He shook his head. 'My parents weren't ones for animals.' At least he'd had that to be grateful for. One less thing to worry about.

'Goodness.' She shrugged. 'Oh well, it takes all sorts I suppose.' She slammed the washing machine door shut and poured detergent and fabric softener into the appropriate compartments. 'The kids are in the garden,' she informed him unnecessarily. 'They need to burn off some energy. Isla pretends she's too sophisticated to play but even she needs to get out once in a while, and there are some amazing hiding places in the garden. I think she's planning to build a tree house as an escape from the others.'

Jackson tried not to sound appalled. 'How old is she?'

'Thirteen this week.' She paused, a child's dress in her hand, and shook her head. 'I can't believe it. Me, a mother of a teenager. I know, I don't look old enough do I?'

She laughed and turned back to the laundry basket, dividing its contents into piles.

Come to think of it, no she didn't, especially when she laughed. If she hadn't already told him she was thirty-seven he wouldn't have guessed.

'Surely she's too young to build a tree house?' He felt the anxiety surge through him at the thought.

She gave him a scathing look. 'You're kidding right? She wouldn't be building it alone, obviously, although she's exceptionally good at woodwork. Gets very high marks for it at school.'

'But—but it's dangerous!'

Abbie straightened, frowning. 'I'm hardly going to give her a saw and tell her to get on with it am I? Lord, you look worried. Did you never do anything like that? Climb trees, build dens? Besides, it's all theoretical at the moment. We have a lot more to think about before we get around to tree houses. I think the garden will be way down on our list of priorities, as I'm sure you can see for yourself. I don't know.' She glanced around her and pulled a face. 'Maybe what I really need is a demolition expert.'

'It's that bad?' He had to admit he'd had the same thought. She had the attention span of a goldfish he thought, watching her dividing cottons from synthetics, but he couldn't deny that she had a hell of a lot on her plate. He felt a slight stirring of sympathy for her and an even greater one for the children. 'What made you choose this house, though? I mean, with so much on your plate already, not least such a demanding job, surely it would have made sense to buy a more practical house?'

'I'm surprised you haven't asked what brought us to Bramblewick,' she admitted. 'Everyone else seems bewildered.'

'Who's everyone?'

She sighed. 'My parents, my children, my ex-husband. But when I saw the job come up at Bramblewick Surgery it seemed like fate. I'd been desperate to get out of the city. Our old house was on a main bus route and the stop was just outside our house. All the passengers would gawp in, and the neighbours could see into our back garden too, which I hated. I loved The Gables the minute I saw it. That quiet lane at the front, and the garden at the back with all those trees. No noise at all really except for the birdsong.'

'And your children and dogs,' he reminded her with a rueful grin.

She blushed. 'Yes, I know they're a bit noisy,' she admitted. 'Still, it seems like the perfect place for them to grow up. All that space and freedom, and that lovely garden. At least,' she added, 'it *will* be lovely when it's cleared. I want my children to be brought up in the countryside. I thought the fresh air and open spaces would be good for them—for all of us. We were all a bit stressed you see, what with the divorce and everything.'

He nodded, his eyes soft with sympathy. 'I can imagine.'

'I thought I was making the right choice. When I got the job I was so excited, but the kids didn't react at all how I'd imagined they would. Isla's struggled the most. I thought I was doing the right thing by her, but maybe I was being selfish. I don't know.'

'You lived in Kearton Bay to start with didn't you?'

'Just outside it. It was all I could find at short notice, and it was cute enough. We loved the location, but it was a bit of a drag getting the children to school and myself to work, and the cottage was far too small. Besides, I wanted to buy not rent. We were so lucky when The Gables came up for sale.'

'I heard it had stood empty quite a while.'

She shrugged. 'Two or three years I think. The owner was elderly and moved in with her daughter. She intended it to be temporary, but when it became clear she couldn't manage alone and the daughter could no longer meet her needs, she went into a nursing home. The house went up for sale to pay the fees, which is terribly sad. For her at least. I feel quite guilty admitting that her loss was my gain, but I could never have afforded a house like The Gables if it had been well-maintained.' She pushed her fringe from her eyes, looking self-conscious. 'I know I must seem very stupid to you, Mr Wade, for buying something that needs so much work doing to it.'

'Jackson,' he said again, 'and I don't think you're stupid, Abbie. I just think you've got a heck of a lot of responsibility on your hands. I believe your husband is working abroad.'

'My ex-husband,' she corrected him. 'And yes, he's in New York.'

'That must be hard for you. No help from him with the children I mean.'

She shrugged. 'It was a wonderful opportunity,' she said. 'I didn't blame him for wanting to take it.'

'What does he do?'

'He's in advertising. He was always going to be a huge success, there was no question about it. When the agency in New York headhunted him, I was probably less surprised than he was. I urged him to go for it. He was doubtful, worried about leaving me with the children, but I told him we'd manage just fine. He video calls them regularly, and they're going over to stay with him for a couple of weeks during the summer holidays. That will be a big help,' she admitted. 'I've managed to book a fortnight off work in August, and with them being in the States for two weeks that means Janie will only have to look after them for a fortnight. It's so good of her to offer. I don't know what I'd have done…' Her voice trailed off and she shuffled uncomfortably, then reached for her drink again. 'I was more organised in Hull,' she finished, sounding defensive.

'The children are going to New York?' he raised an eyebrow. 'How are they getting there? Are you going with them?'

'No, Nick's coming over to collect them,' she said.

'They've done it before. He had them for a week before Christmas and they loved it. They're very impressed with his swish apartment, and it was snowing so they thought it was a magical place.'

'It's good that you get on so well,' he said. 'Many parents don't. I've seen some very distressed children during my career I can tell you.'

'That's the last thing we want,' she said fervently. 'They come first, always. We've always got on, Nick and me. There was no big, dramatic bust-up or anything like that. It just ran its course. We both want what's best for our kids, and we have joint custody so there's no problem with them going over to stay with him. None at all.'

Jackson felt his shoulders sag in relief. Here were two parents who clearly cared about their children's welfare. Abbie may be a bit disorganised, and her house was evidently in need of some tender loving care, but her kids were her priority. That made him look at her in a whole different light.

'Look, I've talked the hind legs off a donkey,' she said, finally heading over to the table. 'Are you sure you don't want a drink?'

'Quite sure.' He glanced at the pile of dirty pots on the draining board and felt a wave of nausea at the thought.

She followed his gaze and her mouth tightened. 'Dishwasher hasn't been plumbed in yet,' she said, 'and I've been busy. Planning a splurge of housework this afternoon, as a matter of fact.'

'I wasn't judging,' he assured her, not entirely

truthfully.

She smirked. 'Sure you weren't. I haven't always lived like this you know. Believe it or not I do have some standards. Our old house was immaculate, but I needed to find somewhere to buy that was close to the surgery, and this was affordable, and it had a big garden, which was essential for three kids and two dogs so...'

'You really should get some gates up at the front.' Why on earth had he said that? His mouth seemed to be on a mission of its own. 'I just mean that your children could run straight out into the road couldn't they? The little one at least.'

She dropped into a chair and pushed her hair back from her face. 'You may find this hard to believe, but I'm not the sort of mother who just lets her two-year-old out into the front garden without keeping a very tight grip on her hand.'

Jackson held up his hands. 'I'm not accusing you, Dr—Abbie. Just trying to help.'

She flushed and looked away, her gaze sweeping the garden through the large, picture window. 'I suppose the gates *are* a priority. I was going to sort it all out, but I've been a bit busy...'

With what? Not doing housework, that's for sure.

'I could help if you like.' He mentally clapped his hand over his mouth.

She gave him a suspicious look. 'Help? How?'

'I—I have experience in renovation. I'd be happy to fix the gates for a start and then maybe I could do some work around the house. Fix it up a bit.'

She looked as astounded as he felt. He hadn't meant

to offer but the thought of her children living like this had compelled him to speak up.

Her fingers tapped on the laptop. 'What do you mean, *fix it up*?'

Maybe get a bulldozer and pull the whole lot down?

'Nothing major. That is—I'm assuming you got a full structural survey done when you bought the place?'

Her lips pursed. 'Obviously. I'm not stupid. There's nothing wrong with the building. It just needs some tender loving care that's all. I mean, don't we all?'

She reddened, as if she'd just realised what she'd said, and he shifted uncomfortably.

'I can give your house that,' he mumbled.

'Really?' She wrinkled her nose. 'You don't look the type to get your hands dirty. No offence meant.'

He wasn't convinced by that. It seemed to him she'd meant plenty of offence. He looked down at his smooth hands and acknowledged that he couldn't really blame her.

'I'm sorry,' she said, sounding awkward. 'That was rude of me. Look, I do appreciate—'

The kitchen door flew open, and Bertie hurried in. 'Mum, you'll never guess—oh!' He skidded to a halt and stared at Jackson, his eyes wide with shock. 'What are you doing here?'

'Bertie! Manners!'

Jackson nodded. 'Hello, Bertie. I was just talking to your mum about—' He broke off, not sure that his mother would want him to know what they'd been discussing.

Luckily he didn't have to worry about finishing the

sentence. He reared back in alarm as a black Labrador bounced up to him. It gave him a startled look and let out a loud bark, then jumped up, placing its paws on his knees, and staring at him as if waiting for an introduction.

'That's Albus,' Bertie informed him. 'He's only being friendly so don't be scared. And it wasn't him who messed up my homework, so don't blame him. It was Willow who did that. She's ever so naughty, isn't she, Mum?'

'She's—a character.' Abbie looked ruefully at the pool of slobber that had suddenly appeared on Jackson's trousers and shook her head. 'What were you gabbling on about, Bertie? What wouldn't I guess?'

'Oh, yeah.' Bertie looked doubtfully at Jackson. 'Well, er, it's just that Poppy's done something a bit yucky.'

'Poppy?' *Another dog?*

'My youngest,' Abbie responded. 'What's she done?'

'She scoffed a beetle,' Bertie said, unable to hide his glee. 'A proper big fat juicy one.'

'Bertie! Why didn't you stop her?'

He shrugged. 'She was too quick. Anyway, she didn't choke so that's good.'

Jackson felt his stomach lurch and put his hand to his mouth, feeling sick. 'That's disgusting.'

Abbie gave him a scathing look. 'Given the huge mixed grill you devoured the other night I know you're not a vegetarian.'

'No, but—'

'It's only protein. She'll be fine.'

He gaped at her. 'She'll be fine? She's just eaten a beetle!'

'Do you have children, Mr Wade?'

He straightened, on alert at the use of his "formal" name. 'No, but—'

'I thought not. Between the ages of one and three, children have a propensity for putting anything and everything in their mouths.'

'I'm sure they do. And I'm equally sure it's up to the parents to make sure they don't eat anything they shouldn't.' He paused for effect. 'Like dog food for example.'

She reddened again and gave Bertie a reproachful stare.

'I've brought Poppy in. She's being disgusting.'

Jackson turned and saw a young girl, evidently Isla, the about-to-be-teenager, holding in her arms a toddler with blonde curly hair. He had to admit the little one didn't look any the worse for her misadventures. In fact, she was beaming quite cheerfully.

Isla was like her mother in miniature, with the same tawny-coloured hair and blue eyes. She plonked the child down on a chair and said, 'You'd never think she'd not long had her dinner, would you?'

Abbie sighed. 'It's not hunger. It's curiosity. She'll grow out of it, I've told you.'

'Well, I wish she'd hurry up about it,' Isla muttered. She stared pointedly at Jackson, obviously waiting for an introduction.

'This is Mr Wade,' Bertie informed her. 'He's my teacher.'

Isla eyed him curiously. 'Oh, yes? What's Bertie done?'

Jackson stood, brushing down his trousers to rid himself of the dog hair and cringing as his hand brushed the drool. A pretty Blenheim Cavalier King Charles spaniel came trotting into the kitchen and began to yap furiously.

'That's Willow,' Bertie told him. 'She's the one who muddied up my English homework.'

'I'm afraid Willow has small dog complex,' Abbie said. 'She likes everyone to know she's just as fierce as any large dog, so she barks a lot. She'll settle down in a minute.'

He didn't want to wait that long. He'd made his apology to Abbie and hopefully that was the end of the matter. It was time for him to leave before he developed a headache.

Abbie led him to the front door, and he noticed the shabby, cheap wallpaper in the hallway and the threadbare carpet on the stairs. The house needed so much work doing to it, it was making his teeth itch. Clearly, she had no time to do it herself and the whole thing was overwhelming her. In the meantime those poor children were living like savages.

'Look, it's pretty obvious—' he stopped, appalled with himself as he realised how insulting he would sound if he voiced his thoughts.

'It's pretty obvious, what?' She was waiting, and he didn't have a clue how to get out of it now.

'I just mean, you clearly need some major help here.'

Her mouth dropped open. 'Pardon?'

'I'm sorry,' he said hastily. 'I really don't mean to insult you. It's just that, you've only just moved in and, as you've said yourself, there's a lot of work that needs doing to the place. I wasn't just being polite. I'd be happy to help honestly. Fixing houses up is kind of my thing. I like working on them, bringing order from chaos.'

'Chaos?' She took a deep breath and opened the front door. 'Well, thanks very much for that, Mr Wade. I can assure you that any work that needs doing will be done.'

Mr Wade again? What happened to Jackson?

'What about just letting me do the hallway at least?' He couldn't help but cast another look at the shabby wallpaper, but even as he did so he realised he was doing himself no favours.

'I don't think so.'

'If you're sure...'

She glared at him. 'Quite sure. Thank you.'

'If you change your mind you know where to find me.' *Honestly, have I got a death wish or something?*

'I most certainly do. Bye, Mr Wade.'

He stepped out into the drive and the front door swung shut before he even had time to look back at her. He winced, half expecting the door to rock on its hinges and fall off entirely, but it stayed shut.

Sighing, he walked back to his car and climbed in, trying not to think about the enormous project Abbie Sawdon had taken on, the mess the children were living in, or the state of the garden that surrounded him. It was nothing to do with him. She'd made that very clear.

What happened to the Sawdons now was entirely their problem.

Chapter 6

'Oh, he's absolutely gorgeous! And didn't he behave well at the church?' Abbie couldn't resist stroking the baby boy's cheek as Nell proudly held him in her arms.

'Not a murmur.' Nell smiled as her baby's hand curled around her little finger. 'Can't believe he slept through it all. I was really worried he'd scream the place down and spoil the service. I nearly didn't go.'

'Well, he was quieter than Eloise,' Rachel said, laughing. 'You'd have thought the vicar was trying to drown her the way she protested.'

'Bless her.' Nell dropped a loving kiss on her son's head then gave Rachel a pleading look. 'You couldn't get me a sandwich could you? I'm starving. I didn't even have time for breakfast this morning.'

'Course not. What do you fancy?' Rachel glanced over at the large table that stood at the far end of the dining room in Chestnut House. It was positively groaning under the weight of the enormous buffet that Anna had prepared for the christening guests. 'I think there are about five different fillings to choose from, not to mention all the other stuff on there.'

Nell hesitated. 'Oh to hell with it. Get me a bit of

everything. The diet can wait another day.'

Rachel grinned and hurried off to fill a plate for their hungry friend.

'How old is this little fella now?' Ash wandered over, looking a bit lost since Izzy was in the garden with fellow godparent Riley, and the entire Blake family. They were having their photographs taken and, judging by how long they'd been out there, they were planning on filling an entire album.

'Four weeks,' Nell said. 'But it feels as if we've had him forever.'

'Is he sleeping well?'

Abbie grinned. Ash was clearly trying to be polite and show an interest bless him.

'Not too bad.' Nell stifled a yawn then laughed. 'That made me out to be a liar didn't it? No, honestly, he's good as gold. I have no complaints.' She wrinkled her nose and added, 'Apart from the baby bulge he's left me with. Tell me honestly, Abbie, does this dress look too tight?'

Abbie was quick to reassure her. 'You look lovely, and no, it's not too tight.'

She wasn't saying it to be kind. Nell was wearing a pretty print cotton dress with a matching bolero cardigan, and she looked in fine form for a woman who'd only given birth a month ago. Abbie wished that women didn't get so hung up about such minor issues. She thought back to the days after she'd had Poppy and shuddered inside. If only excess weight was all she'd had to think about back then. Nell had no idea how much she had to be thankful for.

Nell leaned towards her, her voice dropping to a whisper. 'Have you seen those two?'

As she inclined her head slightly, Abbie followed the direction of the nod and noticed Holly and her boyfriend, Jonathan, standing by the kitchen door. Holly was clutching a bag to her while she stared at the floor looking thoroughly miserable. Jonathan, meanwhile, was scrolling down his mobile phone.

'Looks like they've had a row,' Ash said. 'I'm sure they'll be fine.'

Abbie and Nell exchanged knowing glances. Holly had been surprisingly subdued throughout the entire service, and the fact that she wasn't currently fussing round Baby Aiden said it all. She certainly wasn't the happy bunny they'd come to know and love.

Rachel arrived back with her fiancé, Xander, each bearing fully loaded plates of food, just as Izzy and Riley, finally discharged of godparent duties, joined the group. Nell promptly handed her son over to his father and took one of the plates with a grateful smile.

'What were you all talking about?' Izzy queried, obviously curious about seeing them all huddled together in a conspiratorial fashion.

'Guess,' Ash said, rolling his eyes.

Izzy tutted. 'Holly? Something's up isn't it? Do you think we should go over there and say something to her?'

'Best leave it be,' Xander advised. 'If she wants to talk to you she knows where you are. Don't make things worse.'

Nell looked crestfallen. 'I suppose you're right.'

Izzy laughed. 'Not often you accept defeat so easily, Nell. Motherhood's mellowed you. Aw, and look at Baby Aiden. He's such a handsome boy aren't you?'

The baby, who appeared to have fair hair like Nell's, rather than Riley's red curls, blinked and sneezed as Izzy tapped him gently on the nose.

'Bless you,' Izzy said, laughing. 'He's gorgeous. I guess it will be his christening we're all gathered at next?'

'That depends doesn't it?' Ash said, nudging her.

She squealed. 'Oh, yes! Er, guys, any ideas when you're getting him done?'

'Done?' Riley pulled a face. 'What a way to describe it!'

'Oh, you know what I mean,' Izzy said. 'Just that, we're planning to throw an engagement party and we don't want the dates to clash so—'

'Engagement party!' There were squeals all round, causing poor Baby Aiden to jump and wave his arms in alarm.

Nell grabbed Izzy's hand. 'You're engaged! When? Why didn't you tell us?'

'Well, I think I just did,' Izzy said, beaming as everyone crowded round to admire her engagement ring. 'Though I'm amazed you didn't notice this little beauty straightaway.'

'Does Anna know?'

'Of course. She was the first person I told, but don't worry. You lot were next in line.'

'Apart from Jackson,' Ash reminded her.

Abbie's lips pursed as Izzy nodded. 'Oh, yes. Apart

from Jackson. But then, he is your best man so that's only fair.'

So Jackson Wade was going to be best man at the wedding? Lord, it didn't say much for the rest of them. Well if she got an invitation maybe she'd find an excuse to decline it.

'When were you thinking of having the party?' Nell asked.

'Probably mid to late August, before term starts again,' Ash said. 'Would that be okay with you two?'

'Oh, aye,' Riley assured him. 'It'll more than likely be a while before we get around to organising the christening for this wee one.' He gazed down at the child in his arms and smiled. 'But we will get around to it, little man. Never fear.'

'We have to make sure Riley's family can get down here from Scotland,' Nell explained. 'It will more likely be October time, so go ahead and throw your party. Where were you planning on holding it?'

'At The Bay Horse,' Ash said, 'and you're all invited, obviously.'

Abbie groaned inwardly. The Bay Horse, of all places! And no doubt Jackson Wade would be there. If he so much as attempted to tell her how badly she was failing as a parent again she'd throttle him.

'We're hoping to get married before the end of the year,' Izzy added. 'No point in hanging around. I've already started looking at venues.'

Nell nudged Rachel's partner, Xander, who was standing quietly beside her. 'Are you listening to this? Don't you think it's time you made an honest woman of our Rachel?'

Rachel blushed. 'Nell!'

Nell shrugged. 'Well, you've been engaged for months and no mention of a wedding yet. I don't blame you for not wanting to make a song and dance about it,' she told Xander, giving him an understanding look. 'I can imagine the palaver there'd be if news got out and the paparazzi turned up. Weddings are bad enough as it is. Why don't you just sneak off and get married on the quiet like me and Riley?'

Xander, who was a well-known actor with countless adoring fans, laughed. 'Always says what she thinks doesn't she? Believe me, Nell, we have plans. All in good time.'

'Ooh! When—' Nell began but was cut off as Anna and her stepdaughter Gracie hurried over to them.

'That's the photos done,' Anna said, sounding rather glad about it. 'I hope you're all tucking into the food. I think I've done enough to feed the entire village.'

She looked stunning Abbie thought, noting Anna's elegant cream dress coat. She glanced over at Connor's mum, Dottie, smart in a peppermint green suit, cooing over the beautiful baby in an immaculately-turned-out Connor's arms. They were the perfect family.

She thought of her own family. The children were at Folly Farm with Janie and Janie's gentleman friend, Merlyn. Isla had thrown a huge tantrum, stating she was too old to need a babysitter, and was probably sulking right now and driving Janie to distraction. Nick was thousands of miles away in New York, living a life entirely separate from them. Her parents were busy professionals working in a London hospital and hadn't seen her for nearly a year. How she envied the Blakes.

Dottie and Connor joined them, cooing over a smiling Eloise.

'Wasn't she a good girl?' Dottie said, beaming. 'Weren't you proud of your little sister, Gracie?'

Gracie shrugged. 'Can I watch *Paddington 2* now?'

There was a brief exchange of glances and Abbie saw the sympathy in Nell's and Izzy's eyes. She remembered that Gracie was on the autism spectrum, and that Anna and Connor had mentioned that she showed little interest in her sibling, which they found quite hard to deal with. Everyone had something to cope with she thought, feeling guilty for being so envious of them just moments ago. No one's life, after all, was that perfect.

Connor's voice was light as he replied, 'Would you like to watch it upstairs in our room, Gracie? You can take a plate of food up with you if you like.'

After handing Eloise to her mum, he led Gracie towards the table so she could select some of the limited foodstuffs she would eat. Anna gave a big sigh.

'Is she still not showing much interest in Eloise?' Nell asked, her eyes soft as she took Aiden back from Riley, who was looking longingly at the buffet table.

Anna shook her head, wincing as Eloise tugged happily on a strand of her hair. 'Not really. She glances over at her sometimes, and she talks to her in passing as if she's some annoying visitor, but she rarely bothers with her. I don't think she quite knows what to do with her just yet. Maybe as Eloise starts to walk and becomes a bit more interesting she'll take more notice. She's never been nasty to her or anything like that,' she added hastily. 'I'm sure she loves her. Gracie just doesn't really show affection. Not to any of us.'

'But it doesn't mean she doesn't feel it,' Ash said gently.

'Exactly.' Anna smiled. 'She's been doing a lot better lately. Interacting with us more. She asked me about wearing makeup the other day, can you believe. She's got a bit friendly with a girl in her class and it seems to be bringing her out of herself a little. She's eaten with us at the table now and then too. It's just that gatherings of people like this can be a bit overwhelming for her.'

'And you and Connor understand that which is good,' Dottie told her. 'No pressure or fuss. If Gracie wants to take her food upstairs and watch *Paddington 2* in peace while all this is going on around her, then that's fine.'

'We just want her to be happy,' Anna said, sounding wistful.

'I'm sure she is happy,' Ash said. 'She's a bright young girl with a real talent for singing and dancing, and she has a loving, supportive family around her. She'll be okay, Anna. Any more thoughts on buying her that puppy she wants?'

They began to discuss various options, with Anna telling Ash the breeds that Gracie kept mentioning and Ash throwing in suggestions about alternative breeds that might be better suited to the family and suggesting rescue centres and older dogs rather than a puppy.

He certainly seemed to have given the matter a lot

of thought. Having once been Gracie's teacher he evidently still cared what happened to her. Anna had been right it seemed when she'd assured Abbie that the local primary school was a good one, with excellent teaching staff. It was one of the things that had persuaded her to buy The Gables. Of course, she hadn't met Jackson Wade then...

'Penny for them?' Rachel offered her the plate of sandwiches, sausage rolls and other tasty treats, then grinned. 'Not the sandwiches. I mean your thoughts. You look miles away. What's up?'

Abbie blinked. 'Oh, nothing. Nothing. Just thinking about Anna and Gracie. Wondering how I'd deal with it.'

Rachel glanced over at Anna who, with Nell, was heading over to the sofa for a well-earned sit down. 'I know, but Gracie really has improved a lot even since I've known them. They're a close little family. Don't worry.'

'I suppose all families have problems,' Abbie mused, taking a sausage roll from the plate. 'Kind of a relief to know it's not just mine.'

'You okay, Abbie?' Rachel put her hand on Abbie's arm. 'If you want to talk I'm a good listener.'

Abbie glanced round but Xander and Ash were deep in conversation, Riley and Connor were still at the buffet table, and Izzy had headed over to talk to the depressed-looking Holly.

'It's nothing really. Just that bloody Jackson Wade making me feel like a total failure as a mother and a human being.'

Rachel frowned. 'Jackson Wade? What's he said?'

Abbie tutted. 'First he was frosty with me on our disastrous blind date. Made it crystal clear that he didn't want to be there, which was a bit harsh. Okay, I didn't want to be there either, but I would never have said so if he hadn't made his feelings so obvious. Then he told me off like a little kid when I went to pick Bertie up. Apparently, Bertie hadn't handed some homework in and it's the end of the world as we know it. I merely pointed out that, in the grand scheme of things, one missed English Comprehension wasn't that big a deal and he looked at me as if I'd committed some heinous crime against education.'

Rachel pulled a face. 'The school is pretty hot on homework I know. I'm always having to get on at Sam about his. And there's that flipping home school diary thing to check every night. It's all right if you've nothing else to do, but when you've been at work all day and you've got a million animals to feed and goodness knows what else to think about—I mean, I have Xander and Mum to keep an eye on Sam. I can't imagine how you manage with three kids and no other adult to help.'

'Exactly!' Abbie chewed her sausage roll furiously. 'And the thing is,' she added, after swallowing it down with some difficulty, having not really chewed it enough, 'to make matters worse, he had the cheek to come to my house to apologise—'

'Oh well that's something,' Rachel said.

'But he ended up insulting me all over again!' Abbie grabbed a cheese sandwich, suddenly realising she was starving. 'As if implying that I was failing Bertie wasn't bad enough he then lectured me because Poppy ate a beetle.'

Rachel's eyes widened. 'She didn't! Oh dear. From what I know about Jackson that wouldn't have gone down too well at all.'

Abbie grinned. 'Maybe not, but the beetle did.'

Rachel burst out laughing, just as Izzy returned looking a bit worried.

'What are you laughing at?' Izzy demanded, nudging Rachel.

Quickly, Rachel filled her in on their conversation and Izzy laughed, too.

'Bless him. Poor Jackson.'

'Poor Jackson nothing,' Abbie said crossly. 'You should have seen him giving my house dirty looks. All right, it's not the neatest place in the world right now, and yes, it needs a lot doing to it, but do you know he actually said it was chaotic?'

Izzy bit her lip and Rachel gasped. 'He didn't!'

'He did! He said I ought to let him help sort the place out because he was good at bringing order out of chaos.'

Rachel laughed again, while Izzy shook her head, her eyes twinkling in amusement.

'Sorry, Abbie, I can imagine why that would rile you up but don't take it personally. Look, Jackson has a bit of a thing about neatness and cleanliness. It's a real problem for him.'

'Neat freak,' Abbie muttered.

'No, seriously.' Izzy's twinkle vanished. 'He really

struggles with any kind of disorder. It's not easy for him.'

Abbie felt a pang of guilt. 'Oh, I see. Well, that's different I suppose...'

'You've got him all wrong you know,' Izzy assured her. 'He's a lovely man. I know he can come across as a bit of a control freak and a bit bossy, but he's such a kind and generous friend. Ash thinks he's the bee's knees. Under that gruff exterior there's a surprisingly charming, funny man. You ought to give him a chance.'

'And if he offered to help you with The Gables why not let him?' Rachel suggested. 'After all, you said yourself it's more of a project than you'd realised, and you haven't got the time or energy to deal with it all yourself.'

Abbie helped herself to a ham sandwich. 'Maybe I don't,' she admitted. 'And maybe, just maybe, he's not as bad as I think he is. Even so, he's the last person I'd want in my house, telling me what to do and trying to organise my children like soldiers in a barracks.'

Izzy shrugged. 'Your decision of course, but he really is one of the good guys.' She smoothed her hair then leaned towards them her voice suddenly lower. 'Anyway, what's Holly doing now? Don't look!' she added, as both Abbie and Rachel turned to look in their friend's direction.

'Then how are we supposed to tell you?' Rachel asked.

'Well, be discreet then,' Izzy whispered.

Rachel turned her head slightly then said, 'She's talking to Anna. By the looks of it she's saying goodbye.'

'And where's Jonathan?'

Rachel made no show of discretion that time as she scanned the room looking for Holly's boyfriend. 'Gone. Must be waiting for her outside.'

Izzy wrinkled her nose.

'What's going on?' Abbie enquired, feeling some concern for the usually bubbly receptionist she'd already grown very fond of.

'She wouldn't tell me, but I think they'd had a row. They certainly weren't talking anyway. Poor Holls sounded so miserable and wretched. I hope she's going to be okay.' Her eyes brightened and she raised her hand in a wave. 'Oh, bye, Holly! See you soon.'

Rachel and Abbie looked round and caught sight of Holly heading towards the door. They returned her wave then turned back to Izzy.

'You're right, she looks dead miserable,' Rachel said with a sigh. 'I hope she's okay.'

'Young love,' Abbie said. 'It never runs smoothly does it?'

Though come to think of it, even in your thirties love could falter, especially when life pulled the most terrible tricks on you. Didn't she know it.

Chapter 7

Abbie switched off the engine and sat for a moment, her hands on the steering wheel. She had five minutes before Bertie left school and she needed every single one of them. She'd not had a moment to herself all day, what with an endless stream of patients to see and visits at lunchtime.

She sighed and leaned over the steering wheel, resting her head on her arms. She was so tired. All she wanted to do was go home to bed and sleep, but there was no chance of that. It was Isla's birthday and she'd promised to take her out for tea.

It was the least she could do, given that Isla had refused a birthday party.

Abbie had been sure that she'd enjoy having her new friends over for something to eat and a few games. All right, so Isla was now a teenager, but it would be good for her to spend time outside of school with some of her classmates. She knew it had been hard for her daughter to adjust to life in a small, rural village.

The Sawdons had lived in Hull since Isla was a toddler, and she'd grown up used to living in a small city with shops and buses and busy streets. Bramblewick had come as quite a shock to her, and she'd protested about the move quite loudly and persistently.

'It will be good for us,' Abbie had told her repeatedly. 'All that fresh, country air and open spaces. No stress, Isla. Just calm and peace.'

Huh! Well, that was a joke wasn't it? Despite her best efforts, her stress levels weren't going down and the move to the countryside wasn't doing any of them as much good as she'd hoped it would. What with Bertie missing his homework, Isla resenting leaving her old schoolfriends behind, and the difficulties of juggling childcare and work without the support network she'd built up in Hull ... She sighed. Maybe she'd not thought it through. She'd got carried away with the idea of a fresh start and a healthier lifestyle. Perhaps she should have given the practicalities more consideration.

There was a very irregular bus service in Bramblewick, so when Isla wanted to visit her friends she'd probably rely on her mother to taxi her everywhere, and there wasn't a nursery in the village that took children under three, and Poppy's third birthday was still a couple of months away.

She shivered at the thought of it and pushed it from her mind. She had other things to worry about after all. Isla's little outburst for one. She'd been in such a good mood since the day of the christening too. It had turned out that, despite all Abbie's fears, Isla had enjoyed herself at Folly Farm, and had not only cleaned out the guinea pigs but had ridden one of the farm's residents, a pretty chestnut pony called Ginger. She'd been in a good mood when she got home, and Abbie had hoped that she'd turned a corner at last. It seemed she'd been a bit premature in that. Isla had looked aghast at her mother's suggestion.

'Bring my friends here for a birthday party? You're joking aren't you?'

Abbie shook her head, puzzled. 'I thought it would be nice to meet them. It won't be anything babyish, Isla, if that's what you're worried about. No pink iced buns or unicorn birthday cake, promise. A proper grown-up afternoon tea. I'll keep Bertie and Poppy out of the way and—'

'You just don't get it do you?' Isla burst out. 'As if I'd bring anyone back here! Are you blind?'

Abbie had looked around helplessly. 'Look, I know it's a bit of a mess, but I'll give it a good splurge I promise. I'll clean up the kitchen and living room and the bathroom. I'll get the bleach out and—'

'And replace the carpets? And paint the walls? And get rid of that tatty wallpaper in the hallway? And put blinds up at the windows? And do something with that front garden? Wow, Mum, you're going to be ever so busy.'

Abbie had faltered, seeing the look of fury in her daughter's face. 'Are you saying you're ashamed of the house?'

'Of course I am! Open your eyes, Mum. It's a slum. I'd never bring anyone back here. I'm just glad that none of my new mates live in Bramblewick. I'd die of shame if any of them came to visit me. Why did we have to move here anyway? Our old house was so nice.

So normal!'

Normal maybe. But The Gables was so spacious, so airy, so beautiful. It could provide her kids with the idyllic childhood she so longed for them to experience. Well, once the work was done.

If it was ever done.

And that was the problem wasn't it? How was she ever going to find the time to do it all?

She closed her eyes, too tired to try to work it out now. It would all have to wait. She'd had enough for today.

The loud rapping on the car window made her jump and she sat up, her heart thumping.

'What the—!' Seeing Jackson Wade peering in at her, her fury sparked. 'Are you mad?' She wound down the window and glared at him. 'What do you think you're doing? You nearly gave me a heart attack.'

He looked strangely relieved. 'You're all right then. I was worried.'

'Worried? About what?' Abbie swallowed, suddenly noticing that Bertie was standing beside him, his expression one of tearful concern. 'Bertie, are you all right? What's the matter?'

'Abb— Dr Sawdon, you do realise the time?'

She glanced at the clock on the dashboard and paled. 'Oh, my God! How did that happen?'

Twenty-five past three! Isla would be on the school bus already and she hadn't even set off to collect Poppy yet!

'I'm sorry, I must have...' Her voice trailed off and she flushed with shame. 'I was here early, really I was.'

'I know. One of the parents told us when we were standing at the door waiting. She said your car was parked up and had been when she walked through the gates. It worried me so I thought I'd come and check up on you.'

'Bertie, I'm ever so sorry.' She felt tears prick her eyes and blinked them away. How could she have fallen asleep, for goodness' sake?

Bertie shrugged. 'Shall I get in?'

'What? Oh, sorry, yes.' She released the child locks and Mr Wade opened the back door so that Bertie could climb in and fasten himself into his child seat. Abbie twisted around, checking he was doing it properly.

'It won't happen again,' she promised, not sure if she was making that promise to Bertie, Mr Wade, or herself.

'Dr Sawdon—Abbie—are you sure you're well enough to drive?' Mr Wade leaned into the car, his face showing his anxiety. 'You look exhausted.'

'I'm fine, really I am. I just...' She swallowed down the tears and pushed her hair away from her face. 'I just have a lot to do that's all. It's Isla's birthday and I'm supposed to be taking them all out for tea, and I haven't even picked Poppy up from Folly Farm yet.'

'I wish there was something I could do to help.' His voice was soft, and she could hear the concern in it. 'I know it's not much in the scheme of things, but if you change your mind about the house I'm more than happy to—'

'Really, it's fine.' She wound up the window and

started the engine, biting her lip in an effort not to cry. Isla would be panicking if she was late again, and Abbie really couldn't deal with her anxious questions and inevitable anger.

Isla.

She thought about her daughter's impassioned outburst and her obvious loathing for The Gables. If there was something she could do to make her happy, wasn't it her duty to do it?

Abbie hesitated then wound down the window. 'Mr Wade!'

Jackson Wade, who had turned and started to head back to the school building, stopped and looked round.

'Maybe—maybe if you're really certain, I could take you up on that offer.'

He walked back to the car and folded his arms, considering her. 'Are you sure?'

'Not really.' She gave a half laugh. 'But you're right. I need help and no one else is offering.' She looked him up and down, unable to hide her doubts. 'And you really know how to decorate and stuff? Really?'

He nodded. 'I really do. Look, why don't I tackle the front gates and your hallway first, just to see what you think. If you decide I'm not as capable as I think I am we can forget it, but if I do a good job, well maybe I can help with some of the other rooms. Like I said, it's something I enjoy doing.'

'I remember,' she said ruefully. 'Bringing order out of chaos.'

'Hmm.' He looked embarrassed and she thought maybe he wasn't as pompous as she'd assumed. He'd made a kind offer after all, and he certainly didn't have to.

'I suppose it wouldn't hurt to let you loose on the hallway,' she said. 'Not like it's complicated, like the bathroom would be.'

She was sure she saw his mouth twitch in amusement. 'I take it your bathroom needs doing too?'

Abbie sighed. 'To be honest, nearly every room in the house needs doing, but the hallway and bathroom are my pet hates right now. The hallway is the first thing anyone coming to the house sees and it's a disgrace. As for the bathroom—' She shuddered. 'The kids have been sneaking in to use the small one off my bedroom and I can't say I blame them. I won't use the main bathroom either. It's disgusting. No matter how much I scrub it and clean it, it's got this awful dingy, grubby feel to it.'

'Hmm. Well, maybe I could tackle that along with the hallway,' he said. 'But the gates need putting up at the front first. The children's safety is the priority. Anyway, leave it with me.'

Why was he being so kind to her? It was a bit bewildering, but Abbie was in no position to turn him down. 'And you really don't mind taking time out of your summer holidays, Mr Wade?'

'Not if you promise to call me Jackson,' he said. 'And no, not at all. Give me a call next week and tell me what day you want me round.'

'You may regret this,' she told him, surprised when he merely laughed.

She manoeuvred the car out of the car park and

drove as fast as she dared to Folly Farm, where Janie already had Poppy ready and waiting for her.

'Thought you'd be in a rush,' she explained. 'Taking Isla out for her birthday tea aren't you?'

That was something to look forward to, thought Abbie. She had a feeling her daughter wouldn't appreciate the effort at all. Maybe when she told her that the hallway, at least, was about to be decorated at last, she would cheer up. Providing of course that Jackson Wade really was up to the job. Thinking of his soft hands she really couldn't imagine that he was the handy type.

Maybe this was going to be yet another big mistake.

***

'If it wasn't so tragic it would be the funniest thing I've heard all week.' Tyler paused in his task of chopping a red pepper. 'But this is you we're talking about, and we all know where this could lead. How on earth did she manage to con you into it?'

Jackson scowled at his brother. 'She didn't con me into anything. For your information I offered. She clearly needs help, and I can provide that help. With a bit of assistance from you of course.'

'Might have known I'd get dragged into it,' Tyler grumbled.

'It's nothing much,' Jackson assured him. 'Her dishwasher needs plumbing in, but I can manage that myself.' He hesitated. 'It's just that, she's probably going to need a new bathroom suite—'

'What? Oh, so nothing much at all then!'

'It might not happen yet, and if it does it won't take you long will it? And I'll pay you the going rate. Come on, who else am I going to ask, if not the best plumber in Yorkshire?'

'Flattery will get you nowhere,' his brother said firmly.

'But you'll do it, right?'

'Of course he'll do it.' Jackson's sister-in-law, Jeannie, wiped away tears as she diced onions on the big, wooden chopping board, 'And at mate's rates too. It's the least he can do. I think it's really kind of you. Not many men would volunteer the way you have. I'm impressed.'

Jackson squirmed, feeling suddenly uncomfortable. 'It's only a gate. And a hallway,' he muttered. 'And maybe a bathroom.'

'Only, he says. And that's for now,' Tyler said. 'Are we taking bets on what comes next? Wow, she saw you coming.'

'Don't be mean,' Jeannie told him. 'I'm sure she's really nice. From what Jackson has told us, it can't be easy for her, eating humble pie and accepting help from her son's teacher of all people. And it's not even as if they got off to a good start is it?'

'You can say that again.' Jackson puffed out his cheeks, remembering their tricky blind date and all that had followed since. 'I don't really know how I got involved in all this.'

Tyler lowered the knife and turned to face him, his brow furrowed. 'Don't you? Bet I could hazard a guess.'

Jackson decided a change of subject was called for. He put down his cup of coffee and pushed away from the worktop he'd been lounging against. 'Do you two need a hand, by the way? Here I am, watching you do all the work. Sorry.'

Jeannie and Tyler exchanged glances.

'Talk about deflection,' Jeannie said. 'I can finish up in here. Why don't you two leave me to it?'

Jackson groaned inwardly. He knew what that meant. Jeannie was basically telling his brother to take Jackson away and give him "the talk". Or yet another variation on it.

Sure enough, Tyler picked up his own coffee and nodded at Jackson. 'Living room?'

'Really?'

'Oh I think so, don't you?'

Jackson knew when he was beaten. Giving Jeannie a despairing look he took his drink and followed his brother through to the living room which, to his relief, was unusually neat and tidy. Sometimes when he visited it was a horrible mess of children's toys and books, and the floor was often littered with Lego bricks. At least he could relax today, since his brother's boys were at a friend's house for a sleepover.

Lounging on the recliner, his brother sipped coffee and eyed him sternly.

Jackson perched on the sofa and waited. He knew what was coming.

'So,' said Tyler, 'should I be worried?'

How to respond to that? Jackson felt a flash of irritation. He wished his brother would stop seeing him as some sort of wounded, vulnerable charity case, who needed his help and guidance every five minutes. It was a bit galling, especially since Tyler was four years younger than him. It made him feel stupid, needy. And he wasn't.

'I don't know why you worry,' he said slowly. 'I've told you before, I'm absolutely fine.'

'So if I was to tip the contents of the boys' toy box onto the carpet, put this coffee cup down without a coaster underneath it, and leave the dishes scattered over the draining board after we've eaten, it wouldn't bother you in the slightest?'

Jackson tutted. 'That's just being a slob. You couldn't stand that, and I'm pretty sure Jeannie would have a fit.'

Tyler laughed. 'Well, probably,' he admitted, 'but you know where I'm going with this don't you?'

'Where you always go,' Jackson said, narrowing his eyes. 'Over the top.'

'Come on, Jackson. Think about this. You barely know this woman yet suddenly you're offering to do up her house for her. For nothing! I mean, what's wrong with you? Don't you see what you're doing?'

Jackson set his coffee down on the table. He had half a mind to put it on the wood without using a coaster, but when it came to it he couldn't bring himself to do it. He felt a stab of frustration at his own behaviour but pushed it away, intent on proving his brother wrong.

'There's nothing wrong with offering to help someone out. I don't see what's wrong with offering to decorate the house. It's something I enjoy doing. You know that.'

'And it's not as if you have anything else to do?' Tyler sighed. 'All I'm saying is, don't fall into the old pattern okay? Be honest, if she didn't have the kids would you have been so keen to help her?'

Jackson's hand traced the line of his scarred lip, the way it always did when he was tense or deep in thought. He remembered his brother pointing that out to him once and dropped his hand hastily. 'Maybe,' he hedged.

Tyler shook his head, clearly exasperated. 'I doubt it very much! Look, I know you're only trying to do what's right for those kids, but you must remember they're not your responsibility. You're not obligated in any way.'

'For goodness' sake! I know they're not my responsibility. Okay, so maybe I want to help give them a better home, but what's wrong with that? Anyone would feel the same surely? I'm just filling in some spare time over the summer holidays doing something I enjoy. It's my project that's all. There's nothing more to it than that.'

'You're sure about that? Because honestly, I'm only saying this because—well, you know—I… you know. You know that don't you?'

Jackson's tension ebbed away. 'Aw, admit it. You love me.'

Tyler pulled a face. 'Oh, shut up. So what if I do? Look, I just don't want you to take that role on again. That's all. If this woman is so irresponsible—'

Jackson felt a pang of guilt for Abbie. 'She's not!

That is, not in the way you mean. I honestly think she's just taken on too much. I'm sure she loves her children, and at least they go to school every day and she collects them on time. Mostly. The very fact that she's agreed to accept my help surely proves that she's not...'

His voice trailed off and Tyler gave him a sympathetic smile. 'I'm sure she's not like *her*, Jackson. I'm willing to give her the benefit of the doubt, of course I am. I'm just concerned that you don't end up worrying yourself sick about something that's really none of your business. I don't think it will help you, falling back into that position again. Taking on that role. I'm scared it will make your anxieties even worse.'

'I don't have anxieties!'

'Okay, okay. Not anxieties then.' Tyler shrugged. 'What do you call your behaviour? This overwhelming urge to make everything neat and tidy? To have cupboards that are full-to-bursting with food you rarely eat? To have complete order in your life?'

Jackson said nothing, not able to think of a response that would make his brother pipe down once and for all.

'I suppose it's a waste of time asking if you've arranged counselling yet?'

When Jackson didn't respond he gave a big sigh. 'Course it is. Well, you can't say I haven't tried.'

Jackson felt a stirring of sympathy for his brother who, after all, was the only one who really understood him. He knew Tyler loved him deeply and just wanted him to be happy. He wasn't lecturing him to be annoying, even if that's how it came across.

'I honestly don't feel I need counselling,' he said quietly. 'I'm getting on with my life just fine, and I'm better than I was. Really, I am!' he protested, seeing the look of doubt on his brother's face. 'This is just a summer project to keep me occupied throughout the school holidays. What's the alternative? Six weeks on my own, doing nothing?'

'You have friends,' Tyler protested. 'You said you were going to be best man at Ash's wedding, so that must mean you've got a pretty close relationship. And you have your music. Why don't you join some sort of society or club? Volunteer to play the piano at a nursing home or something? There must be something you can do that doesn't involve you taking on the responsibility of someone else's family.'

'Tyler, I'm not taking on the responsibility. I'm just helping, that's all. Please don't worry about me.'

Tyler's eyes were full of anxiety, which made Jackson feel terrible.

'I can't help it,' Tyler said. 'I'm always going to worry about you. You're my big brother, and I owe you everything.'

'You don't owe me anything,' Jackson assured him wearily. How many times had they had this conversation?

'We both know that's not true. God only knows where I'd have been without you. I'll never be able to pay you back so please, don't ask me to stop worrying because you're my brother and I—yeah, well, we've already established I care about you. I'd do anything to see you happy.'

'I *am* happy,' Jackson said, wanting nothing more than to take the burden of fear away from Tyler. 'Now drink your coffee and stop being such a wuss.'

Tyler laughed. 'Yeah, all right. Less of the cheek.'

Jeannie popped her head round the door. 'Safe to come in?'

'Of course. Lecture is over,' Jackson told her.

'Glad to hear it. Did it do any good?'

'Well, at least now I know my brother cares.'

'As if that was ever in any doubt,' she said, glancing affectionately at her husband. 'The kids and I come a very poor second to you, Jackson.'

He was quite certain that wasn't true, but it was nice of her to say so. Tyler, Jeannie, and the children were a tight family unit, and he couldn't be happier that his brother had managed to overcome everything and make such a wonderful life for himself. He knew that all Tyler wanted was the same for him.

Jackson wanted to believe that his time hadn't passed, that he hadn't missed his chance, but there was a nagging little voice in his head that kept telling him he would never have what his brother had. The truth was, however much he tried to reassure Tyler, he knew he had issues, and he really couldn't imagine any woman in her right mind wanting to deal with them.

Chapter 8

Jackson's first day at The Gables didn't get off to the best start. He arrived promptly at eight o'clock that Monday morning to discover a pair of brand-new wooden gates already installed at the entrance to the front drive. He'd planned for the gates to be his first job, so he wasn't best pleased about it, and evidently Abbie could read his annoyance in his face, as her welcoming smile when she opened the front door soon faltered.

'I see someone beat me to it.' He hoped he'd managed to keep the irritation out of his voice, but even he could hear the edge to his tone.

Abbie looked embarrassed. 'Oh, you mean the gates. Well the thing is—look, come in. Let's start the day with a cuppa before I have to go to work.' She yelled up the stairs, 'Isla! Bring Poppy down please. I need to get you all ready or I'll be late for surgery.'

Trying not to scowl, Jackson followed her into the hallway, only to be pounced upon by two noisy, excitable dogs.

'Albus! Willow! Get down,' Abbie called, not bothering to stop and drag them away from him.

'They're only saying hello to you, Mr Wade.' Bertie

trudged down the stairs, his eyes heavy with sleep and his hair ruffled as usual. He was wearing Avengers pyjamas and had clearly just tumbled out of bed. 'I'm starving, Mum. What's for breakfast?'

The black Labrador trotted after him as he shuffled into the kitchen. The Cavalier on the other hand wasn't going to let Jackson off so lightly. She stood squarely and watched him through bulbous brown eyes, yapping continuously. Jackson decided that any length of time in her company was going to be torture and wondered if he was strong enough to face it.

'Willow, come on! Breakfast!'

Willow turned at the sound of Bertie's voice, then glanced back at Jackson. She seemed to be torn between the twin pleasures of food and tormenting her guest. Luckily food won, and Willow eventually trotted into the kitchen on her dainty little feet.

Jackson groaned inwardly and followed her. Now that the dogs had shut up he could hear the music blaring from the radio and all his nerves jangled in protest.

Abbie was busy at the worktop, pouring cereal, popping teabags in cups and buttering toast, while doing a little jig to the music.

'Have you eaten?' she enquired.

Jackson confirmed that he'd had breakfast and didn't want any toast and jam or Coco Pops if it was all the same to her.

'I can see you're annoyed,' she said, turning to face him as she handed Bertie his cereal, 'but I was trying to do you a favour.'

'Funny,' Jackson said, 'because I thought it was me who was doing you one.'

Abbie's eyes narrowed. 'I'm well aware that you're doing me a favour, Jackson. All I was trying to do was give you one less thing to worry about. Xander had been having some fences installed at the farm because of the alpacas—'

Jackson held up his hand to interrupt her. 'Sorry, did you say alpacas?'

She rolled her eyes. 'Long story. So, the man who was doing the fence got talking to us, and Xander was telling him about the work I was having done and about me needing double gates for the front of the house. Before I knew it he'd offered to whip round and give me a quote. I didn't like to say no because he was so nice, and Xander said he was very reasonable. Anyway, he turned up and gave me a good price and said he would fit me in the next day as a special favour, since I was a friend of Xander's and had a toddler and dogs to keep safe, so...' She gave him an apologetic look. 'It seemed easier to go along with it, and I did think it was at least one thing ticked off your list. I'm sorry if I've annoyed you. I was trying to help.'

Jackson felt a prickling of shame. It was her house, her money. She had every right to employ whoever she chose to help her, and he had no call to be so rude to her. He had to admit that it had sent him into panic mode. He'd had his list all carefully written out, knew exactly what he was supposed to be doing that day, and finding out that things had changed had thrown him. He didn't like change, but that was his problem, not

Abbie's.

'It's fine,' he assured her. 'You're right. It will save me a job. I was going to measure up and then go to a wood yard I know of near Farthingdale, but I can be getting on with something else now. It's not a problem. Besides, the main thing is that the gates are in place. I feel a lot better knowing your children and dogs can't get onto that lane.'

Abbie rewarded him with a beaming smile, and he was surprised to realise how much pleasure her approval gave him.

'Oh, that's great. So before we do anything else you must have a drink. Tea or coffee?'

Feeling a bit stupid for making such a fuss, he reluctantly agreed to have a coffee and sat down at the table opposite Bertie, who was slurping Coco Pops and watching him warily.

'Everything okay, Bertie?'

Bertie shrugged. 'S'pose.'

'You don't sound too sure about it.'

'Well, it's a bit weird that's all. I mean, you're my teacher. Feels funny having you at home.'

'I'm not your teacher any longer,' Jackson pointed out. 'As of last Friday school is out, and your teacher is Miss Turner.'

Bertie pulled a face. 'She stinks.'

'Bertie!' Abbie looked mortified and Jackson hid a smile.

'I'll pretend I didn't hear that,' he said, although he knew what Bertie meant. Kirsty Turner smoked like a chimney and the smell of nicotine followed her wherever she went. It wasn't pleasant.

Isla pushed open the door, her face set in a scowl. She wore a blue stripy dressing gown over lilac pyjamas, despite the warm weather, and held the youngest child's hand in hers.

'Why do we have to go to Folly Farm?' she demanded. 'Can't I stay here and get some peace?'

Peace? Jackson wondered how Isla could consider The Gables peaceful, what with the radio blasting out and the dogs constantly barking and yapping. Frankly his head was already beginning to hurt.

'Because, my angel,' Abbie said, after she'd dropped a kiss on the cross-looking teenager's head and scooped Poppy into her arms for a hug, 'You're all too young to be left unsupervised and Janie has very kindly offered to take care of you all. Now, Poppy, egg and soldiers?'

Poppy nodded and her blonde curls bounced. 'And juice.'

'Juice coming right up.' Abbie fastened her into a highchair, eyeing Isla warily. 'You okay, Isla?'

Isla shrugged and slumped onto a chair. 'S'pose. Was looking forward to a lie-in for once. You shouldn't be working full-time. We don't see you often enough, and besides it's too much for you since—'

'If you want us to live on the poverty line that's fine,' Abbie interjected. 'But if you want a decent lifestyle then I have to work for it.'

'*Decent lifestyle*? When does that start then? Besides, you know Dad would help if you needed money. He said so enough times.' She twisted a strand of hair between her fingers. 'He doesn't like you working full-time either. He's worried that—'

'Isla! Will you just accept that you're going to Folly Farm and that's that, for goodness' sake!'

Isla tutted and gave Jackson an appealing look. 'Can't we stay here since you're going to be about? You're a responsible adult.'

'How kind of you to say so,' he replied, crossing his fingers that Abbie would dismiss the idea out of hand.

'Mr Wade is here to work on the house, Isla,' Abbie pointed out. 'He's not the hired childminder. Now that's enough of that subject, thank you very much.'

Isla tutted and glared at Jackson, as if it were all his fault that she had to go to Folly Farm. 'You're here early enough,' she observed. 'You must be mad giving up your holidays to come here to do more work.'

'I don't mind at all, and I thought I'd come here early since I have a lot to be getting on with,' he replied, trying not to take offence that she clearly wasn't keen on his presence.

'Not the gates,' she told him. 'So that's saved you some time. How long are you planning to be here anyway?'

'Isla!' Abbie gave her daughter a despairing look.

'I'm only asking,' Isla protested.

'As long as it takes,' Jackson replied, determined not to rise to the bait. 'We want to get this house in some sort of order don't we?'

Isla tucked her hair behind her ears. 'Well, *we* do,' she said. 'Not sure why it matters to you though.'

'I'm just doing a friend a favour,' Jackson assured her.

'And Mum's your *friend,* is she?'

Bertie looked puzzled. 'Are you and Mr Wade friends, Mum?'

'I wouldn't have thought you'd have wanted to do anything for her after your awful date the other week,' Isla announced.

Abbie spun round, butter knife in her hand. 'What are you talking about?'

Isla smirked. 'I heard you talking to Rachel about it at the farm. You said it was a disaster and that neither of you could wait to leave. You said it was bad enough being set up with Bertie's teacher, but if you'd known he was as miserable off duty as he was in the classroom you'd never have bothered.'

'Oh, for goodness' sake!' Abbie looked distraught. 'Why do you have to be so—so—'

'Honest?'

Jackson decided to put Abbie out of her agony. 'It's okay. Your mum's right. I was pretty miserable that night. I felt pushed into going on the date and I wasn't in the mood for it. I wasn't good company.'

'Yet here you are.' Isla clearly wasn't convinced.

'Here I am,' he acknowledged.

'What I don't get,' she continued, 'is why. If you didn't get on that night, why are you here helping Mum out now? What's in it for you?'

Abbie closed her eyes as Bertie stared up at Jackson, obviously trying his best to follow the conversation but not quite sure what to make of it.

Poppy let out a bellow of rage.

'Mummy, want juice! And egg and shoulders!'

'Sorry, sweetie. Coming right up.' Abbie turned away, probably relieved to have something to distract her, while Jackson faced down the defiant-looking teenager.

'I apologised to your mum for the way I behaved on our date, and we've had a few conversations since then. When I visited that day, I could see The Gables needed some work doing and, as I was at a loose end during the school holidays, I offered to help. Simple as that.'

'But what can you actually do?' Isla persisted. 'You're a teacher. What do you know about real work?'

Jackson heard Abbie make a funny sort of noise and wondered if she was smothering a laugh or a cry of despair.

'It may surprise you,' he said calmly, 'but teachers have lives outside the classroom. I renovated my current flat, and I've worked on a couple of properties before that. I buy them cheaply and improve them, then move up the ladder each time. I enjoy it. I find DIY very soothing.'

Isla folded her arms and pursed her lips but said nothing.

Bertie blinked as if he'd just caught up with the conversation. 'You went on a *date* with *my mum*?'

The shock and disgust in his voice was too much. Jackson tried his best to hide his amusement, but it proved impossible. Despite his best efforts he started to laugh.

Abbie, her eyes wide with surprise, began to laugh too, and Poppy whooped with delight, momentarily forgetting she was desperate for juice. This seemed to be the signal for both dogs to start jumping around and barking again unfortunately.

Bertie grinned. Jackson suspected that his pride at making them all laugh had surpassed his disgust at his teacher's friendship with his mother. Only Isla continued to stare at him, her face showing nothing but mistrust.

'What would you like for breakfast, Isla?' Abbie said, laying a hand on her daughter's shoulder.

'Scrambled eggs on toast,' Isla muttered.

'Please,' Abbie reminded her.

Isla rolled her eyes. 'Please. So,' she said, leaning forward suddenly and resting her elbows on the table, 'what are you actually going to be doing here? The gate's done so what's your job now?'

'Well, the hallway's the real reason I'm here. Having said that, your mum's desperate to get the main bathroom sorted out as she thinks it's a complete eyesore.' He reached into his rucksack and pulled out some brochures.

'What are those?' Isla queried.

'They're for your mum to take to work today, so when she's on her lunch break she can look through them and choose a new bathroom suite.'

Abbie's face lit up. 'Ooh, Isla, isn't it exciting?'

Isla tutted but Jackson thought he detected a brief flash of pleasure in her expression.

'I thought it would be cheaper and quicker if you went for an off-the-shelf suite from the local DIY shop, otherwise you could be waiting ages if you went with a specialist company. My brother's promised to do any plumbing work,' he told them all. 'He has his own plumbing business and he's on standby.'

'So when you said you liked doing up houses, you meant your brother did the work and you just paid him?'

Jackson silently counted to ten. Isla was evidently determined to take a swipe at everything he said.

'Not at all. There are some things, however, I won't mess with—electrics being the main thing. As for plumbing and joinery, I've dabbled and I've assisted, but we're talking about a new bathroom that your mum will be paying for, and I don't want to risk damaging anything. I'll happily assist if needed, but I don't see why I should take a chance on ruining things when I have a reliable tradesman to call on. Do you?'

Isla stared at him for a moment, and he waited for a sarcastic comeback. He gave an inward sigh of relief when she nodded and said, 'S'pose not.'

'Good. So,' he said, trying to sound cheerful, even though the effort of being around disapproving children and two noisy dogs, while sitting in an extremely messy kitchen with the radio blaring out pop music, was already exhausting him, 'I'm going to start in the hallway today, as we agreed, Abbie.'

'What are you doing to the hallway?' asked Bertie, clearly interested.

'Firstly,' Abbie said, 'get rid of that awful old-fashioned wallpaper. You should be very glad about that, Isla,' she remarked, 'since you so forcefully pointed out how much you hate it.'

Isla looked a bit shamefaced and Jackson mentally

congratulated Abbie on finally getting one over on her petulant teenage daughter.

'Isla! Not at the table please. We've had this discussion.'

Jackson saw Isla roll her eyes and shove a mobile phone back in her dressing gown pocket.

'Nice phone,' he said, trying to be pleasant.

She tutted. 'Yeah, Dad got it for my birthday. Not that I ever get the chance to use it,' she added, glaring at her mother.

Abbie's face clearly said that she wasn't impressed with Isla's present.

'You're not turning into one of those girls who has their phone welded to their hand. You know what I think about it all. I'm furious with your father for buying it for you and I'll be telling him so when I see him. We'd agreed... Well, anyway, the point is there's a time and a place for them and at the breakfast table isn't one of them.'

She placed a plastic cup of juice, and a plate with a peeled, soft-boiled egg in an egg cup and a few strips of bread and butter, on the tray of Poppy's highchair, earning an appreciative smile from her youngest daughter.

'Egg and shoulders!'

The tension in Abbie's face lifted and she ruffled Poppy's hair affectionately. 'That's right, Poppy. Eat it all up, there's a good girl.'

Jackson felt a stirring of affection for the little girl, who looked so delighted with her breakfast that she quite melted his heart. Her little hand closed around one of the "shoulders" and she dunked it into the egg yolk, before cramming it into her mouth, a blissful expression on her face. She was a sweetie really—even if she did eat beetles and dog food, given half a chance.

'Don't worry,' Abbie whispered. She'd obviously noticed him watching Poppy and mistaken his look for concern, 'I'll never ask you to babysit. Janie has very kindly said she'll have all three children during the holidays. It was such a relief I can't begin to tell you.'

He imagined it had been, but he couldn't help feeling that the children deserved better. Isla clearly didn't want to go to Folly Farm, and since she'd been wrenched away from her old schoolfriends in Hull it seemed unfair to him that she'd got nothing more to look forward to during the summer holidays than cleaning out animals and hanging round with her eight-year-old brother and his friend.

But he couldn't get involved. Tyler was right, they weren't his responsibility. He just had to decorate the hallway, spruce up the bathroom, and leave the Sawdons to get on with their own lives, while he got on with his.

***

'Are you still looking at those brochures?'

Holly leaned over and snatched one of them from the table where Abbie was sitting, sandwich in one hand, flicking through a glossy catalogue of bathroom suites and shower units.

'Leave her alone.' Joan, who although only working

at the practice on a temporary basis felt like one of the team, gave Abbie a knowing look. 'Tricky business, isn't it? Like choosing a kitchen. Always worried that you choose the wrong one. I know I did.'

'What? Worry, or choose the wrong kitchen?' Holly demanded, plonking herself down next to Abbie and opening the brochure she'd taken.

'Got the wrong kitchen,' Joan admitted. She put the cup she was washing on the draining board and sighed, gazing at the wall ahead as if seeing her kitchen laid out before her. 'Dunno what I was thinking, honest I don't. All that dark wood in my poky little house. Should've gone for something lighter. But there you go. You live and learn. How did your Isla's birthday tea go, love? Did she have a nice time?'

Abbie gritted her teeth. Yes, she had, and had forgiven her mother for everything it seemed, when she'd opened her presents over tea at The Hare and Moon pub in Kearton Bay and discovered the mobile phone.

When they'd got home Nick had video called Isla to wish her a happy birthday, which had put a big smile on their daughter's face, and Abbie had presented her with a birthday cake which, admittedly, she hadn't baked herself but had purchased from Spill the Beans. Even so Isla had seemed grateful and pleased, so Abbie had gone to bed that evening feeling relieved and a lot happier with herself.

She smiled at Joan. 'Yes thanks. She had a great birthday.'

Holly turned the pages of the brochure, her

expression wistful. 'I wouldn't mind any of these. My bathroom's a right dump. Must have been fitted about thirty years ago now. Honestly, it should be featured on the Antiques Road Show.'

'Well, get your landlord to replace it then,' Joan said.

Holly laughed. 'Yeah, right. Have you met my landlord? He doesn't even do repairs, never mind replacing something that still works, even if it does look like it should be condemned.'

'I've never understood that mentality,' Abbie said. 'Surely if you've invested money in a house you want to keep it looking nice and in good condition? It's your own investment you're neglecting otherwise.'

'Not with the amount of rent *he* charges,' Holly said. 'Reckon I've paid off his flipping mortgage for him twice over.' She looked longingly at Abbie's chicken sandwich. 'Is that nice? Looks ever so tasty.'

'You're not still on this daft diet?' Joan clucked like a mother hen, all concern, and hurried over to the table. 'Look, I'm off to Spill the Beans in a sec. Let me bring you something back, eh?'

Holly shook her head. 'No thanks. I'm determined to lose this weight if it kills me.'

'It might just do that,' Abbie said. 'Dieting doesn't mean starving, Holly. You should eat lunch. Here, have this other sandwich.'

'Aarrggh! Don't offer me that! It's got mayonnaise on it. I love mayonnaise.' Holly pulled a face and quickly snatched up the brochure again. 'So, which bathroom do you have in mind?'

Tutting, Joan exchanged worried glances with

Abbie. 'Right, well I'm off for me dinner. See you in half an hour. You sure you don't want anything from the café, Holly?'

'Quite sure,' Holly assured her.

Shaking her head, Joan left the kitchen.

Abbie felt guilty eating in front of Holly, but she was starving. It had been a busy morning in the surgery, and she'd been relieved to have only one visit to carry out. It meant she could hurry back to the practice and eat her sandwiches in peace while trying to make a final decision on which bathroom suite to choose.

The problem was settling on one. There were so many styles to choose from.

'I love that one,' Holly said, pointing to a roll-top bath with an ornate central tap.

'Is that what you'd have in your house?' Abbie enquired.

Holly shook her head. 'No. My bathroom's too small. I live in one of those little cottages at the opposite side of the village to you, just before you reach the sign for Bramblewick. You know, Honeysuckle Terrace.'

Abbie wrinkled her nose, thinking. 'Is that near Mrs Drake's house?' she said. 'The lady with the leg ulcers?'

Holly smiled. 'Yes, Lulu. She's in Cuckoo Nest Cottage a bit further along on its own. My cottage is the end terrace just before her place.'

Abbie nodded, able to place Holly's home in her mind at last. She could see why Holly had said it was small. Those cottages were basically two-up two-downs.

'How long have you lived there?' she asked, taking her second sandwich from its pack, and trying not to feel awkward that Holly wasn't eating.

'All my life. Ooh, I like that one. Very swish.' Holly jabbed her finger at a glossy, modern bath. 'Mind you, not with those taps.'

'All your life? I thought you said it was rented?'

'Oh it is. Mum and Dad used to rent it but then they got divorced and Dad moved down south with his new woman, so Mum took over the tenancy. Then when she remarried, she moved to Whitby with her new husband and the landlord let me take over as tenant.'

'He sounds quite reasonable,' Abbie said, surprised.

'Old Mr Sowter? He was. Lovely old bloke. But he went and snuffed it didn't he? His son sold it to a property company about five years ago and they're not lovely at all. Put the rent up every year too. Ah, well.'

Abbie surveyed her with compassion. Poor Holly. She sounded resigned to it all, but it must be a worry. There wasn't much security for tenants, and if you got an unsympathetic landlord she could imagine life could be very difficult.

'So come on, have you got any favourites?' Holly asked.

Abbie blinked and focused on the brochures. 'Yes. I like this simple, modern suite with the built-in cupboards.'

Holly leaned in and had a good look. 'Yeah, I like that look. Elegant without being fussy. The cupboards are a good idea. You have three kids don't you? And two dogs. That's a lot of mud and dirt to wash away. I reckon you'll need storage for industrial sized bottles of shampoo. Next, of course, you have to choose taps and flooring and tiles.'

Abbie pushed the brochures away with a sigh. 'Oh, not now. I'll talk to Jackson later. See what he thinks.'

Holly grinned and nudged her. 'Jackson, eh? Starting to rely on Mr Grumpy, are we?'

'Of course not! Just another opinion, that's all.' Abbie blushed and took a large bite of her sandwich. 'Honestly, you and your imagination,' she managed, despite a mouthful of chicken.

'All right, all right. Just joking.' Holly gave her a quizzical look. 'So, he's not as bad as you thought he was, despite that disastrous first date?'

Abbie swallowed her food and gave Holly a hard stare. 'It wasn't a first date. It was an only date. A one-off. We're just friends. Not even that really,' she considered. 'Just doing each other a favour.'

'And what favour are you doing *him*, Dr Sawdon?' Holly teased.

Abbie tutted. 'Giving him something to do with his time. Six weeks can go on forever if you haven't got a job to do, and he doesn't seem to have any hobbies or anything so...'

'Except the piano.'

'Sorry?'

'He plays the piano. Didn't you know? He's in charge of the music at school. When Izzy and Ash put on the school play at Christmas, Jackson organised the soundtrack and played the piano for the carols. He does the music in assemblies too, and any events that need a piano player. Izz said he's very good, and apparently he loves it.'

'Well,' she said. 'I never knew that about him. Interesting.'

'Aw,' Holly giggled, nudging her, 'you're finding out new things about him all the time.'

'Oh, shut up,' Abbie said, laughing despite herself. 'Here, you pick me out some decent tiles. I'll put the kettle on before the madness starts again.'

Chapter 9

Woodchip, thought Jackson, was the very devil to shift, and this stuff seemed to have been in place for decades. He was in the hallway stripping off the last of the wallpaper, which had proved to be a much more troublesome task than he'd expected. It was practically welded to the walls, and there were multiple layers of paint on top of it by the looks of things.

Jackson had taught himself to skim and plaster, and it seemed his skills were going to be needed. Along with much of the wallpaper, great lumps of wall had come off too. Abbie didn't want the hallway repapering, so if it was going to be an emulsion job, the walls would have to be repaired first.

'You're making a proper hash of that aren't you?'

He gritted his teeth as Isla plonked herself down on the bottom step and stared up at him. He was halfway up the flight of stairs, his forehead prickling with sweat as he worked the paper scraper. The whole wall had been steamed but it hadn't made it much easier. If he'd known, he mused, he might never have offered.

'Looks like the paper's been on for years,' he said, trying not to show his annoyance.

'Huh.' One word, but it was loaded with meaning.

Jackson stopped scraping the wall and stared down at her. 'If you think it's so easy, why don't you come and show me how it's done?'

Isla stared back. 'No, you're all right thanks.'

He smirked. 'Talk's cheap. Actions are what count. If you're not going to try it yourself, don't sit there criticising me.'

'All right, Mr Touchy,' she said, leaping up and holding out her hand. 'Give me that scraper then.'

'Seriously?' He hadn't bargained on that. What would Abbie say if she got back and found he'd got her thirteen-year-old daughter labouring for him?

Then again, it might do Isla some good to have something constructive to do. Janie, apparently, had been unable to have the children that day as she had a routine hospital appointment, followed by a meeting of her local book club, so Abbie had tentatively asked Jackson if he would mind keeping an eye on the two eldest children. She'd arranged for her friend, Anna, to look after Poppy, which was something of a relief to him, as he couldn't imagine getting any work done at all with a toddler to see to.

After two days of peace, working alone in an empty house, the shock of having two children around had been immense.

Bertie had been cheerful enough, following him around, watching him scrape the paper, and asking questions. He'd just gone downstairs to load the dishwasher which Jackson had plumbed in the previous day, unable to bear the thought of all those dirty pots piling up a moment longer. At least, he thought, that would keep Bertie occupied for a short while. And reassuringly he hadn't heard any crash of falling dishes.

Isla, though, worried him. She seemed to have spent most of the day in her room, or moping around making sarcastic comments and sighing a lot.

He handed her the scraper. 'Now, just be careful how you do this. You don't want to dig it into the plaster and—'

Isla gave him a withering look. 'Are you serious? Have you seen the state of this wall? Besides, I *have* done this before you know.'

'You have?'

She climbed a couple of steps until she was standing on the one beneath his. 'At our old house. Dad wanted to get the nursery done for when Poppy arrived, so we all helped...'

Her voice trailed off and she turned to the wall and began working furiously.

'Whoa,' Jackson said, alarmed. 'It's not a race! Maybe your dad was in a hurry to get the nursery done but there's no great rush with this.'

She scowled. 'You want it doing, don't you? The sooner all these jobs are done, the sooner you can stop coming here.'

'Charming.' Jackson tried hard not to feel offended, but it wasn't easy. Isla seemed determined to dislike him. She radiated unhappiness, which saddened him. She was young and it was summer. She should be outside, having fun with her friends.

'Won't you be seeing your friends over the holidays?' he enquired, determined to make some sort of headway with her somehow.

'Doubt it,' she replied, scratching away at the wall, her brow furrowed as she worked.

'Why not?'

She flicked her hair back and tutted. 'Just won't.'

'Ah. You just won't. Right. I see.'

She gave him a sideways glance. 'What do you mean, you see? What's that supposed to mean?'

'Just that, obviously you haven't been here that long. You probably haven't made any friends at your new school yet.'

'I've made loads of friends actually,' she said. 'So that's all you know.'

'Sorry.' He stuck his hands in his pockets, wondering how to reach this spiky child. 'So, don't you want to meet up with them over the holidays then?'

She didn't reply, and he watched as she continued to work furiously, clearly venting some frustration on the wall.

'Well, while you're doing that, I'll just go and see how Bertie's getting on,' he said, realising he was getting nowhere fast with Isla.

Getting no response he smothered a sigh and headed downstairs into the kitchen. Bertie was happily rinsing plates under the tap, which rather impressed Jackson, who'd assumed the youngster would simply dump them in the dishwasher with all food residue in place.

'How's it going?' Jackson queried, plucking pieces of woodchip from his hair, and dropping them in the waste bin.

'I've stacked the cups,' Bertie said. 'That was easy. Flipping egg's hard to shift from these plates though.'

'You're doing a great job,' Jackson assured him. 'Maybe your mum will make you chief dishwasher-stacker.'

'I wouldn't bet on it.'

Jackson looked up and felt a flash of irritation upon seeing Isla peering into the dishwasher.

'I thought you were stripping wallpaper. That didn't last long.'

'I got bored.' She strolled towards him and handed him the scraper. 'You've put the cups in upside down,' she told Bertie.

'They're supposed to be upside down,' Jackson pointed out. 'Otherwise they'll just fill with water.'

'That's what I meant,' she said. 'Upside down to the way they're supposed to be stacked. He's put them the right way up.'

Bertie's brow wrinkled. 'Huh?'

'Look, I'll show you,' Isla said.

Bertie put the plate on the draining board, wiped his hands on his trousers and went over to have a look. As Isla showed her younger brother how to correctly position the cups in the upper rack, Jackson thought how patient she suddenly seemed. If only she would be this kind and reasonable all the time.

'Why don't you both leave the housework and go out into the garden with the dogs?' he suggested, aware that the sun was beating down outside, and they really ought to be getting some fresh air and Vitamin D.

Isla pushed her hair behind her ears and gave him

an incredulous look. 'Have you seen that garden? You may never find us again.' She narrowed her eyes. 'Unless that's the plan.'

Jackson grinned. 'Never thought of that, but now you mention it...' He glanced out of the window, realising that the grass that had already been overgrown when he'd first visited The Gables would now be practically waist-high on Bertie. The bushes and shrubs and trees gave the whole area a jungle feel. No wonder there was no sign of either Willow or Albus. 'Hmm. Great place to make a den though.'

Bertie's eyes widened. 'Did you ever make a den when you were little, Jackson?'

Had he ever made a den? He almost laughed out loud at the idea. He'd had other things to do when he was Bertie's age, and having fun wasn't one of them.

'Not really,' he said.

'Isla's going to make a treehouse,' Bertie informed him.

Jackson remembered only too well. 'Is she?' He glanced at Isla whose face had gone pink. 'Are you?'

'I only said I might,' she protested. 'It was just to shut him up.'

Jackson recalled that Abbie had said Isla wanted a treehouse herself, for some privacy if nothing else. When it came right down to it, moods and petulance aside, she was just a child and she'd been through a lot. Moving to a new area, a new school, two new homes in the space of a few months, and then there was the divorce. He considered for a moment. Poppy was only almost three after all. The divorce must be a fairly recent event.

He felt a stirring of compassion for Isla. That was an awful lot for a young girl to deal with in such a short space of time. If he was being honest, her spiky behaviour reminded him of his own teenage self. He'd been rude, petulant, and sulky, but that attitude had hidden a whole world of pain. He needed to give Isla the benefit of a doubt.

'I'm sure you'd make a great job of it,' he told her. 'Maybe you can start drawing up some designs?'

'Don't think so,' she muttered. She wandered over to the cupboards and threw open a door, peering inside. 'For god's sake!'

'What's up?' Bertie queried, his forehead puckered.

'There's nothing in again! Why doesn't she do a big shop? We're always running out of stuff to eat. I'm sick to death of cereal.' She turned to Bertie, her eyes wistful. 'Remember in Hull? We used to have crisps and biscuits in the house then, and yoghurts in the fridge, and fresh milk that hadn't gone off and there was always bread.'

'I suppose it's 'cos there was a shop nearby,' Bertie said sagely. 'If mum forgot anything she could just nip to the top of the street. It's a bit further here and she's busy all the time, isn't she?'

Isla folded her arms. 'Her memory's shocking. Do you think she's getting worse?'

Jackson surveyed her, his curiosity aroused. Isla sounded strained, the tone of her voice veering between belligerence and anxiety.

Bertie paused, plate in hand. 'What do you mean?

She's just tired isn't she?'

Isla bit her lip. 'Aren't we all?'

Bertie slotted the last plate into the dishwasher rack. 'Have you got any more jobs for me to do?' he asked. 'I can get a bin liner and pick up all the wallpaper off the stairs if you like.'

'That would be great,' Jackson said. 'You've been so helpful today, Bertie. Your mum will be proud of you when I tell her. We really appreciate it.'

Bertie beamed but Isla's eyes narrowed. 'What's with all the *we* stuff?'

Jackson stood stock still, not sure what she was implying. 'Pardon?'

'You! *We do appreciate it*! Since when were you and Mum, *we*?'

He tapped the palm of one hand with the wallpaper scraper and shuffled a little, feeling awkward. 'I didn't mean it like that. It's just a figure of speech, Isla. Nothing more.'

'Huh.' She sat at the table, looking suspicious. 'You don't want to get any ideas about Mum anyway. She's a nightmare to live with. I mean, look at this!' She waved a despairing arm that took in the whole of the run-down and undeniably cluttered kitchen. 'It would drive you mad. It drives me mad.'

'Mum's not a nightmare,' Bertie protested. 'She's lovely.'

Isla appeared not to have noticed him. 'And you don't even like dogs,' she added. 'I mean, as if you'd ever be able to live with us if you don't like dogs.'

'Are you going to live with us, Jackson?' Bertie

gasped.

Jackson felt the blood drain from his face. 'Live with you? What on earth are you talking about? Isla, I don't know what you think is going on here but all I'm doing is helping around the house because I've got some free time. Nothing more.'

'But you went on a date,' she pointed out.

'That was a blind date, set up by friends of ours. Neither of us particularly wanted to do it and we both agreed it wouldn't happen again. You don't have to worry.'

'I'm not worried,' she said, her bottom lip wobbling. 'Just saying that she's not your type. She's not any man's type really. She's in a world of her own half the time, that's what Dad always says about her.'

Jackson bit his lip. *Don't defend Abbie, and don't criticise or correct her ex-husband. This is none of your business.*

'Your mum's a good woman, Isla,' he said, feeling obliged to ignore the warning voice in his head. 'She's got a demanding job and she's trying to raise three children alone. It's not easy for her.'

'I never said it was,' she snapped.

'She's doing her absolute best for you. You do know that don't you?'

Bertie nodded. '*I* know.'

'I'm glad to hear it,' Jackson said.

Isla leapt to her feet. 'I never said she was a bad mother, did I?'

'Well, no you didn't exactly say that, but—'

'She's a brilliant mother. The best in the world. I would never say she wasn't, okay? Don't go putting words in my mouth! I love my mum, so just shut up!'

'I never—' Jackson's mouth fell open as Isla dashed out of the room. He heard her feet pounding on the stairs, then a door slammed upstairs. He shook his head slightly, not sure what had just happened.

'Don't worry about it,' Bertie said with a shrug. 'She often gets like that. Can I have a drink of juice now please?'

Chapter 10

Abbie couldn't help feeling it was desperately unfair that, on the very first day of her two-week holiday from work, she had to get up at the usual time rather than have a nice, long, lazy lie-in.

She wouldn't have felt so fed up about it if Poppy had risen early, but Poppy had never been one of those toddlers who woke at the crack of dawn and demanded to get up immediately. She often slept in until eight o'clock and Abbie would find herself in the unlikely position of having to wake her two-year-old up so that she could get her ready in time before heading off to work.

Bertie usually got up at around half past seven and Isla—well, Isla would stay in bed until lunchtime if she were allowed. Abbie herself was usually up and about by six, since she had three children to get ready for school, breakfasts to prepare, school runs, and dropping off a toddler at Folly Farm before going into work. It should have been a real treat for her to have two weeks off, but instead she found herself in the kitchen at quarter to eight, pouring tea for herself, Jackson, and a man called Lewis Palmer.

It was a knock on the front door that had pulled her

from her dreams and forced her downstairs, wrapping a dressing gown around her as she trudged along the hallway, muttering curses under her breath.

'What on earth are you doing here?' she'd asked, stifling a yawn as she saw Jackson standing on her doorstep. 'I wasn't expecting you. Was I?'

She wrinkled her nose, trying to remember what they'd said on the Friday. The hallway was painted, and a new stair carpet had been laid at last. Jackson had even put up new lightshades in the hall and landing. Job done. He'd spoken to her about getting on with the bathroom if she wanted him to, but they'd made no definite plans as Abbie hadn't liked to push him into doing yet more work, especially since the hallway had taken much longer than expected, thanks to the demon woodchip, and he'd done such a wonderful job of it. Then again, maybe he *had* told her he'd be back on the Monday? She'd been so tired on Friday evening that she could well have missed what he said... Oh, lord! Abbie's eyes widened and she pulled her dressing gown tighter as she realised Jackson wasn't alone.

'I'm so sorry, I didn't know you'd brought someone with you.' She ran a hand through her dishevelled hair and blushed as the young man standing just behind Jackson stepped to one side and smiled.

'Lewis Palmer,' he said, holding out his hand. 'Very pleased to meet you, Dr Sawdon.'

'Oh, er, pleased to meet you too. Who are you exactly?'

Jackson cleared his throat. 'I hope you don't mind but I noticed, the other day, how overgrown your garden was. We couldn't even see the dogs, and the children can't really play out with all that wilderness, so Lewis here has agreed to tackle it. He was highly recommended by several people when I made enquiries. I think he'll do a great job of clearing all the weeds and overgrowth out there.'

He was a gardener? Abbie ushered them in, wishing Jackson had warned her so she could at least have got dressed and brushed her hair. Plus the kitchen was a tip as usual.

If Lewis noticed though he didn't show it. Abbie had never given much thought to what a gardener would look like, but if she had she was sure she would never have pictured anyone like this polite, well-spoken, and rather attractive young man. If anything, she'd have expected a middle-aged to elderly chap, with a checked shirt and wellies, weather-beaten face, and a broad Yorkshire accent. Sort of a budget Alan Titchmarsh.

'Please, take a seat,' she said.

Lewis duly obliged, sitting down at the table, and pulling out his mobile as a message notification pinged.

Abbie pulled Jackson over to the sink.

'Are you sure he's a gardener?' she whispered to him as she reached for the kettle. 'He doesn't look like one. Or sound like one for that matter.'

'What should gardeners look and sound like?' he whispered back.

As she made the tea, she quietly filled him in on her idea of a gardener. He reared back in mock alarm. 'Abbie! That's gardenerist!'

'Idiot.' She giggled and handed him a mug of tea. 'Sugar, Mr Palmer?'

The young man put away his mobile and held up his hands. 'Please, call me Lewis. Mr Palmer's my dad. And yes, one sugar please, Dr Sawdon.'

Abbie grinned. 'If you're Lewis, then I'm Abbie, okay?'

'Okay.' He smiled back and she thought what an affable young man he seemed. There was something appealing about him, with his cropped fair hair and blue eyes, even though he was probably on the skinny side for someone of around six foot three. He had an unusual face, rather than conventionally handsome, but he spoke with a deep and rather sexy voice that made her wish she'd brushed her hair and got dressed after all. Being a gardener in a remote moorland village seemed an unlikely occupation for someone like him. She'd have pictured him working in banking or being "something in the city" if not for his faded jeans, grungy t-shirt, and work boots.

Jackson raised an eyebrow as she reluctantly turned away.

'What?' she mouthed.

He shook his head. 'Any biscuits on the go? I haven't had breakfast.'

Jackson Wade was, she thought, as she headed to the cupboard for the digestives, behaving very strangely. He never asked for *anything*. Casually requesting biscuits wasn't his usual sort of behaviour at all.

Not that she was complaining. She didn't begrudge

him anything since he'd already gone above and beyond the call of duty.

'What are you doing here anyway?' she said, rummaging around in the cupboard and keeping everything crossed that Bertie hadn't finished off all the biscuits. 'We hadn't arranged anything had we?'

Jackson shrugged. 'We need to make firm plans for the bathroom. I thought I'd measure up for the flooring and tiles then we can go into Helmston and choose what we need. You might make a final decision on the bathroom suite if you see them on display, rather than in a brochure.'

'Seriously?' She stared at him, shocked. 'What about the kids?'

'They could come with us,' he said. 'They might have some good ideas. Well, maybe not so much Poppy, but I'm sure Bertie and Isla would appreciate having a say. My brother's happy to fit the suite as soon as it arrives, so the sooner you make your choice the better.'

Abbie hardly knew what to say. She'd have been floundering for months without Jackson's help. As her hands found the packet of digestives she breathed a sigh of relief and thrust them at him.

'Help yourself,' she said, thinking it seemed a pretty poor reward for all his help, but he was still refusing to take payment.

Jackson took a biscuit and they smiled at each other. He had a lovely smile, she thought. He ought to do it more often. It spread right into his eyes, lighting up his whole face.

Blinking, she forced herself to look away. 'Digestive,

Lewis?' she asked, feeling a bit dazed.

Lewis, who had evidently given up waiting to be handed his cup of tea and had gone to fetch it himself, shook his head. 'No thanks, I've had breakfast.' He wandered over to the window and studied the garden, a frown creasing his brow. 'I understand you don't want me to do any landscaping or planting for you? Just clearance. Is that right? Because I could do a lot with that space you know.'

Abbie stood beside him, still clutching the half empty packet of biscuits. Now that he'd brought it up she wished she could hand over the whole project to him. Her priority had been to simply clear away all the weeds and rubbish in the garden and make it look tidy, but Lewis was brimming with ideas. As she listened, he began to talk with increasing passion about landscaping and zones, which all sounded rather lovely, but prohibitively expensive.

'My prices are very reasonable,' he assured her, almost as if he sensed her trepidation. 'Just think about it. What sort of look would you like for your garden?'

If money was no object? For a moment, Abbie allowed herself to imagine all sorts of wonderful things. Probably totally unrealistic but so what? Life was for living. That was one thing she'd learned if nothing else. They had, after all, moved away from Hull to Bramblewick to experience nature in all its beauty. Why not focus as much attention and love on the garden as the house?

'I'd want lots of colour,' she said thoughtfully. 'And scents. I'd like to be able to close my eyes and smell the flowers, and hear bees buzzing and birds singing, and maybe the sound of water.'

'Water?' Lewis nodded. 'You mean a pond, or just a water feature?'

'Oh, not a pond,' she said quickly. 'Not with Poppy around, not to mention Willow.'

'Sorry?'

'Poppy is her toddler,' Jackson explained, standing next to Abbie. 'Dr Sawdon has three children you see. The eldest is a teenager now.'

Abbie glared at him. No need to rub it in was there?

'Willow, on the other hand, is a very bossy little dog. Where is she anyway? And the other one, come to that.'

'In Bertie's bedroom,' Abbie said, pretending not to notice when he winced. Jackson, no doubt, thought allowing dogs upstairs was disgustingly unhygienic, but tough. The dogs adored Bertie and he adored them. Having them sleep in his bedroom made them all happy so what did a few dog hairs matter? 'Obviously, it would be nice to have somewhere for the children to play,' she continued, turning back to Lewis. 'A nice, lawned area. But I'd quite like a wildflower patch too.'

'For someone who just wanted the land cleared you're doing very well.' Lewis laughed. 'You see? Now, would you like me to come up with some quotes for you?'

She shook her head regretfully. 'Sorry. It would be wonderful but I'm on a tight budget and I must make the house the priority for now. If you could just clear the jungle that would be wonderful. Well,' she conceded, 'not wonderful, obviously, but enough. For now at least.'

Lewis leaned towards her, his eyes twinkling. 'Fair enough. For now. But when you're ready I'll be waiting.'

'I'll bear that in mind,' she told him, a mischievous smile playing on her lips.

She glanced around, startled, as Jackson rummaged noisily in the packet of digestives, almost knocking them out of her hand.

'Sorry,' he said, eyeing her steadily. 'I didn't realise how hungry I was.'

She tutted. 'Biscuits aren't exactly a healthy breakfast. Would you like me to make you something to eat?'

To her astonishment he nodded. 'If it's not too much trouble. I'd love one of your breakfasts. They always smell so good.'

What had come over him? Abbie frowned, feeling a little out of her depth. 'You mean a cooked breakfast?'

'Isn't that what you were offering?' he said, colouring slightly. 'The one you made the kids the other day looked really tasty, but if it's too much bother toast will do fine.' He nodded at Lewis. 'She makes good toast too. Seeded bread. Delicious. And real butter and strawberry jam.'

Abbie surveyed him, wondering what had happened to him. 'Er, Lewis, would you like anything to eat?'

Lewis drained his cup and put it on the draining board. 'No thanks, Dr—Abbie. Like I said, I've had breakfast. Just going to my van to get some tools and I'll make a start. Is the side gate unlocked?'

'I'll unlock it,' Jackson offered.

Abbie smiled uncertainly as Lewis left the kitchen and Jackson turned to look at her.

'Don't bother with the breakfast. That digestive has filled me up more than I realised. I think I'll start measuring up the bathroom now.'

'*What?*' She really didn't know what to make of his weird behaviour. 'Look, you don't have to do this you know. There's really no need.'

'Abbie, there's one thing you should know about me. I always keep my promises.' His fingers tapped lightly on the worktop as he seemed to hesitate, a slight frown on his face. 'Right,' he said eventually, 'I'd better go and unlock the gate for Lewis. Nice chap isn't he? Even if he wasn't what you were expecting.'

'Very nice,' she agreed. 'Rather attractive too.'

'Really?' Jackson shrugged. 'Don't worry that he won't do a good job, by the way.'

'I wasn't,' she assured him.

'Just that, with him being *so* young, don't think he's inexperienced. He's got a good reputation around here, despite his age.'

'Good to hear,' she said.

'Not all youngsters are immature,' he added.

Abbie wrinkled her nose, perplexed. 'I'm not worried honestly. I trust your judgment.'

He looked at her uncertainly. 'You do?'

'Of course. Now, shouldn't you go and open that gate?'

'What? Oh, yes, right. I'll do that now.'

Jackson strolled out of the kitchen leaving Abbie staring after him in confusion. Honestly, sometimes men could be quite bewildering.

Chapter 11

'Are you absolutely sure about this?'

Bertie hurtled past his mother and practically leapt into his car seat, fastening it with superhero speed. Funny that, since he usually took forever and a day to get himself sorted, thought Abbie wryly. Of course, that was when they were going to school, or shopping; not to the seaside to play on the beach, picnic on the sands and just have fun for once.

She glanced warily at Jackson, wondering if Bertie's enthusiasm had made him think twice, but he was still smiling, which was an encouraging sign.

'Seriously, you don't have to do this. It's ever so kind of you but—'

'I'm not doing it to be kind,' Jackson insisted. 'I really want to go with you all. It's ages since I had a day at the coast, which is crazy when you think how close I live to it. It will be fun.'

She wondered if he realised what he'd let himself in for. When she'd wearily agreed with him after he'd commented that the children needed to let off some steam, she certainly hadn't expected him to suggest that they all went to the coast. She'd been further surprised when he offered to drive them in his own car.

'It will save you driving,' he'd said. 'You can just sit back and enjoy the view for once.'

'But your car's too small to take the dogs,' she'd pointed out.

His expression had changed to one of shock, but only fleetingly. 'I forgot about the dogs,' he admitted.

'We always take them with us,' she confessed. 'Bertie would never leave them behind.'

She watched him as he clearly wrestled with the urge to call the whole thing off, but to her amazement he'd finally nodded. 'Okay, so what if I drive your car? I'm insured to drive any car, and that way you can still get to relax, and the dogs can come too.'

She'd wanted to protest, but the thought of being able to chill out and maybe even close her eyes for ten minutes or so while they travelled was too irresistible to turn down.

'It's so good of you,' she murmured, her gratitude increasing as he lifted Poppy into her car seat and patiently fastened her in.

Willow and Albus were happily settled in the boot of the estate and their bright eyes and eager expressions showed they'd already realised they were heading out for some fun.

Poppy, her fair hair in plaits, her pudgy little hands clutching a bucket and spade in anticipation, beamed up at him as he strapped her in. 'Make sandcastle with me?'

Abbie rolled her eyes. The last thing she could imagine Jackson doing was going onto the sands and helping Poppy with her masterpiece.

'I don't see why not,' Jackson told the little girl. 'You'll have to show me how to make them though. It's been a long time since I tried.'

Poppy giggled while Bertie tutted in disgust.

'Anyone can make a sandcastle! It's easy peasy. Even you can do that, Jackson.'

'Don't count on it,' Jackson told him, grinning. 'Now, where's that sister of yours?'

'Here.'

Isla strolled to the other side of the car and climbed in, making Bertie yowl as she clambered over him and plonked herself down in the middle of the back seat.

'Shut up,' she told him. 'I didn't touch you.'

'You squashed my legs,' he protested.

'Don't be a baby. Think yourself lucky. You get a whole big seat to yourself, and you're near the window. Here am I, all squashed in between you both.'

'Are you comfortable enough?' Jackson sounded seriously worried and Abbie decided an intervention was necessary.

'She's absolutely fine. Don't worry about it.'

Isla usually sat in the front seat next to Abbie, and probably resented being relegated to what she termed "the baby seat". Her eldest daughter, she decided, just liked to moan these days. She'd changed so much from the cheerful, happy girl she used to be.

'Great. So, are we all set?'

'Ugh! What's Pops eating?' Bertie squealed.

'Oh, lord, what's she got now?' Abbie clambered onto her knees in the passenger seat and leaned over, gently coaxing Poppy's mouth open. She could feel

Jackson eyes on her back and knew he'd be appalled.

'It's a jelly baby!' Abbie was thoroughly perplexed. 'Where did she get a jelly baby from?'

Isla gave her a wicked grin. 'Don't you remember? Bertie had some last week. Must've dropped one between the seats. Poppy's ever so good at finding things to eat,' she told Jackson, her voice sounding far too smug for Abbie's liking.

Abbie shot him an embarrassed look and fastened herself into the passenger seat. 'Can't do anything about it now,' she said. 'She's swallowed it.'

She saw him blanch and bit back the impatient retort she longed to make. He couldn't help it after all. He had... issues. To his credit, he made no comment as he took his place and started the engine.

She gave him top marks for his attempt at a smile as he said, 'Right then. Starfish Sands, here we come.'

She could hear the tension in his voice and wasn't at all surprised. A day out with three young children was probably way out of his comfort zone, and Poppy's antics hadn't got the day off to a good start.

She really couldn't imagine why he'd offered to take them when he could have taken a well-earned day off and spent some time at his own place for once. Abbie had been rather anxious about it, but he was adamant, saying it would do him the world of good to be outside too, and they were doing him a favour letting him tag along.

Abbie really didn't know what to make of him. He was the kindest man she'd ever met.

After much debate, they'd settled on Starfish Sands,

which was a small village not too far from Filey. Although it wasn't as popular a resort as Filey itself, or Scarborough for that matter, it had one huge advantage. Dogs were welcome on its beach all year round, and that was the most important thing to the Sawdons. They'd visited it many times before when they lived in Hull.

Abbie had packed a picnic and a couple of rugs to sit on, plus towels so the children could get dry after paddling or swimming. She mentally ticked off her list: water bowls and water for the dogs; sandwiches, sausage rolls and drinks for the humans; bucket and spade for Poppy; swimming costumes and trunks for the children; book to read in the unlikely event that she had a spare ten minutes where one of the children wasn't shouting for her attention; a comic for Bertie; sun cream; sunhats; sunglasses; parasol. She couldn't think of anything else offhand and could only cross her fingers that there wasn't something essential that she'd forgotten.

At least there was a shop in Starfish Sands. It might not be huge, but it sold the usual seaside stuff. She couldn't imagine there'd be any reason to terminate their trip early.

The pretty little village, which consisted mainly of a caravan park and a few cottages, perched on a cliff top with a steep and winding path that led down to the beach, was surprisingly busy.

'It's the free parking that does it,' Abbie told Jackson, as he drove round and round the car park looking for an empty space. 'All the other resorts charge, so people come here for a freebie stay.'

'And the dog-friendly beaches,' he reminded her, looking a bit wary as his gaze took in what seemed to be an endless stream of spaniels, hounds, and terriers on leads, eagerly pulling their owners towards the beach path.

Abbie smiled. 'Don't worry. It's a big beach.'

He finally found an empty space and pulled in, much to the children's delight. Abbie climbed out and unfastened Poppy's straps while Isla helped Bertie with his.

Bertie's first thought was to release the dogs, which led to them making a leap from the car boot and galloping full pelt towards the path.

'Get back here now!' Abbie hollered, feeling her stress levels already beginning to rise.

Isla looked at her in surprise. 'What's up with you? They know where they're going don't they? You know they'll only be waiting at the bottom of the path for us, like they always do.'

It was true, but Abbie was suddenly uncomfortably aware that Jackson wouldn't understand the way she did things. Letting her dogs run free would no doubt stress him out. He was already clearly nervous about all the other dogs that were around. He wasn't used to this sort of thing.

Jackson, however, made no comment, other than to remark that Albus and Willow had made it safely to the path and did Abbie want him to get the bags?

Clutching Poppy's hand tightly, Abbie led the others towards the path where Bertie and Isla immediately began to run ahead.

'Be careful! You can slip on the sandy surface!' Abbie yelled, knowing full-well that they wouldn't take a bit of notice of her warnings.

Poppy tugged restlessly on her hand, but Abbie tightened her grip. 'Oh no you don't,' she told her youngest daughter. 'You're staying with us.'

Jackson was carrying the bags and looked around him in surprise as they walked down the wide, sandy path. It was quite steep and surrounded on both sides by trees and bushes.

'I've never been here before,' he admitted. 'It seems ridiculous when I only live in Helmston.'

'Lord, you've missed out,' she told him. 'We've been coming here for years because of the dogs. It's not so bad up until May, but then most of the beaches around here are off-limits to dogs 'til the end of September. It was a real blessing to find this place. Wait 'til you see the beach. It's gorgeous.'

His face, when they finally rounded the last bend of the path and stepped onto the beach at Starfish Sands, said it all. He gazed in amazement at the wide expanse of sand, and the huge skies.

In the distance to their left lay the outstretched arm of Filey Brigg, a long narrow peninsula that, so legend had it, was made from the bones of a dragon who had drowned while diving into the sea to wash Yorkshire parkin from its teeth.

When she relayed this piece of information to him, in front of a wide-eyed Bertie, she was quite enchanted when he blew out his cheeks and exclaimed, 'Wow!

Poor dragon. Mind you, I'm not surprised. Have you ever tasted Yorkshire parkin? Sticky as anything. No wonder he needed to rinse his mouth in the sea.'

Bertie looked delighted. 'I've never tasted Yorkshire parkin, Jackson. What is it?'

'You've never tasted Yorkshire parkin?' Jackson looked appalled. 'Only the finest, stickiest, gooiest ginger cake ever. We'll have to get some for you to taste. Mind, you'll have to give your teeth a good brush afterwards, so best wait until you're at home. We don't want you sticking your head in the sea do we? Not after what happened to that poor dragon.'

Bertie nodded and Isla rolled her eyes, but Abbie was pleased to note that she was smiling. Being out in the sunshine seemed to be affecting her already. Abbie hadn't seen those dimples for far too long.

Of course, she'd expected that Jackson would struggle with certain aspects of their day out, and it proved to be so.

They'd found a fairly remote spot on the beach, as far away from other people as they could manage, but now and then a beach ball would come flying in their direction, showering sand at them and setting the dogs off chasing after it. Although the owners of the ball didn't seem to mind, Abbie could see that Jackson was on edge, perhaps worrying that there would be complaints about the dogs' behaviour.

He got quite nervous when Bertie wanted to go off and explore some rocks too, and insisted on accompanying him, even though Bertie had done that activity alone many times in the past and wouldn't be out of their sight for a moment. Luckily, Bertie didn't seem to mind and the two of them spent half an hour clambering over rocks, digging in the sand and examining rock pools together.

When they returned, Jackson tried to relax, but the dogs repeatedly bounded up to him, bursting with excitement. He tried very hard to be polite, but although he could cope better with Willow, who basically just wanted a bit of attention, Albus was more demanding. He wanted "kisses" from his new friend, and he wanted to give them in return. Unfortunately, the one thing Jackson really didn't like was a dog licking him, so he faced a constant battle to avoid Albus's long, slurpy tongue. Abbie knew she shouldn't laugh, but it was amusing to see poor Jackson do his level best to dodge the Labrador's attempts at affection, while minding his manners. Instead of telling Albus to go away and pushing him back, Jackson ducked and dived and pleaded, 'No, don't do that, Albus, there's a good boy.'

I should really tell him that won't work, she thought, seeing that Albus was viewing Jackson's actions as an entertaining new game.

Should I say something? She hesitated, then settled herself down on the rug and picked up her book. *Nah. Best he figures it out for himself.*

Poor Jackson found the picnic particularly trying. Abbie laid out another rug and spread plastic tubs of food and flasks of drinks upon it. The children gathered round eagerly. Unfortunately, so did the dogs, and she flinched inwardly as he made a valiant attempt at hiding his disgust, while discreetly trying to protect the food from them.

'Albus, Willow, sit down!' she commanded, taking pity on him.

The dogs gave her an incredulous look but obeyed, and she rewarded them with some cooked chicken breast. The children tucked in happily, and Abbie pretended not to notice as Jackson examined every morsel of food for sand or—horror of horrors—dog hairs.

He seemed to have made it his mission to be Poppy's protector too. She noticed that he checked every piece of food she had in her hand, and when she dropped anything—which she did on several occasions—he whipped it away quickly and put it in an empty bag before she could eat it. It was, she had to concede, rather sweet, although he must be exhausted being on such high alert all the time.

Despite his guard duties, she was gratified to see him devour several sandwiches, some cooked chicken, a sausage roll, and some biscuits, all washed down with a mug of hot tea from one of the flasks.

When everyone had finished, Isla and Abbie sunbathed while Bertie read a comic and Jackson, rather nobly, helped Poppy to make sandcastles.

'Not a bad job, if I do say so myself,' he said, sounding quite satisfied as he surveyed the finished construction, complete with four turrets between sand walls and topped with a variety of seashells.

Poppy had clearly enjoyed herself thoroughly, but wasn't particularly interested in the end product, a fact she demonstrated by smashing her fists through it and destroying it all.

Jackson wailed. 'Oh, no! Look at that!'

Poppy giggled in delight. 'Again!' she demanded.

Jackson frowned. 'Seriously?'

'You've done it now,' Abbie warned him. 'That's your job for the next hour or so until she gets bored.'

He gave her a worried look. 'Really?'

'Don't worry. She'll probably want a nap soon.'

Poppy, indeed, grew tired of building sandcastles and began yawning within twenty minutes.

'Let me put some more sun cream on her,' Abbie said, 'then she can have a nap.'

After smoothing the lotion onto Poppy's face and every visible square inch of her, they moved the rugs over to the shelter of the cliffs and found a nice shady spot where she could nap for a little while, positioning the parasol carefully to make doubly sure that she wouldn't burn.

Bertie joined her, while Isla decided to go in the sea, where dozens of other people were already paddling or floating or splashing each other, their shrieks of joy echoing across the sands.

'Are you sure? You won't go far will you?' Jackson said, clearly alarmed at the idea.

'I'll stay in the shallows,' Isla promised him. 'I'm a good swimmer, don't worry.'

But Jackson was obviously worried in the extreme. He sat upright, his jaw tense, his eyes scanning the horizon as he watched Isla's every move.

Abbie was quite touched at his concern and moved

to sit beside him, after casting a glance back at her youngest two children who were still sound asleep under the parasol.

'I can't stand this,' he confessed. 'I feel I should be out there with her.'

'There are plenty of people out there with her, and she's a sensible girl,' Abbie said. 'We can see her from here. It won't take a moment for us to get in the water if we need to, but she's a strong swimmer and she's done this plenty of times.'

Jackson's brow was furrowed. 'I know you must think I'm a real worrier,' he began. 'It's just—'

'I think you're very sensible,' she assured him. 'I also think you're a kind man who cares about the welfare of my children. I'm very grateful.'

He turned to her, surprise apparent in his expression. 'Really?'

'Of course.'

He opened his mouth as if to speak, then turned away again, his gaze once more focused on Isla as she dunked up and down in the sea, laughing.

'Thank you.'

He spoke so softly that she strained to hear him.

'Thanks for what?'

'For not making fun of me,' he said, not looking at her. 'Some people find me a bit—a bit too much, shall we say.'

'How long have you been like this?' she asked. 'With all this anxiety and obsessive behaviour I mean.'

He sighed. 'Is that how you see me? Some sort of medical case?'

'Of course not, Jackson, but I'm not blind and I'm obviously aware of what you're dealing with. I see many patients in my job who are just like you.'

'Crazy people.'

'People who are trying to cope with life the only way they know how,' she corrected him firmly. 'Have you thought about counselling?'

He groaned. 'Oh, not you too. My brother's always nagging at me to go.'

'But you haven't?'

He shook his head.

'Why not?'

He was silent for a moment, his focus seemingly all on the shoreline where Isla was now sitting, allowing the waves to lap over her, relaxed, totally unafraid.

'I'm sure counselling helps some people,' he said eventually, his voice halting, 'but for others it's probably best to just let the past stay in the past.'

She raised an eyebrow. Just what had been in his past that still caused him so much anxiety?

'I was thinking,' he said suddenly, 'about your kitchen.'

She smiled. Talk about changing the subject! 'What about it?'

'I know you said you can't afford to buy new units, but what about freshening up the ones you have? I could sand down the doors and repaint them, any colour you like. And with a coat of emulsion on the walls and some cheap and cheerful new accessories—a new wall clock for example—you could really ring the changes in there for a few quid. What do you think?'

'But, Jackson, that would be even more work for you to do,' she protested. 'Haven't you done enough already? You're already going to be tackling the bathroom and that's a big enough job.'

He waved his hand dismissively. 'Not really. My brother will be doing the main job of fitting the new suite.'

She didn't know what to say. It seemed a terrible imposition on his good nature to agree, yet she had the feeling that this was something he needed to do for his own sake. Was being at The Gables, filling his days with work, serving a greater purpose for him than it was even for her? What demons was he trying to keep at bay, she wondered.

'Are you sure your brother doesn't mind helping out?' she questioned, wondering if she could steer him onto the subject of his family.

'Tyler?' He laughed. 'Well, he grumbled a bit, but he doesn't mean anything by that. He's a kind-hearted man and he'll be happy to do it.'

'Are you very close then?' she pushed. 'Is he younger or older than you?'

'Four years younger,' Jackson replied, somewhat curtly. 'And yes. We're very close.'

Abbie laughed as Isla bobbed up and down in the water and gave them a cheery wave. She waved back, her heart melting as Jackson gave a hesitant wave too, almost as if he wasn't sure that Isla would want one from him.

'I do envy you, having a brother,' she said. 'I was an only child. That's why I was determined Isla wouldn't be. Do you have any other brothers or sisters?'

Jackson shook his head. 'Just me and Tyler.'

'And your parents?'

There was a long silence and Abbie winced. Had she said something out of turn? What if Jackson's parents had died in some horrible tragedy?

'They're abroad,' he said eventually. 'Travelling.'

'Oh.' That wasn't what she'd expected to hear, and it rather closed the conversation. Abbie scooped up a handful of sand and let it run through her fingers. 'My parents are in London,' she told him. 'They're high-flying consultants. Not lowly GPs like me.'

He looked at her. 'Nothing lowly about being a GP,' he said sharply. 'It's a wonderful profession.'

'Try telling that to Mum and Dad,' she said. 'They've never got over the disappointment.'

He shook his head. 'Some parents are—' He broke off and buried his fingers in the sand, his attention seeming fixed on the activity for a moment. 'Ignore them.'

'Oh I do. I've strived all my life to be nothing like them.' She gave him a half-smile. 'I suppose that's why I desperately wanted my kids to have a bit of freedom and not live in what amounted to regimental barracks.'

He glanced up at her. 'Regimental barracks?'

'They were very neat and tidy, and everything had its time and place. Punctuality was God. I guess I rebelled a bit,' she admitted. 'They'd have loved you. You'd have been their ideal child.'

He looked doubtful and she giggled to show him she wasn't being serious, although, when she gave the matter deeper thought, she realised it was probably true.

'Were your parents like that?' she said, desperate to probe a little further into his background.

He gave a short and rather scornful laugh. 'Not in the slightest. My parents were, shall we say, bohemian and leave it at that?'

'Oh.' What did that mean exactly? Were they hippies? 'Did you live in some sort of commune?'

He picked up a pebble and threw it across the sands. Albus, who'd been half snoozing beside them immediately leapt to his feet and bounded over to retrieve it, while Willow opened one eye and, clearly deciding it was nothing worth getting excited about, returned to her nap.

Jackson took the pebble back from Albus and patted him distractedly on the head. 'Not a commune, no. Well, not exactly.' He threw the pebble again, shaking his head slightly as Albus galloped after it once more. 'They weren't the ideal parents for me,' he admitted grudgingly. 'I think my anxieties stem from living in that sort of atmosphere. I think—I think children need some sort of structure. I don't mean they should feel as if they're in the army, or anything like that, but routine and order is more important than most parents realise. It all contributes to a feeling of wellbeing and safety. Well,' he gave her an apologetic look, 'that's what I think anyway, but what do I know?'

Albus, having dropped the pebble at Jackson's feet and getting no response, decided to join Isla in the water. Isla squealed as he bounded through the waves, splashing her thoroughly in the process.

Abbie hugged her knees, thinking. Maybe he had a point. She'd so wanted her children to have a different childhood to herself and after—after what happened she'd wanted it even more strongly, until it had become almost an obsession. She'd wanted to throw away the rulebook, stop the clocks, let them just live freely and without restraint. Maybe she'd gone too far.

She thought about Isla refusing to invite friends around. She remembered the scorn in her face and voice when she talked about the house, and the flashes of anger when she discovered the empty freezer or moaned that they'd run out of butter or milk yet again.

Abbie had wanted to foster a feeling of calm and relaxation at The Gables. When she thought about it though, she had to wonder if her "What does it matter" attitude was causing more stress rather than decreasing it. Was Jackson right? Did children respond to and thrive better with some discipline and routine?

She knew for a fact that she'd used the last of the bread making the sandwiches for the picnic. They'd had a lovely lunch, but dinner would be potluck again. Nothing was going to plan. She was making a real hash of things.

'Jackson?'

He didn't look round, his attention focused on Isla who was now floating on her back, Albus paddling nearby.

'When we leave here, would you mind looking after the children for an hour while I go to the supermarket and do a big shop?'

He turned to her, and she saw the surprise and pleasure in his face. He'd obviously heard the children's complaints about the empty fridge enough times to realise that this was a big deal.

'Of course. I'd be delighted.'

'Thank you.'

She felt a sudden overwhelming desire to rest her head on his shoulder and had to fight it with every ounce of determination she possessed. She didn't think Jackson Wade would take too kindly to such blatant shows of affection. But affection it was that was driving the desire. She wasn't sure how it had happened, but this man had become a very dear friend to her. She simply couldn't imagine life without him.

Chapter 12

Abbie hadn't meant to fall asleep, but somehow, despite the mess around her and the sound of Jackson hammering in the dining room and Poppy throwing her toys around, she'd managed to do so. It was Isla who woke her up.

'Mum, come on! We're supposed to be going out remember?'

Abbie's eyes flickered open, and she groaned as her daughter's face loomed over her. 'What time is it?'

'Nearly one. You said we were going out at half twelve, but you fell asleep.'

The hammering had stopped she realised. She struggled to sit up, feeling a flush of embarrassment as she noticed that Jackson was standing by the door, Poppy's hand in his.

'What's wrong? Is she okay?' she demanded, alarm bells ringing when she realised she'd left Poppy unsupervised in the living room as she slept.

'She's fine. She was just hungry. I hope you don't mind but I made them some sandwiches.'

'You did what?' She blinked, confused. Had he really just said that he'd made her children lunch? The crumbs on Bertie's t-shirt confirmed that he'd eaten.

'And you.' He gave her a faint smile. 'Bertie said you liked ham and tomato, so I made you some sandwiches too. They're on the table next to you,' he added, nodding at the small occasional table that stood beside the sofa. 'You've got plenty of ham left,' he added, a distinct twinkle in his eye. 'Those cupboards and that fridge are full to bursting.'

Abbie sat up straight and pushed her hair out of her eyes, glad that she'd earned his approval for something since she'd blotted her copy book by falling asleep. She hoped her mascara hadn't smudged. She probably looked an absolute fright, and what must he think of her? She couldn't even say the nap had done her good, because she felt, if anything, even worse. She longed to go to bed and sleep the entire afternoon.

'Mum, are you okay? Are you feeling all right?'

Abbie heard the fear in Isla's voice and waved a hand, dismissing her daughter's anxieties. 'I'm fine. I was just having forty winks that's all. Don't fuss.'

Isla stepped back, a worried frown on her face, but Bertie showed no such concern as he pushed his way past her, clearly keen for his mother to get a move on.

'Mum, hurry up and eat your sandwiches. We need to go.'

They'd all been promised new clothes for their trip to New York, which was only a couple of days away and were straining at the leash to get to the shops.

'Bertie, let your mum wake up properly first.'

Jackson sounded surprisingly gentle she thought. She'd have expected him to point out her failings as a mother, falling asleep before feeding her children and leaving her toddler to play alone. Maybe he had a more understanding nature than she'd given him credit for.

'Did you get the unit put together?' she asked, suddenly remembering what he'd been doing before she slept. She'd seen a large storage unit online that she'd thought would be perfect for putting the children's toys in and had ordered it for the other reception room. When she'd told Jackson about it, he'd immediately offered to come around and put it together as soon as it arrived, and she'd wanted to tell him she could do it herself. Because she could really. At a push. She just thought that he could probably make a better job of it and, realising she had all the energy of a flat battery, she'd finally accepted his offer. She doubted he'd expected her to fall fast asleep while he worked though.

He nodded and sat down on the chair, lifting Poppy onto his knee. Abbie felt a strange fluttering of something unexpected at the action. Poppy beamed up at him and he absent-mindedly stroked her hair as he told Abbie how easily the storage unit had been put together and how neatly it fitted against the back wall of the room.

'It's looking a bit bare in there though. You'll need to buy more furniture.' He shook his head. 'Got to say, this is a big house. What are you using that empty middle room for by the way? An office?'

Abbie hadn't really made up her mind. It was true that The Gables was a large place; double fronted with two large front rooms of identical size, a big kitchen, a dining room, and a spare room that, as Jackson suggested, would make an ideal office. She didn't particularly feel the need for an office though. Then upstairs there were four good-sized bedrooms, and a family bathroom. Abbie's own room was at the back of the house. She'd chosen it because it had an en suite and, more importantly, a balcony that looked over the garden. When the garden was in full bloom it would be a wonderful view, she thought, imagining opening the French doors in a morning and breathing in the scent of flowers. Very different to her functional and tidy bedroom at the house in Hull, which looked out over a tarmac road and a row of neat, nineteen-thirties houses very similar to her own.

'I'm not sure what I'm doing to be honest,' she admitted. 'I'm just shoving things in any old room until I make up my mind.'

He looked puzzled. 'Didn't you have it all set out in your mind before you moved?'

'Not really. It was all a mad rush you see. I had to find somewhere else to live unless I wanted to renew my lease on the rental cottage in Kearton Bay. I didn't want to be in rented property for another six months, so I snapped this place up without really sitting down to question if I needed such a large place and what I was going to do with it. I don't regret it though,' she added defiantly, in case he was thinking what an idiot she was. 'It was a good price, and it's a lovely house.'

Isla rolled her eyes at that statement and Abbie said firmly, 'It will be. Just you wait and see.'

'Suppose it will,' Isla admitted grudgingly. 'It's getting better now already. At least that hallway looks decent at last, and the kitchen looks great since Jackson painted the walls and the units.'

'And Mum did the ironing!' Bertie burst out.

Abbie blushed, embarrassed that his mother picking up an iron was a noteworthy event in her son's life. She had to admit, though, that clearing the ironing pile had made a huge difference. The kitchen looked as if it had a complete makeover. It was amazing what a paint job and a bit of tidying up could do.

She took a bite of her ham sandwich and leaned back in the sofa. It was tempting to close her eyes, but she mustn't. If only this exhaustion would just go away. Sometimes she felt absolutely fine. Other times she could barely get dressed. It was so frustrating.

'Of course, what I really need now is another wardrobe,' Isla pointed out. 'I'm sick of sharing mine with Bertie. There's not enough room for all my stuff, and I'm sick of having piles of clothes folded up on the chair in my room.'

'We'll get your room sorted soon,' Abbie promised. 'Just be patient a little while longer.' She smiled at Jackson. 'This is yummy. Thank you so much. I'm ever so sorry for falling asleep. You really didn't have to make the kids their lunch you know. You should have woken me up.'

'But you looked so peaceful lying there,' he said, 'I didn't want to disturb you. Besides, it was no problem. Not at all.'

His eyes were warm, and his tone was kind. Abbie wondered when he'd morphed into this understanding and reasonable human being. It seemed to have happened gradually, without her noticing. She liked it. He was very different to the man she'd met on that ill-fated blind date. If he'd been like this that night at The Bay Horse, who knows what might have happened. She realised she was staring and looked away hastily, taking another bite of her sandwich.

Jackson stood up and put Poppy on the chair where he'd been sitting. 'I'd better get back to work,' he said, his voice sounding rather gruff suddenly.

'What are you doing next?' Isla enquired.

'Removing the old bathroom tiles,' he said. 'By the time you get back from the States you'll have a beautiful new bathroom, Isla. Just think of that.'

'I can't wait,' she admitted. 'It will make a load of difference.' She looked up at him, a shy expression on her face. 'Thanks, Jackson. You've been great.'

Abbie almost choked on her sandwich. Was that Isla being *grateful*? Good grief! She glanced at Jackson, who was looking rather stunned himself.

'Well—er—you're welcome,' he mumbled. 'Anyway, must get on.'

Abbie waited until he'd left the room and closed the door behind him, then she rounded on her daughter. 'What was that about?'

'What?'

'You, being all nice and grateful to Jackson Wade? You've been really offhand with him ever since he started here.'

'Yeah, well.' Isla looked uncomfortable. 'It's all coming on isn't it? He's really made a difference already, and besides, he's been here loads more than I expected, and he works non-stop. It's taken some of the pressure off you hasn't it? Got to give the bloke some credit.'

Abbie smiled. 'Well, yes. Right, let's get Poppy and Bertie cleaned up and changed and then we can have a lovely afternoon shopping, shall we? America in two days.'

'And Dad will be here tomorrow,' Isla reminded her, her eyes shining with excitement.

Yes, there was that to deal with. Even though she and Nick were still friends, it would feel strange seeing him in person again. He'd asked if he could collect the children a couple of days early, as he wanted to take them to see his family in Berkshire before they headed to America. He was due to arrive around this time tomorrow, and she wasn't sure how she felt about it. It was bad enough that he was taking the children away with him for two whole weeks, although she couldn't begrudge him that. After all, she had them for most of the year.

She supposed a lot of her trepidation was wondering what he'd make of The Gables. Even with the improvements done so far it wasn't exactly the ideal home. Would he think she'd been an idiot for buying it? It was so different to their marital home, and he might worry it wasn't suitable for his children. She was glad that Jackson had done such a great job tidying the hallway, and that Lewis had hacked down the tangle of weeds that was smothering the garden. At least Nick would realise she was trying. He'd have no cause to worry that she wasn't coping, that it was all too much for her...

She dropped her half-eaten sandwich back on the plate and stood. 'Come on, let's get ready.'

She would prove to Nick that he needn't be concerned. She could look after her family, she really could. The children would have the home they deserved, and Abbie would show that she could take care of them as well as hold down her job. All she needed to do tomorrow was make sure she didn't fall asleep on him.

***

'I gather you're the man I have to thank for helping transform the house.'

Jackson hesitated, then shook the hand of the broad-shouldered, sandy-haired man who stood opposite him, a wide smile on his face.

'It was no trouble,' he said. 'You don't have to thank me honestly.'

Not least, he thought, because it really had nothing to do with him. He might be Abbie's ex-husband, but this was her house, and he'd done the work for her and the children, not for him. Why was he thanking him, as if he still had something to do with it?

'Oh, but I really appreciate it,' Nick said. 'It's a weight off my mind, knowing she's got someone helping her. I know Isla was really worried about the place, and I thought maybe Abbie had bitten off more than she could chew, but I can see you've taken control and it's a work in progress. Some way to go obviously, but still...'

Jackson risked a sideways glance at Abbie, who was standing with an excited-looking Willow in her arms. She looked, as he'd expected, quite annoyed by this conversation.

'I'm not the one in control,' he assured Nick. 'I'm merely doing what Abbie instructs me to do. She's the one who put the plan into action. I'm merely the hired hand.'

Nick pushed an eager and inquisitive Albus aside and gave Jackson an appraising look. 'Hired hand who won't take any money I believe,' he said. 'That's quite a big favour to do someone you hardly know.'

'Not really,' Jackson said, sensing a sudden edge to Nick's voice. 'I was at a loose end over the summer holidays. I needed something to do. This came at just the right time and was a welcome relief. I like renovating and decorating houses, so it was no bother.' He felt a flash of irrational delight as Albus abandoned the unresponsive Nick and headed over to him instead, earning himself a rare but heartfelt pat on the head.

'Even so.' Nick glanced over at his ex-wife and shrugged. 'Seems you struck lucky, Abbie. Not many men are as noble as Jackson here.'

Abbie stiffened. 'I know that,' she said. 'But if I hadn't found Jackson I would have found someone else. I always intended to start the work this summer, whatever Isla told you.'

Isla looked embarrassed. 'I didn't say it was that bad,' she protested.

Nick pulled a face. 'Hmm. I could show your mum some of the texts, but I'll let that go. I'm just glad it's not as awful as I'd feared, and that work is progressing. It will be a great house when it's finished. I'm sure you'll all be very happy here.'

He slipped an arm around Abbie's shoulders and Jackson felt the muscles in his own shoulders tighten. 'You're doing okay, though, Abbie? It's not all too much for you?'

Abbie, Jackson noticed, looked visibly flustered and he wondered why. Was it the physical contact from her ex that was having that effect on her? Or was it, as he hoped, that she was thoroughly annoyed with his patronising attitude towards her? Seriously, where did this Nick bloke get off, talking to her like a child?

'Of course it's not too much for me,' she said firmly, moving, Jackson was pleased to see, away from his embrace by making a great show of putting Willow down. 'I'm managing absolutely fine.'

'You're sure?' Nick was nothing if not persistent. Jackson would have hated him if not for the fact that his concern seemed genuine. His tone was gentle, and there was a look in his eyes that said he was asking because he cared, not because he wanted to put her down.

Abbie gave Jackson a brief but clearly nervous glance.

'Quite sure,' she said. 'You don't have to worry about me any longer okay?'

Why would he be worried? And why was Abbie so obviously edgy? Jackson frowned as he puzzled out this strange conversation. It was none of his business anyway. Abbie had told him he didn't have to come in today if he would rather not, but he'd insisted that he may as well make a start on fitting the new flooring in the bathroom until Nick arrived.

He'd intended to be gone before her ex-husband turned up, but Nick had reached Bramblewick slightly earlier than expected and Jackson couldn't help wishing he'd not bothered going to The Gables at all today. He wasn't sure he really wanted to know how good-looking and well-dressed Nick Sawdon was. It was bad enough that he had a well-paid and high-flying career in New York. This was like rubbing salt in the wound.

He realised that he was thinking like a jealous new boyfriend and the shock made him look away sharply. He'd had a similar feeling about Lewis. A gut-twisting sensation as the young gardener and Abbie playfully flirted that had shaken him to the core. What was he doing? What did he care about any of this? He was just here to do a job, nothing more.

'I'll get off now,' he said, thinking the sooner he left here the better.

'Oh yes, thanks, Jackson.' Abbie sounded highly relieved, which he couldn't help feeling depressed about.

'When will you be back?' asked Bertie. 'Only we're leaving for Grandma and Grandad Sawdon's tomorrow morning. Will we see you before we go?'

Jackson turned around and saw the two eldest children plus both dogs staring at him expectantly. A strange feeling washed over him, and his throat felt suddenly full.

'I don't think so,' he said regretfully. 'I'll be thinking

of you all. Have a wonderful time in New York.'

'Oh, we will,' Bertie assured him. 'See you when we get back, Jackson.'

Jackson nodded and smiled. 'See you then.'

Isla raised a hand. 'Bye, Jackson. Look after Mum, won't you?'

As Abbie tutted impatiently, Jackson hesitated, but he'd heard the faint note of pleading in Isla's voice and his curiosity increased. Why did Abbie's family seem so set on treating her as some incompetent fool?

'Of course,' he said, not meeting Abbie's eyes. Goodness only knows what she was thinking, and he didn't want to antagonise her any further. 'Although I'm pretty sure she doesn't need looking after. She seems to have everything well under control.'

'I'll see you out,' Abbie said and practically pushed him out of the living room and into the hallway.

'Thank you for that,' she whispered as they neared the front door.

'For what?'

'For saying I don't need looking after.' She smiled as he turned to look at her. 'They do seem to think I need it, and I really don't.'

'Well,' he said slowly, 'I wouldn't have thought so. No.'

'They're just very protective,' she explained. 'Nick probably just feels guilty for leaving me and the children here when he went to America. Not that he needs to feel guilty of course. We were already divorced, and I totally encouraged him to leave. And the children try to replace him I suppose. There's no need for it but what can I do?'

'I suppose it's quite nice that they care so much,' he said.

She nodded. 'I suppose it is.'

'And your ex-husband seems like a decent man.'

'Oh, he is!' She sounded desperate that he should believe it. 'Really, he's one of the best.'

Jackson couldn't help wondering why on earth they'd ever got divorced, since Nick clearly still worried about Abbie and Abbie still seemed to think so highly of him.

'I hope the kids have a great time. I'll not come here tomorrow, or over the weekend. Give you all chance to spend time together and say your goodbyes. I'll be back on the Monday,' he promised.

'That's probably for the best,' she agreed. She leaned against the open door, resting her head wearily on it and sighed.

'Oh! I'll see you tomorrow night anyway,' he said, suddenly remembering. 'That's if you're still going?'

'Going where? Oh!' Clearly Abbie had forgotten, too. 'Of course, the engagement party. Yes, I'll see you there. If I'm still in the mood to go after saying goodbye to my children that is.'

'It might help take your mind off it,' he suggested.

'I suppose so.' She didn't sound too convinced. 'It's going to be so empty here without them. I'll miss them so much.'

He could well believe it. Funnily enough, he'd grown quite fond of them all, and had to admit that even he would find the house quite strange without their presence. 'Maybe—' He stopped and shook his head.

'Maybe what?'

He paused, then said in a low voice, 'Maybe we could do something for them while they're away.'

'Do what for them?' she said, her eyes wide with surprise.

'Well, what about fixing up their bedrooms?' he suggested. 'Isla especially is really longing for her own space and a room she can feel at home in. Why don't we spend the next two weeks while they're away getting all three bedrooms ready for their return?'

'But will you have time, with the bathroom to do?'

'I've already started laying the flooring. Once Tyler's fitted the suite it's just a case of tiling. That won't take me too long. We'll have plenty of time to finish the bedrooms.'

Abbie's eyes shone with excitement. 'That would be perfect! I'll have a think tonight about what we can do.'

'And at some point during the week we can go shopping one evening, after you finish work. Get the stuff we need for the bedrooms. What do you say?'

'Oh thank you, Jackson! They'll love it. And it will make me feel better about them being away for so long. I was dreading it to be honest, but if I'm going to be doing this as a surprise for them it will fly by.'

Jackson's stomach fluttered as she beamed up at him, her face alight, dimples on display. He had to force himself not to reach out and touch her face. That would be a catastrophe. Their friendship had been hard-won and there was no way he was going to risk losing it for something that had no chance of even beginning.

Because it *would* have no chance. Abbie was bright and beautiful and would have no time for someone like him, with all his hang-ups and insecurities. And he really couldn't blame her for that.

'Get looking online for ideas,' he whispered as he stepped outside. 'And remember, it's a secret.'

'Our secret,' she promised.

He felt a vague thrill at the words and something inside him screamed in alarm. Things had changed—at least for him. But absolutely nothing could come of it. What on earth was he going to do now?

Chapter 13

The engagement party was a fairly intimate affair, held in the function room at The Bay Horse. Izzy was having a fine old time, flashing her sparkling engagement ring under the noses of every person in the pub, and beaming as they congratulated her and admired the beautiful diamond solitaire.

'Ash chose it,' she kept telling everyone. 'All by himself. Didn't he choose well?'

Everyone agreed he had, and Ash stood, pint of his favourite Lusty Tup beer in hand, looking very smug, much to Jackson's amusement.

'Should've brought my sunglasses,' Jackson said, as Ash accepted yet another compliment on his superb choice of jewellery.

'Huh?'

'Your halo's dazzling me.'

Ash grinned. 'Hey, not often I get this much praise—especially from women. Let me wallow in it for a while, eh? Anyway, you can talk.'

Jackson raised an eyebrow. 'Me? What have I done?'

'Don't play the innocent! The knight in shining armour who rode to the rescue of *that nice Dr Sawdon, and he's doing all that work on the house for her for free and taking her and them kiddies out an' all.* What a hero.'

Jackson shuffled uncomfortably. 'Who's saying that?'

'Everyone in the village, mate. They're all talking. Course, they don't think you're doing it out of the kindness of your heart. They all think something's going on between you.'

'Tell me you're joking!'

Ash shook his head. 'Nope. It's all round Bramblewick. What did you expect when you decided to take them all out to the seaside? Did you honestly think you'd get away with that round here? As far as the villagers are concerned, you and that lovely doctor are an item. I'm guessing you're not?'

Jackson tutted. 'Don't be ridiculous. We're just friends, that's all.'

'Ooh.' Ash gave him a meaningful look. 'Well that's a step up. You were barely acquaintances, last I heard. Friends now are you?'

'Shut up.' Jackson was feeling increasingly uncomfortable. 'I've been working there, on and off, for a month now. Of course we're friends. How could we not be?'

'Well, it's a start I suppose.'

'For goodness' sake!' A sudden thought occurred to Jackson, and he stared at Ash in dismay. 'Abbie hasn't heard about this has she?'

'I have no idea. It wouldn't surprise me. You know how chatty people are here, and she does have to make her visits after all, not to mention all the locals popping into the surgery with their aches and pains. Someone's bound to have mentioned something, surely?'

'Oh, no.' Abbie hadn't arrived at the party yet, and Jackson felt his stomach lurch in dread. If everyone here in this room thought they were an item they would be watched all night, their every move scrutinised. Abbie was bound to pick up on it, if she hadn't already, and how would she react? It might scare her off. She might push him away altogether, ask him not to continue working on The Gables. He was appalled at how depressed that thought made him feel.

'So, the lovely doctor hasn't arrived yet then?'

Jackson blinked then pulled a face as Xander wandered over, his wide grin revealing that he too had heard the gossip.

'Don't you start.'

'So it's not true? You and Abbie Sawdon, you're not an item?'

'Of course we're not! I'm just helping her out, that's all.'

'Well, obviously. But the question is, what are you helping her out *with*?'

Jackson glared at him and Xander held up his hands. 'Sorry, sorry. Clearly a sore subject. I won't mention it again.'

But it was too late, because now that he was aware of what people thought it became clear to Jackson that he was getting sly glances from just about everyone in the function room. It seemed to him that there were huddles of people everywhere, whispering, dissecting his behaviour, speculating...

'I think I should go home.'

'What?' Both Ash and Xander looked stunned. 'Don't be daft, mate. Look we won't say anything more about this, will we, Xander?'

'Of course not. Sorry, Jackson. I know what it's like when every detail of your private life is picked over. The subject is closed. Anyway, I'd best be getting back to Rachel. She's been accosted by Sandra about some medical problem. That's why I came over here in the first place. Maybe I should rescue her. So... yeah...' He wandered away, clearly wishing he'd never left Rachel's side, and Jackson and Ash looked at each other, a questioning look on the latter's face.

'You're not really going are you? Just over a bit of gossip. Surely you can ignore that?'

Jackson shook his head. 'I can, yes, but what if Abbie hears about this? What's she going to think?'

'Well,' Ash frowned, 'she knows the truth of it, so I'm sure she'll just laugh it off. What else can she do?'

What else *could* she do? React with horror he guessed. Why wouldn't she?

'Are you okay?' Ash eyed him over the rim of his glass. 'Is there something I'm missing?'

'No of course not. I just—' Jackson broke off and his mouth went dry as he saw Abbie walk into the room. His heart thumped. He'd never seen her look like that before, with her hair pinned up, tawny-coloured tendrils falling loosely at the side of her face. She'd put on makeup—even lipstick—and was wearing an elegant black dress with a lace inset at the neckline and lace sleeves. It was on the tip of his tongue to say, "Wow!" but, luckily, he stopped himself in time.

As she moved towards the other end of the room where Izzy, Anna and Nell were gathered, Jackson's eyes followed her automatically. He realised his heartbeat had speeded up and groaned inwardly. Was this what he feared? Was this how love felt? He'd never experienced it before and had no idea how to react. After all this time, how had it even happened? And so unexpectedly too.

'I think you'd better tell me the truth.'

'What?'

Ash's eyes narrowed. 'Don't play the innocent. It's written all over your face.'

'Is it?' *Was it?*

'You like her don't you? I mean, you *really* like her. So *are* you an item or what? Is all this indignation a charade? Are you seeing each other?'

'Don't be ridiculous! I've told you, we're just friends.'

'But you'd like to be more? Oh come on, Jackson, don't look at me like that. We've known each other long enough for me to be able to tell when you're covering something up.' He glanced around then moved a little closer. 'I won't say anything, mate, trust me. This is between you and me.'

Jackson hesitated, but he knew he could rely on Ash and, besides, hadn't his friend confided in him when he'd been pining for Izzy? Maybe that was what friends were for. He wasn't sure, having never had a friend other than Ash. His brother had always been his only confidante and he'd got used to keeping things from Tyler anyway, never wanting to burden him, always keen to protect him. It was his default setting. Protect

Tyler at all costs.

'She's—' He paused, wondering whether to go on. 'She's grown on me.'

Ash smirked. 'You don't say. Is that Jacksonese for *I fancy her rotten?*'

Jackson closed his eyes. 'Don't. Just don't.'

Ash's tone altered. 'This is serious, isn't it?'

The concern in his voice made Jackson finally meet his gaze. 'I don't know what to do. I've never felt this way before.'

'What, never?'

Jackson swirled the beer round in his glass and gazed into its dark amber depths, feeling bewildered. 'No. Never.'

'Phew!' Ash was quiet for a moment, considering. 'Is it love, do you think?'

'How would I know? How did you know when you were falling for Izzy?'

Ash thought about it. 'I guess she was all I thought about. Couldn't think about anyone else.'

Jackson sighed. 'Tick.'

'Couldn't concentrate on anything.'

'Tick.'

'Made any excuse I could to be near her.'

Jackson swallowed hard. 'Tick.'

'Wanted to touch her—just brush against her even.'

This was too much! He felt pathetic. He looked away, unable to answer.

Ash blew out his cheeks. 'Oh, dear. You're in love, mate.'

'Well, what do I do?' He heard a hint of panic in his

voice and tried to rein in the anxiety. 'How do I get over it?'

Ash looked puzzled. 'Why would you want to get over it? Why don't you embrace it instead?'

'Embrace it?' Was Ash completely mad? 'What do you mean, embrace it?'

'Well, have you told her? Have you so much as hinted how you feel?'

'Of course not!' Hell, he'd rather die.

'Then how do you know she doesn't feel exactly the same about you?'

'Abbie? Are you crazy?'

'What's crazy about that?' Ash's expression softened. 'Come on, mate, why shouldn't she? You've been hanging around her house for a month now and she hasn't got sick of you. That's got to mean something.'

'Yes, it means she needs the house finishing.'

'Oh, come on. She could hire someone if it were that bad. You've been good to her. Maybe it's made her see you in a positive light. Why wouldn't it? You have a lot to offer her.'

Jackson spluttered with laughter. 'Yes, right, course I have.'

Ash looked genuinely puzzled. 'What do you mean?'

'Well, for god's sake! Me, with all my hang-ups and anxieties? Abbie's a free spirit. I'd drive her mad. And besides...' His voice trailed off as he contemplated revealing his innermost fears to his friend.

Ash surveyed him curiously. 'Besides what?'

Jackson took the plunge. 'Well, this.' He made a

circular motion around his lower face, not meeting Ash's eyes.

'What?'

Jackson tutted impatiently. 'Don't play games. You know perfectly well what.'

'I genuinely don't have the first—oh! Oh my word, is this about that bloody scar again?'

Jackson felt wounded. 'Don't say it like that! As if it's nothing.'

'But it is nothing! Blimey, Jackson, it's no more than a scratch and you're seriously still banging on about it as if you're the Elephant Man or something.'

'It's—it's ugly.'

'Mate, seriously, it's not even noticeable. I only saw it after you pointed it out to me, and why you felt the need to do that I've never understood.'

'You were staring at it,' Jackson protested. 'I knew you had questions.'

'That, my friend,' Ash assured him, 'was absolutely one hundred per cent in your head. I hadn't spotted it. I was actually admiring your beard and wishing I could grow one. I just don't have that ability. I can go days without shaving and it's embarrassing.'

'Not as embarrassing as a cleft lip,' Jackson muttered.

'But you haven't got a cleft lip anymore,' Ash said, sounding exasperated. 'You told me yourself, you had the operation when you were just a toddler. Bet you can't even remember before that.'

'Well, no,' Jackson admitted. 'But I do remember starting school and all the kids making fun of the scar and staring at me, laughing at me.'

'But the scar would have been quite new then,' Ash pointed out. 'And you know what kids are like. They try to find anything different about anybody. It's been decades, mate, and honestly that scar's barely visible.' He sighed. 'That's why you keep the beard isn't it? Camouflage.'

Jackson looked away, feeling the emotions well up inside him. 'I don't want to talk about this anymore, Ash. I'm sorry.'

Ash made a noise, as if he were about to say something, but evidently thought better of it. 'Okay, fair enough. But that doesn't change anything about Abbie. I'll bet you anything you like that she hasn't even noticed the scar. If you like her so much you ought to approach her. Why not?'

Jackson shrugged. 'Can we change the subject now?'

Ash looked as if he were about to argue the point, but luckily Izzy wandered over at that moment and threw her arms around her fiancé's neck.

'Are you having a good time? I am. Everyone loves the engagement ring and quite right too.' She smiled at Jackson. 'Are you having a good time, Jackson?'

Jackson gave her a stiff smile. 'Absolutely.'

'Good. You should.' She waved her hand in the air. 'Abbie's over there you know. Go and see her. Bet she's waiting for you.'

Ash cleared his throat. 'No sign of Holly, I see,' he said, demonstrating a masterclass in changing the subject.

Izzy's smile vanished. 'I know. Nell tried calling her,

but she didn't answer. I'm a bit worried to be honest. She loves a party usually. Do you think she's all right?'

'I'm sure she's fine,' Ash reassured her. 'Don't worry. Maybe she's just running late.'

'I hope you're right,' Izzy said. 'I suppose you are. She'll probably be here any minute.'

***

Holly, however, never turned up. Rachel tried ringing her, then Izzy tried an hour later, but the phone wasn't picked up.

'Maybe she's not very well,' Anna said, sounding unconvinced.

'She could at least have called me to tell me she'd changed her mind about coming.'

Izzy was clearly hurt, Abbie realised, and even though she'd only known Holly for a relatively short time, she too was a little concerned. Holly had definitely said she was going to the party, so it was strange that she hadn't turned up, especially given how close she was to her little group of friends.

'She's probably having a night of passion with the divine Jonathan instead,' Anna said eventually.

Rachel looked doubtful. 'You think? Are they getting on okay?'

'They were very loved up last week,' Abbie admitted. 'She was acting really soppy about him at work.'

'I suppose she might be,' Izzy said. 'Still think she could have rung me though. Anyway,' she grinned suddenly and nudged Abbie, 'talking about being loved up, what's this I've been hearing about you and Jackson?'

Abbie frowned. 'What about me and Jackson?'

'Told you she'd deny it!' Anna giggled. 'Look at her face! Miss aspirin-wouldn't-melt-in-her-mouth.'

'You're not fooling anyone you know,' Nell told her, her blue eyes twinkling. 'The whole village is agog. That lovely doctor from Bramblewick Surgery and that gorgeous teacher from the primary school. You're this month's star couple.'

'What on earth are you all talking about?' Abbie felt a weird clutching feeling in her stomach. 'Where have you got this from?'

'You and Jackson? Like I said, it's the talk of the village.' Nell reached for a sandwich from the plate that was lying on the table. 'Everyone's discussing how Mr Wade is spending each and every day of his holidays up at The Gables.'

'Doing work!'

Rachel tilted her head to one side. 'So there's nothing in it? Really?'

'You don't have to sound so disappointed,' Abbie muttered. She felt nauseated at the thought that everyone had been discussing her private life. Oh lord, what if Jackson heard about it? He'd be mortified! 'Jackson's just been really kind, that's all.'

'But he's been there a month, Abbie,' Anna persisted. 'Surely you've developed some sort of bond by now?'

'A friendship, that's all.' Abbie could feel the butterflies flapping frantically around in her stomach.

'There's nothing else going on, nor will there ever be.'

'But you all went to the coast for the day! You must be more than just friends,' Nell persisted.

'Why? Do you never go anywhere with your friends?'

Nell looked thoroughly disappointed. 'Well, yes but…oh, why not? Jackson's a good-looking bloke. You could do worse.'

'Hmm, maybe he is good-looking,' Rachel said, 'but he's a bit—er—sullen, isn't he?'

'No, he's not!' Izzy and Abbie burst out at the same time and Rachel, Nell and Anna exchanged knowing looks.

'Ooh, defending him there, Abbie,' Anna said, helping herself to a sausage roll. 'He *has* got a bit of a reputation though. Good-looking he may be, but he's not exactly chatty at school is he?'

'He's just a bit shy,' Izzy protested. 'Once you get to know him he's a great bloke.' She smiled at Abbie. 'That's true, isn't it? He's lovely, isn't he?'

'I—yes—I mean, yes he is.' Abbie wished she'd never opened her mouth. Was it getting hot in here? She fished in her bag and brought out a tissue, dabbing at her face.

'You've gone ever so red,' Nell observed.

Abbie had had an awful feeling about that. She could feel the tell-tale prickling sensation in her scalp and groaned inside. Not now! Not tonight, with everyone focusing on her.

'Would anyone like another drink?' she managed brightly, hoping to deflect interest from her obvious discomfort.

'You're not even drinking,' Anna pointed out.

'None of us are except for Izzy,' Nell said, grinning. 'What with you and me breastfeeding and Rachel driving. What's your excuse, Abbie? With your kids away I'd have thought you'd be in a real party mood, not having to get up early with them for once.'

'I just don't like the taste of alcohol,' Abbie said. 'So, do you want a drink or not?'

'I'll come with you,' Rachel offered. 'Same again, ladies?'

They all confirmed the order and Rachel steered Abbie towards the bar.

'Are you okay?' she asked, as they leaned on the counter and Abbie dabbed frantically at her forehead. 'You seem a bit flustered. Is it the Jackson thing? *Are* you seeing him? Because I can keep a secret you know.'

Abbie took a deep breath and tried to calm her nerves. 'I know you can, Rachel, and I would tell you if there was anything going on, but there's not. Really there's not.'

'Shame.' Rachel tapped a beermat on the bar top as she considered her. 'I thought maybe—well, you must admit he's been at your place a lot, considering the plan was only to tidy up the hallway for you. I've got to wonder why he's so intent on finding new things to do for you. What's he trying to prove to you?'

'He's just bored and looking for something to do,' Abbie protested. 'You're looking for something that isn't there.'

'Or you're refusing to see something that is.' Rachel

raised an eyebrow. 'You could do with a bit of love in your life, and he is rather sexy isn't he?'

'Is he?'

Rachel nodded in a vague direction somewhere over Abbie's shoulder. Abbie spun round and gulped as she saw Jackson standing near the door, deep in conversation with Ash. He was wearing black trousers and a black shirt, and by the look of it he was taking something very seriously, as there was a deep frown on his forehead.

She wanted to turn away but found she couldn't do it. She supposed, when she came to think about it, Jackson *was* rather handsome. And she certainly couldn't deny that he was kind and generous. He'd been nothing but helpful to her, that was for sure, and he'd even managed to win Isla over.

Beside her she heard Rachel giving their order to Ernie, and wanted to turn around to face him, but something was locking her gaze in Jackson's direction. Like a scene from a horror movie, as if in slow motion she saw Jackson turn his head slightly and look over in her direction.

Every fibre of her being was screaming at her to turn away quickly, but she was frozen. Jackson's eyes met hers and for a long moment they stared at each other. He gave her a faint smile and nodded at her. Her mouth felt dry, and her legs were shaky. She managed a brief nod back then turned thankfully to face Ernie, leaning heavily on the counter as if she'd been drained of all energy.

'Are you all right?' Rachel looked at her in alarm.

'Yes, I just—' Abbie shook her head, not sure what had happened. Why was she suddenly seeing Jackson Wade in a whole new light? It was bewildering. When she'd arrived at the pub, he'd just been a kind man who was doing her a favour. A friend. Nothing more.

Now suddenly he was the most desirable man in the village, and her heart was thumping just knowing he was across the room from her.

How had that happened? What was she going to do about it? Had she actually gone and fallen for him?

She felt a flutter of panic. Now what? Jackson Wade would be appalled if he suspected her feelings. She was, after all, his polar opposite. His life was controlled, organised, calm. Her life was messy and chaotic. She had three noisy children and two energetic, hairy dogs. He still pulled a face if he got a dog hair on his trousers. What would he ever see in someone like her? Especially when... She shuddered. He must never know about that. Never. *Stop it, Abbie. Don't think about that.*

Well, she thought grimly, this was just great. Of all the messes to get herself into, this was just about the biggest. As if she didn't have enough to cope with.

'Can you manage some of these?' Rachel asked, nodding at the glasses that Ernie had placed on the bar. 'Only you look ever so hot and bothered.'

'I'm okay,' Abbie assured her. Because after all she would have to be, wouldn't she? She wasn't the weak and incapable woman that Nick seemed to think she was. She knew he worried about her, and she appreciated that, but she would show him that she was fine and could deal with anything that life threw at her.

She could keep things on a level footing and be completely normal around Jackson Wade. He would never so much as suspect that her feelings for him had changed. Irrevocably. Dramatically. Catastrophically.

Oh damn. She really, really wished she could drink.

Chapter 14

Abbie had made up her mind. Jackson Wade must never know that she had feelings for him. He mustn't have the faintest glimmer of suspicion. She knew enough about him to realise that it would make things so awkward that he'd probably decide it would be better to stop working at The Gables.

No doubt he would be polite and kind, but he'd find it impossible to continue visiting the house each day. His anxieties would grow and that wouldn't be fair to him. It wouldn't be fair to her either, quite honestly. It was tough enough seeing him every day, smiling, making polite conversation, working alongside him at the weekends, but it would be even tougher if she didn't see him at all.

Which was what she'd finally realised after a long and largely sleepless night following Izzy's engagement party. Lying awake in her bed, staring up at the ceiling, she'd wondered what to do. Should she come up with some excuse to send him away? But what? And how could she do that without hurting his feelings, or making her seem like a heartless, ungrateful monster?

Going over and over it in her mind, she'd eventually concluded that the problem lay with the fact that she didn't *want* to tell him to leave. She wanted to see him every day, even if it was torture pretending not to care.

She did her best when he arrived at The Gables that Monday morning to act as she usually did. It proved harder than she'd imagined, and she was glad to dash away to work, only to find she spent the entire day trying her best not to think about him.

He'd finished laying the bathroom flooring by the time she got home and had already made a start stripping the wallpaper in Isla's bedroom. Feeling a mixture of gratitude and guilt she ordered them both a takeaway, against her better judgment, and they ate together in the living room, from trays on their laps. She thoughtfully shut the dogs in the kitchen so he wouldn't be freaked out by them trying to steal food off his plate.

'If it's okay with you, I'll stay on for a couple more hours,' he said, in between forkfuls of chicken chow mein. 'I'd really like to get on with the bedrooms as fast as possible, since I'll have the tiling to do in the bathroom after my brother's fitted the suite.'

'I'll help,' she offered immediately.

He looked doubtful. 'Are you sure? You've been at work all day as it is.'

'So have you,' she pointed out, a fact he couldn't deny. She couldn't help feeling a little discouraged that he didn't seem thrilled at the prospect of her working with him, but she tried to ignore the disappointment, making bright and chatty conversation as they worked.

She watched him out of the corner of her eye as he stood in Isla's bedroom, stripping wallpaper. Her stomach fluttered as she noticed little things about him: the way he rolled his sleeves up so neatly and evenly; the frown of concentration on his face as he worked; the way his hand held the paper stripper so firmly; the shape of his fingers as his other hand tore off the paper that had come loose. She wondered how on earth she hadn't noticed all these things before. To think he'd been at her house for a month, and she'd wasted all that time! She couldn't fathom it out.

'Do you want to make a start on Bertie's room?' he queried, evidently noticing that she was doing nothing of any use.

Abbie reddened. Now he'd think she was lazy. 'Oh, yes. Right. Good idea.'

Her heart sinking, she left him to it and took her own paper stripper into the back bedroom, thinking it was going to be a lot less bearable to do such a boring job by herself. It had all been a lot easier when Jackson Wade was just a kind man doing her a favour.

***

After two days of hard work both bedrooms had been stripped, carpets taken up and all the children's belongings piled into her own bedroom, which was now practically inaccessible. Poppy's room hadn't needed as much work as it hadn't been papered and just needed a fresh coat of paint. All three bedrooms were now blank canvases, and Jackson had been pleased to note that the walls didn't need skimming after all. Unlike the landing and hallway, which had all been covered in the dreaded woodchip, the children's rooms had been decorated in one layer of easy-to-remove wallpaper.

Abbie had agreed that painting the walls would be quicker and easier, so the two of them had arranged to go into Helmston on the Saturday morning. They'd be able to get all the paint they needed from the DIY store in town, as well as browse the furniture department, before visiting the carpet shop for new carpets for all three of the children's rooms.

'In the meantime,' Jackson said, 'I'll take the bathroom suite out while you're at work tomorrow, since Tyler's coming to fit the new one on Thursday night.'

Abbie smiled. 'It's so good of him. I'm looking forward to meeting him at last.'

If Jackson wanted her to meet his brother he didn't show it, but then that was Jackson. He simply got on with the work and didn't reveal much of himself at all. He'd already removed the old wall tiles and the bathroom was now ready to be transformed. It was all so exciting, but it also brought home to her that time was running out. The summer holidays would soon be over, and with it the Gables project. Jackson would head back to school and become the distant teacher he'd been just a few short weeks ago. She'd hardly see him—perhaps catching the odd glimpse of him at school events, or the occasional social gathering with Izzy and Ash.

Maybe, she thought dismally, her friends' wedding would be the next real opportunity she had to spend any time with him.

Jackson didn't seem to have given the matter any thought at all. He was in his own happy little world, making lists and ticking things off as each job was completed. He was clearly in his element, and she could see that it gave him a great deal of satisfaction that he'd already made such a difference to the house.

The front door had been painted and rehung, a shiny new letterbox and handle fitted to give it that finishing touch; the hallway and landing were freshly painted and there was a thick new stair carpet laid which made a whole world of difference; the children's rooms were waiting to be transformed; the bathroom had smart new flooring and was just waiting for the suite to be fitted and the final touches to be made with tiles, paint and accessories. Downstairs, the kitchen looked much better, and Abbie was confident that she could make further improvements to the other rooms herself over time. The second reception room had bookcases and toy chests in it, as Abbie had decided to make it into a space for Poppy and Bertie to spend time and create as much mess and mayhem as they wished. The empty middle room had no purpose as yet. Abbie was still wondering whether to turn it into an office—which she didn't really need—or maybe make it a snug. She was in no hurry to decide anyway.

Lewis had cleared the gardens, digging out weeds, strimming, and mowing, and cutting back shrubbery to reveal flowerbeds and a fairly sizeable lawn both front and back. For now, she would concentrate on keeping them that way, but maybe after Christmas she would be able to afford to hire Lewis to landscape the gardens for her. It would make all the difference.

Abbie had to admit that it was a lot less stressful, coming downstairs each morning to a tidy house. The main challenge, of course, would be keeping on top of it all, but maybe it was time she asked Isla for a bit of help. Abbie had certainly been helping her own mother at thirteen. Even Bertie could make himself useful in the garden, and they could both help to keep their rooms tidy.

Despite her desire for them to have the perfect, idyllic childhood, Abbie realised that she had her limitations, and it wouldn't hurt to ask them for help. In fact, it might do them good she mused. Give them a sense of purpose and responsibility. She was pretty sure that, when they saw their new bedrooms, they'd be very keen to keep them looking as good as new.

It wasn't the lifestyle she'd expected when she moved into The Gables, envisioning a rather bohemian existence for them all, but Jackson had made a bit of organisation seem so enticing that she'd had a major rethink. The whole point of the move was to ensure that the children had a happy and carefree childhood. It seemed, against all her expectations, that routine and a bit of discipline was what they needed after all. She'd really got that wrong hadn't she? She wondered how long it would have taken her to realise it without Jackson at her side.

None of this would have been possible without his help. He really had been amazing.

She wasn't sure how to feel as he picked her up in

his car that Saturday morning. Part of her was excited to be spending a whole day with him, but the other part was dreading it. She didn't know if she could hide the fact that she was now completely besotted with him for the entire outing.

What she'd come to realise was, these feelings weren't as out of the blue as she'd thought. When she looked back over the last few weeks, she'd concluded that her feelings for Jackson Wade had been building slowly day upon day. She'd just done an amazing job at not paying attention to them. It was only when her friends had voiced their opinions about their relationship that the truth had dawned on her, and it had hit her hard.

She couldn't see any way to resolve it. Not only was she not Jackson's type, but he wasn't hers. He was everything she was trying to avoid. All about rules and order and reality. He represented the world she'd escaped from. The reason she'd taken the job at Bramblewick and moved her family to this little village on the North York Moors, away from their comfortable home in the ultra-normal street, with its overlooked garden and concrete views.

Jackson, if given free rein in her life, would, once he knew more about her, take over. Nick had been bad enough, but Jackson would be worse. He wouldn't let her bury her head in the sand. He would make her face up to reality and she didn't want to do that. He would fuss and worry, and his anxieties would deepen. How was that fair on either of them? She knew their relationship was a non-starter, but it really didn't stop her fantasising that, somehow, they would find a way to compromise.

Crazy, she thought to herself, as Jackson drove them along the moors' road towards Helmston. *That's what you are, Abbie Sawdon. Completely crazy. Here you are, worrying about how he's going to change your life and he's not even a part of it. Not really. And he has no intention of becoming part of it either.*

She almost laughed out loud at the thought of Jackson's expression if she told him how she felt. She could almost see his lip curl, the alarm in his eyes. That house! Those dogs! Those noisy, messy children!

'What are you smiling at?'

She flushed and glanced at him, her heart thudding as she noticed he was smiling too, his dark brown eyes warm with just a hint of curiosity in them.

'I didn't realise I was,' she admitted. 'I was—er—just imagining the kids' faces when they see their rooms.'

He nodded. 'They're going to love them. Have you got a clear picture of what you want for them?'

She beamed, glad of the distraction. 'Absolutely! I've been thinking about it all week, and I know exactly what they'd like.'

The DIY store on the outskirts of Helmston was huge. Jackson took a trolley, and they began by visiting the paint department.

'Right.' Abbie took a deep breath. 'Here we go.'

'So many choices,' Jackson mused as they stood examining the tins of emulsion. 'Even if you want white, have you seen how many shades of white there are? Have you got any ideas?'

'Jackson! Abbie!'

Abbie spun round and her heart sank as she saw Izzy heading over towards them, basket in hand and a huge grin on her face. 'Oh, hi, Izz.'

'Izzy.' Jackson nodded, his previously relaxed stance completely altered as he surveyed her warily.

'Fancy seeing you here,' Izzy said, grinning. 'Together.'

The word hung in the air and Abbie felt the colour seep into her cheeks. Now Izzy would put two and two together and make three million and seventy the way she always did. This would get around the village in no time.

'What are you up to then?' Izzy enquired, peering at the tin of paint in Jackson's hands.

'I would have thought that was obvious,' he said. 'We're buying paint for the bedrooms.'

Izzy's eyes widened. 'For the *bedrooms*?'

The way she said it, the word *bedrooms* took on a whole new meaning.

'The children's bedrooms,' Abbie said hastily. 'It's a surprise for them while they're away. They're going to get home to a whole new look.'

'Aw, how lovely.' Izzy beamed at them.

'Where's Ash?' Jackson enquired, probably to change the subject.

'He's at home,' she said cheerfully. 'Taking a leaf out of your book and tidying up the house.' She nodded at her loaded basket. 'I've just popped in to get some new towels and a bathmat for the bathroom. We're sprucing it up a bit. Ringing the changes. As you do.'

'Well,' Jackson said evenly, 'don't let us keep you.'

Izzy gave him a knowing look. 'Anyone would think you were trying to get rid of me,' she said, a twinkle in her eyes. 'Okay, I'll take the hint and leave you to it. Great to see you both out and about.' She beamed at them. 'You look so lovely together. I'm so happy for you both!'

Abbie's face burned as she gave Jackson a sideways glance, dreading to see how he was taking Izzy's remark.

Jackson looked as if he'd happily throttle Izzy. His mouth opened and closed but, evidently, he had no words to express his contempt.

'Bye, Izzy,' Abbie said hastily.

Izzy was either being remarkably thick-skinned or deliberately obtuse she thought, as their so-called friend gave them a knowing grin and headed off towards the checkout.

Abbie swallowed, not knowing what to say after such an embarrassing encounter.

'Sorry.'

Nervously, they both started to laugh at the fact that each had apologised to the other in the same breath.

'Don't worry about it,' Abbie said, relieved that Jackson was still hanging on to his sense of humour. 'We all know what Izzy's like. A sucker for a romance, and never mind if there's no truth in it.'

Jackson nodded—rather too eagerly, Abbie thought wretchedly.

'Absolutely. I'm sure no one else has given any thought to us at all. Shall we get on?'

They were in the DIY store for over two hours, followed by another forty minutes in the nearby carpet shop, but at last they were done. The car was loaded up, deliveries were booked, and Abbie felt a real sense of accomplishment.

'Is this what it feels like?' she asked Jackson as they fastened their seatbelts.

'What?'

'To achieve something,' she said. 'To have a list of goals and to tick them all off.'

He grinned and her heart thudded in response. 'Feels good doesn't it?'

'Oh,' she said, 'it really does.' *You have no idea, thank God.*

'Tell you what,' he said, 'why don't we have lunch while we're here? There's that nice little pub off the marketplace that does good food.'

She wrinkled her nose. 'Is that The Fox and Hounds?'

He exhaled sharply. 'Phew, no chance. The Fox and Hounds is booked up for months ahead, sorry. But The Fat Grouse is decent enough. Not as posh as The Fox and Hounds but it's comfy and clean. The food's standard pub grub, but...'

'That would be fine,' she agreed.

'Not that you wouldn't be welcome at my flat,' he added hastily. 'Just, I thought we deserved a treat. Don't we?'

He was looking at her quite intently, and she hoped her face wasn't burning. It certainly felt as if it were. She wondered what his flat was like. Was it wrong that she'd really like to have seen it? She couldn't help wishing that he'd wanted her to.

'I think we do, yes.'

She should have said she needed to get home really. After all, was sitting across a table, staring into his eyes in a pub really the way to convince him, and herself, that this relationship was purely platonic? Anyone would think she enjoyed torturing herself she mused, as they pulled into the car park of The Fat Grouse.

Jackson ordered the food at the bar and returned to the table with two glasses of Coke. He looked a bit flustered himself, which was unusual for him.

'What do you think?' He glanced around the room, his voice enquiring. 'Good enough?'

'It's lovely,' she said. 'I've never been here before. Actually,' she admitted, 'I've never been in any pub around here except The Hare and Moon in Kearton Bay and The Bay Horse, obviously.'

They both stared at each other for a moment, as if, Abbie thought, they were each struck by the memory of that ill-fated blind date. Lord, her and her big mouth!

'It was a bit of a disaster wasn't it?' Jackson said, a rueful smile on his lips.

Abbie was about to agree with him, but when she thought about it, she couldn't. 'It was a bit tricky,' she conceded, 'but it paved the way for all this didn't it? So maybe it wasn't the disaster we think it was.'

His eyes widened and she knew for a fact that, this time, her face was definitely burning. 'What I mean is, if we hadn't gone on that date, maybe you wouldn't have felt able to offer to help me out. We'd still have been just parent and teacher. Strangers really. Instead of—friends.'

He seemed to find this comment extraordinary, and it evidently took a moment or two for him to digest her words. Eventually he murmured, 'I suppose you're right.'

'And anyway,' she added, trying her best to sound nonchalant, 'it wasn't so bad was it?' She looked at him hopefully. 'I mean, we got on okay in the end once we'd relaxed.'

'And admitted neither of us were expecting the date to lead to anything,' Jackson said quietly.

Abbie's heart sank. 'Yeah. That too I suppose.' She took a large swig of Coke and cradled her glass in her hand, not sure what to say next.

They sat in silence for ages. Actually, she realised, it was only for a few minutes, but it felt like eternity.

'The bedrooms are going to look great,' Jackson ventured at last. 'I love what you've got planned for them.'

'Thanks. I had to do a lot of browsing online to get some ideas,' she admitted, relieved to have something else to talk about. 'It was quite easy with Bertie. He loved being near the sea at Kearton Bay, and he'll adore the nautical look. Pops is easy too of course. She'll be happy with anything really. It was Isla who was the trickiest. I don't want her to feel that I'm still treating her like a child, even though in my eyes she is.'

'I think you've judged it just right,' Jackson assured her. 'She's a lucky girl.'

'She's had a tough time of it,' Abbie said, her voice

suddenly thick with emotion. 'I doubt very much that she'd see herself as lucky at all.'

'It's always hard being a teenager.' Jackson was clearly trying to console her. 'And I know divorce can be hard on children, especially ones of Isla's age, but I think you and Nick have handled it really well. You're clearly still friends, and the fact that he keeps in touch and has a say in their lives is so important. It was never going to be perfect, but you've probably made the situation the best it can be.'

'It's not just the divorce though.' Abbie shook her head, wondering why she'd blurted that out.

'Oh?'

She really didn't want to go there. She *couldn't* go there. 'It's nothing,' she said.

He was watching her, obviously curious. 'Are you sure? I'm a good listener.'

She was quite certain that he would be, and he would no doubt be concerned and kind and say all the right things, but she couldn't do it. She didn't want to go over all that again. It was in the past and she wanted it to stay there, buried away, forgotten.

'I hope that food won't be long,' she said cheerfully. 'I'm starving!'

Jackson smiled and took a sip of his Coke, but his eyes showed that he was puzzled, and she knew he would be wondering.

He would have to wonder. Some things should never be spoken about. Not unless they had to be, and she could only pray that would never be the case.

Chapter 15

Bertie's and Poppy's rooms were painted, and Jackson and Abbie were hard at work on Isla's.

It was important to Abbie that her daughter's bedroom was just right. She wanted it to reflect the fact that Isla was now a teenager and not a child and, to that end, she'd ordered her a new double bed, new "grown-up" bedding—not a pop star or Disney character in sight—and soft furnishings. There was a new wardrobe, and a desk and chair had been selected too, so that she'd have space to sit and do her homework in peace. New mixed storage units were ready to be put together, so all Isla's bits and pieces could be either hidden in cupboards and drawers, or left on display in the open shelving, as she wished.

As Abbie and Jackson emulsioned the walls, she wondered how Isla would react when she saw what they'd done. She hadn't been expecting any changes to her room as Abbie had told her it would be months before they got around to doing the bedrooms, so it would be an amazing surprise for her. Isla really needed a comfortable and private space for herself, and she deserved somewhere pretty—somewhere she'd be happy to invite friends to.

Bertie's room looked fresh and rather jaunty, with white walls and red curtains. A set of blue bunk beds, red and white storage units, and a whole box full of nautical-themed accessories were ready to be put in place, once the carpet had been laid. Poppy's room was a pretty picture of lemon and white.

Abbie thought that, really, it was the children's bedrooms that were giving her the most pleasure. The bathroom was fabulous, now that Tyler had fitted the new suite and Jackson had tiled the walls. She loved it, and she knew the children would too, but it was the fact that they would now have their own little sanctuaries that most pleased her.

She thought about her own bedroom and en suite and winced. They really needed doing too, but they were way down on the list of priorities. It would be months—maybe years—before she got around to tackling them, but that was okay. The main thing was Isla would have a home to be proud of, and the children would have space and freedom and a clean and uncluttered home to move around in. She'd been letting them down for far too long.

Jackson's brother had done a wonderful job with the bathroom and for a very reasonable price. Tyler, she mused, had been very different to Jackson and not at all as she'd expected. Unlike his brother he'd been relaxed and chatty, and had taken a real interest in her, making easy conversation with her when she popped upstairs to take him drinks and biscuits at regular intervals.

Jackson had been putting units together in Bertie's

room while Tyler worked, and at one point he'd actually gone into the bathroom to investigate what all the laughter was about. He hadn't looked best pleased when Tyler confessed to revealing some of Jackson's childhood secrets. In fact, she thought, he'd seemed quite annoyed and—maybe nervous? Now what, she considered, could Jackson possibly have to hide? Someone like him, surely, had never done anything wrong?

Tyler certainly hadn't said a bad word against his brother. His admiration and affection for Jackson was obvious, so Jackson really needn't have worried. If there was something shady in his past, Tyler wasn't going to breathe a word about it, that much was clear.

'You'll have to come to ours for dinner one evening when all this is done,' he'd told her, as he finished work and began to pack his tools away. 'My wife would love to meet you.'

Abbie had looked at him doubtfully. 'Would she?' She couldn't see why, although it was kind of him to offer.

He'd laughed. 'I'm not just saying it you know. I'm serious. We live in Moreton Cross. Do you know it?'

Abbie shrugged. 'I know of it. I've never been though.'

'It's a fairly substantial village—much bigger than Bramblewick. It's got Carroll's Confectionery World on the outskirts. You must have passed that?'

Abbie nodded, seeing the factory outlet in her mind's eye. 'Oh, yes. I know where that is.'

'Yeah, we live about five minutes' drive from that.

Get Jackson to bring you. Seriously, I mean it. We'll set a date and arrange it, okay?'

Abbie wondered why he was being so persistent. Did he invite all his clients to dinner? His wife must love him, she thought wryly. 'Fine, okay.'

He'd smiled and picked up his tool bag. 'Great. So, all done. Okay for you? Like it?'

Abbie's beaming smile was genuine. 'I love it. It looks great. Thank you so much.'

'No worries. Jackson will do a great job with the tiling. He's ever so good at it. Handy to have around isn't he?'

The butterflies in her tummy awakened and had a brief practice flight, just to remind her they were still there. 'Yes, he's been amazing.'

Tyler eyed her thoughtfully. 'He's always helping people. He's a much better person than I am, that's for sure. I could never be as unselfish as he is, I'm afraid. I don't know where I'd have been without him.'

Abbie frowned, wondering what he meant but evidently he'd got no intention of enlightening her as he slung his bag over his shoulder and headed out of the bathroom. She had no choice but to follow him down the stairs, wondering all the time what he'd meant by his remark.

'I'm going, Jackson!'

Jackson appeared at the top of the stairs as Abbie opened the front door for Tyler. 'Okay, thanks for doing that. I'll see you soon.'

'You sure will. I've invited you and Abbie to dinner.'

Tyler grinned up at his brother and Abbie flinched

as she saw the look of shock on Jackson's face. He clearly didn't think that was such a great idea.

'You've done what?'

'I know you're busy for the foreseeable future with this place,' Tyler said, raising a hand to ward off all protest, 'but a break will do you good. We'll be in touch with you to set a date.' He grinned at Abbie. 'That's settled then. See you later, Abbie. Jackson.'

'Yes, but—'

The door closed and Abbie stared up at Jackson, feeling awkward. 'What a kind invitation!' she said, keeping her tone light to allay his anxiety. 'Tyler's wife's going to be thrilled. Not.' When he didn't respond she added, 'I don't have to go. I'm sure I can make some excuse if you like.'

He ran a hand through his hair, looking confused. 'Don't be silly. If you want to go, we'll go.' His voice betrayed his uncertainty. 'Did you *want* to go?'

'I—I hadn't really thought about it. Seriously, what about his wife? Won't she object? She doesn't even know me after all.'

Jackson's fingers absently outlined his upper lip. 'No, she won't mind at all,' he said. He spoke so quietly that Abbie could hardly hear him. 'I'll leave it with you. No need to worry just yet until they start coming up with dates. Must get back to work.'

He turned and practically hurtled back into Bertie's room, leaving Abbie feeling a bit wretched.

They hadn't mentioned it again but had thrown themselves into the decorating, until now it was just a case of finishing off the painting in Isla's room and waiting for the carpets.

'I'll do the glossing in here tomorrow,' Jackson said, breaking through her thoughts and bringing her back to the present.

Abbie nodded and picked up her cup of tea. 'Ugh!' She pulled a face after taking a sip. 'This is going cold. Do you want a fresh cup?'

He shook his head. 'I'm awash with tea,' he admitted. He stepped away from the wall and put a hand in the small of his back.

'Backache?' she asked sympathetically.

'A bit,' he admitted.

She eyed him guiltily. 'I'm not surprised. You've not stopped for weeks. I really don't know how to thank you for all this.'

'Don't be silly. Like I said, I've enjoyed it. I can't believe how quickly five weeks have passed.'

'I know.' Abbie studied the lukewarm tea, feeling suddenly depressed. 'You'll be back at work in just over a week. Bet you'll be glad to see the back of The Gables.'

He put the paintbrush down on the open tin of paint and straightened again. 'Not really,' he said quietly. 'It's been fun.'

'Fun?' Abbie laughed. 'You have a strange idea of fun, I must say. This has been a really long, hard slog.'

'It's probably been harder for you,' he pointed out. 'Don't forget I've had nothing else to do, apart from some lesson planning, but you've been doing the day job and then working on the house at weekends and in the evenings. You must be shattered. You look exhausted most of the time. I've been feeling guilty about you.'

'Guilty about me?' She stared at him in surprise. 'It's me who feels guilty about you all the time! You've been a star, Jackson, you really have.'

'Not at all.' He really didn't know how to take a compliment. 'Like I said, if I'd been at home for six weeks I'd have been going mad with boredom.'

'Don't you have any hobbies?' Something nudged her subconscious and she said, 'Music! Don't you play the piano?'

He picked up his half-empty cup and placed it on the windowsill, for no fathomable reason that she could see. 'Yes, but only in term-time. I haven't got a piano as I'm afraid my flat's not exactly piano sized.'

She gave him a sympathetic smile. 'What a shame. Did you ever own one?'

'Oh, yes, but I sold it. Tyler used to look after it for me but once he had children they had no room for it either. I thought about putting it in storage, but it seemed such a waste, so I let it go.' He sighed. 'Never mind. One day I'll have a bigger place and that will be my priority. Till then, I'm lucky that I get to play the one at school so regularly. Sometimes I stay back late and just go and sit in the hall and practise. It's quite soothing.'

'I expect it is,' Abbie agreed. 'And I suppose after a long day teaching hordes of children like Bertie, your nerves are in need of soothing.'

'You could say that.' He laughed and her heart melted. He had such a delightful laugh, and she really wished she heard it more often.

'Jackson, I—' She wasn't exactly sure what she'd intended to say, but whatever it was it didn't matter as she never got the chance to finish the sentence.

As they faced each other they became aware of a blur of black and then Albus was chasing round and round the bedroom, the paintbrush he'd snatched from the top of the paint tin in his mouth, while Willow ran after him, yapping furiously.

'Albus, no!'

Abbie shrieked as the Labrador shot past her, the brush dragging against her leg leaving a thick white streak of emulsion on her jeans.

Jackson made a lunge for the dog's collar, but Albus was far too fast. He shot onto the landing, Willow following behind, clearly relishing the excitement, only to turn tail as the Labrador ran past her and back into the bedroom again, as if taunting them all.

'Come here, boy, there's a good boy!' Jackson's attempts at encouraging Albus seemed to startle the dog, which wasn't surprising given that he rarely spoke a word to them. He usually, Abbie thought, simply stared at them in wary silence or dismay, not being a dog person. Hearing him call for Albus had shocked them all, probably even Jackson himself. Even Willow stopped yapping and turned to look at him in surprise.

Albus trotted over to Jackson and stood facing him, brush hanging from his mouth, tail wagging furiously.

Jackson reached out a hand to take the brush and grasped the handle firmly.

Abbie grinned to herself. Jackson had played right

into Albus's paws.

Sure enough, the dog began to pull back as Jackson tried to take the brush from his mouth.

'Heck, he's stronger than I thought!' Jackson pulled again, while Albus took up his favourite tug-of-war position.

'You've done it now,' Abbie told him. 'This is what he wanted. It's his favourite game.'

'How did he get to be this strong?' Jackson demanded, as his attempts to remove the paintbrush proved futile. Willow danced around his ankles, letting out intermittent yaps and wagging her tail so hard her entire body rocked from side to side.

Abbie put her hands on her hips, so the dogs knew she meant business. 'Albus Dumbledore Sawdon! Behave yourself and give it back now!'

Jackson burst out laughing and let go of the paintbrush. 'Are you serious? That's his name?'

Abbie laughed, too. 'It's a tribute to our favourite wizard,' she protested. 'Don't mock.'

Albus looked from one to the other, his expression mournful. He was obviously wondering why they were no longer playing. Willow seemed to be wondering the same thing. Desperate for attention, she stood on her hind legs and did her circus dog act, circling round and round on her back legs, her front paws in the air.

Jackson shook his head. 'Honestly, you two are crazy.'

To Abbie's amazement he scooped Willow up in his arms and fondled the space between her ears with affection. 'You're clever, okay? We get it. As for you,' he glanced down at Albus who was so astonished he dropped the paintbrush on the floor, allowing Abbie to take advantage and grab it, 'you're a prize pest. Do you know that? But you're a good boy really,' he relented, reaching out a hand to pat Albus on the head. 'As dogs go, you two are probably the nicest I've ever met.'

'They are aren't they?' Abbie put the paintbrush out of reach and bent down, wrapping her arms around Albus's neck and giving him a kiss on the nose. 'Who's my handsome boy?'

She stood up and glanced round at Jackson, surprised to see him staring at her quite intently. The atmosphere in the room changed, the air between them suddenly crackling with something tangible.

'I never thought,' Jackson said slowly, 'that I'd be jealous of a Labrador.'

Abbie's stomach somersaulted as he put Willow gently on the floor and moved towards her. 'Wh—what do you mean?'

'How easily Albus earns affection from you,' Jackson said. 'I wish I knew his secret.'

He stopped within an arm's reach of her but made no attempt to touch her. They stared at each other, neither of them apparently brave enough to take another step forward.

Abbie's heart thudded. One of them had to do or say something or the moment would be lost. Sure enough, Jackson was already beginning to lose courage. She saw his expression change and knew he was about to turn away. Throwing caution to the wind, she cupped his face in her hands, forcing him to keep looking at her. She saw the surprise flit across his eyes, the slight parting of his mouth as if he wanted to say something but had no words, the sudden tension in his shoulders as he waited.

What could she say? How to express what she was feeling?

Abbie felt a panic rising, knowing that any moment now he would lose faith and walk away, and that would be that.

Without warning he pulled her to him and kissed her. Panic gave way to surprise, then to delight, and finally to a passion that startled her with its intensity.

Was this really Jackson? Reassuringly familiar yet astonishingly different at the same time. This was no taciturn, reserved man. There was no sign of hesitation or anxiety in his kiss. It was as if the real man inside had been freed at last, and what was revealed about him was enough to take her breath away.

Like everything else in the world ceased to exist they stood, locked together inside a little bubble, forgetting all about their surroundings or the fact that they had two witnesses.

It was only when Willow yapped and launched herself at Abbie's legs that the bubble burst and Jackson let go, blinking them both back into reality where they gazed at each other in shocked silence. Albus and Willow, she realised, were watching them with keen interest.

She half-laughed, not sure what else to do.

Jackson looked dazed.

'Well,' she said eventually, 'I wasn't expecting that to

happen.'

'No, I—' He shrugged, evidently unsure how to finish the sentence.

He looked quite relieved when his phone rang, and he fished around in his pocket with undue haste. 'It's Tyler,' he said, waving the mobile at her before accepting the call and putting the device to his ear. He turned away from Abbie as if shutting her out of his mind as well as his sight.

She bit her lip, not sure what was going to happen. How would he react now? Would he push her away, pretend it had never happened?

'Wednesday night?' Jackson turned back to look at her, a query in his eyes. She saw him run a finger along his upper lip, the way he always did when he was thinking about something. 'I— I'll have to check. Yes, she's here.'

He pulled a face and whispered, 'We've been invited to dinner on Wednesday night. It's up to you. Feel free to say no if you'd rather not.'

Abbie heard someone shout something and Jackson winced. 'Okay, so you can hear me. Well, so what? I'm not going to bully her into agreeing just because you want—'

'It's fine,' she said quickly.

Jackson raised an eyebrow. 'Are you sure?' he said, sounding doubtful. 'You really don't have to if you—'

'I'm absolutely sure,' she said firmly. 'Wednesday would be perfect.'

Jackson held her gaze for a moment then his lips curved into a smile. 'Tyler? Yeah, okay you heard that too. Yes, we'll be there. About seven? Fine. See you then.'

Abbie's heart was pounding so hard she barely heard her own voice as she reached out a hand to him and, flushed with a sudden and exhilarating courage, said, 'Now, Mr Wade. Where were we?'

Chapter 16

After Tyler's phone call, she and Jackson had followed up the kiss they'd just shared with another. And another one after that. Then, laughing nervously with embarrassment, they'd packed away the paint for the day, rinsed out the paintbrushes and headed downstairs. Jackson had refused a cup of tea and told her he'd better be getting home, since they would be finishing the bedrooms the next day. The carpet fitters were coming the day after tomorrow and he wanted all the paintwork complete well before they arrived.

Abbie could see the sense in that, but when he'd left she'd sank onto the sofa and found herself unable to concentrate on anything. Even her favourite programme didn't hold her attention, as she nibbled her nails and wondered what would happen now. Their relationship had just moved onto another level, and she couldn't help but fear what came next.

As much as she liked Jackson and was attracted to him, she could see that there were huge obstacles in their path. Firstly, she couldn't imagine him being able to cope with ever living in The Gables which—even once its makeover was complete—would never be the pristine gleaming home he seemed to favour. It would always have that "lived-in", family feel. How could it not when there were three children and two dogs living there? And anyway, Abbie didn't want it any other way. She didn't want her children to feel they were up for inspection every morning. She wanted them to feel relaxed and totally comfortable. How could Jackson deal with that?

And then there was the other obstacle. And that, Abbie knew, was something that she wasn't ready to face just yet. Their relationship could never move forward until she had. The problem was her feelings for Jackson were pushing her into a dark place that she simply didn't want to go. She was already beginning to feel cornered because she didn't want to lose him. But keeping him would mean a level of honesty that she wasn't ready for. Not even with herself.

All that day as they'd worked together the sparks of attraction had been flying. She'd been unable to deny to herself that she felt something for him, and it had been a thrilling delight to discover the feeling was reciprocated. Now that they'd kissed it seemed the genie was well and truly out of the bottle and the atmosphere at The Gables was changed forever. Yet they'd discussed nothing. There was no talk of where they went from here. Did Jackson, like her, recognise that it wasn't going to be easy to take their relationship—if that was what it was—much beyond where they were now? Would they ever move on from those shy smiles and gentle kisses?

'Don't you think you're getting a bit ahead of

yourself?' Rachel's eyes sparkled with amusement as Abbie voiced her misgivings the following lunchtime. They were sitting in the kitchenette at work. Holly was away with the wonderful Jonathan—he'd surprised her with a cheap and cheerful week in Majorca, which had only confirmed in her eyes how amazing and brilliant he was and how lucky she was to have him—and Joan had gone, as usual, to Spill the Beans for lunch.

Abbie had done her one, solitary visit, and Connor and Riley, having completed their own visits, had headed back to their respective homes for lunch and to catch up with their infant offspring.

It wasn't often that Abbie and Rachel were the only ones in the surgery, and Abbie had taken it as a sign that it was okay to confide in her friend what had happened and seek advice.

'What do you mean, ahead of myself?' she asked, as Rachel leaned back in her chair, half-eaten tuna sandwich in her hand, a sympathetic smile playing on her lips.

'Well, it's one kiss and—'

'Lots of kisses!' Abbie shook her head, feeling stupid. 'I mean, okay, I see what you mean, but even so...'

Rachel winked. 'Passionate were they?'

Abbie flushed. 'You could say that.' She grinned suddenly. 'Honestly, Rachel, he really surprised me. I never expected he could be like that.'

'Hidden depths, our Mr Wade.' Rachel took a bite of her sandwich and surveyed Abbie thoughtfully. 'Nevertheless,' she said at last, having swallowed the food, 'you're galloping ahead of yourself. Why are you worrying about how Jackson would fit in at The Gables when it's still early days?'

Abbie supposed she was right. 'I'm just not used to all this,' she admitted with a sigh. 'Nick and I were together for fourteen years. It's ages since I did this whole dating thing. I'm not sure what I'm supposed to do.'

Rachel leaned forward, smiling. 'What you're supposed to do is enjoy it. Your kids will be home in a few days. Until then, make the most of every moment. These are the best days! It's all new and exciting and thrilling. Relish every single second of them and stop worrying about what may or may not happen. It's far too early for all that.'

'You're right of course.' Abbie could see the sense in Rachel's words all too clearly. 'The trouble is, we're so different, Jackson and me. It's hard to imagine how we'd ever blend together successfully, especially given his discomfort around dogs, and me having three children who make such a mess, and—'

'Oh, for goodness' sake!' Rachel laughed and dropped her sandwich back in the lunchbox. 'You're doing it again. When will you be seeing him again?'

'After work. He's at The Gables right now, glossing the doors and skirting boards in the children's rooms. The carpets are getting fitted tomorrow afternoon you see, so…'

'Perfect! So tonight, when you get home, go upstairs and seduce him.'

'Seduce him?' Abbie felt a wave of nausea at the

thought of it.

'Absolutely. Just think, no kids at home, peace and quiet, and a man already primed and waiting upstairs for you. Make the most of it. I know I would.'

She folded her arms and gave Abbie a knowing look, but Abbie could only feel panic. Rachel had no idea. It was far too soon to talk about seducing Jackson. She simply couldn't do it.

No, she would have to keep things grounded for a good while yet, until she'd plucked up the courage to reveal the truth to him. Right now, she simply couldn't imagine when that would be.

Chapter 17

'Oh, my word! I can't believe how fabulous it all looks!'

Abbie gazed around Isla's bedroom, unable to wipe the smile off her face. Jackson put his arm around her waist.

'You like?'

'It's fantastic! These carpets are so thick too. The kids are going to love it all.'

She'd already cooed over Poppy's pretty lemon and white bedroom, and grinned delightedly at Bertie's nautical-themed room, but Isla's was the cherry on the cake. Decorated in delicate shades of lilac, grey and white, it was grown-up and feminine without being too girly and Abbie knew that Isla would be over the moon with it.

'Oh, Jackson.' She turned to him, her heart full to the brim with love and gratitude. 'I don't know what to say.'

'You don't have to say anything,' he assured her, his brown eyes sparkling with pleasure. 'Just knowing you like it is enough.'

'But it's not, really it's not.' She sighed and rested her head against his chest, closing her eyes as he wrapped his arms around her and she nestled close, revelling in a happiness that she hadn't felt for so, so long. 'You've done so much for me. How can I ever thank you?'

'You already have,' he murmured against the top of her head. 'Being here with you—it's everything I ever dreamed of. You've made me so happy, Abbie. You've changed my life.'

She put her arms around his waist and held him tightly. If only, she thought, they could stay like this forever. No questions, no difficult conversations… Just the thrill and excitement of holding each other close, being together, the promise of so much more to come.

'Now, much as I'd like to stand here cuddling all night,' Jackson said, interrupting her train of thought as he pulled away from her, 'we have things to do.'

'We do?' She glanced around the room. 'What else is there?'

'Not in the house,' he said. 'I'm talking about dinner.'

She smiled, loving this relaxed, playful version of him. 'I'm not really very hungry,' she admitted coyly.

'You will be,' he told her. 'Especially once you know that I'm cooking for you.'

She peered up at him, astonished. 'You are?'

'I am. I thought—' he hesitated then ploughed on, 'I thought it was time you visited my flat. Saw my home. So I'd like to formally invite you for dinner this evening. Shall we say, eight o'clock?'

Abbie glanced at her watch. 'It's half past six now.'

'Exactly,' he said, grinning. 'So, I'm going to head home now, and I want you to get yourself ready and meet me over there, okay?'

'Wow,' she teased, 'I finally get to see the Jackson Wade domain. I'd better clean myself up hadn't I?'

'Don't worry,' he said, 'there's no disinfectant dip to stand in before you enter the premises. It's not that bad honestly.'

She reached up and stroked the side of his face. 'I wouldn't care if it were,' she told him softly. 'I'd still go. Thank you for inviting me.'

He took hold of her hand and kissed it gently. 'I'd better go,' he said, his voice thick with emotion. 'See you at eight?'

'I'll be there,' she promised.

***

Abbie knocked tentatively on the door before noticing the four doorbells tucked away in the porch. She glanced at her phone, having opened her memo app a few seconds ago to double check the house number. Flat Three. There'd be stairs to climb then. Great.

Pressing the relevant bell, she leaned against the wall of the porch, her stomach fluttering with nerves. This was a big deal. Rachel would be laughing at her now and telling her to just go with the flow, to enjoy herself, but Rachel didn't understand. How could she when Abbie hadn't revealed everything to her? Supposing Jackson pushed for more than she was ready to give him? What would she do then?

He's not like that. The voice in her head was stern. She felt a wave of shame, knowing it was true. He wasn't like that. He would never push her for anything, she was certain of that. But what if—what if she wanted him to? It would destroy everything before they'd even started.

Her heart thudded with panic, and she clenched her fists. Maybe she should just go home? Tell him she felt ill?

A speaker crackled and a voice said, 'Hello?'

Abbie took a deep breath. Too late to change her mind now. 'Jackson?'

There was a moment's silence then his voice, radiating with warmth, said, 'Come right up, Abbie.'

There was another crackle then a clicking noise as the front door evidently unlocked. Abbie pushed it open and found herself in a neat, spacious hallway.

Whenever she thought of flats, she always remembered the sort of places she'd lived in as a student. She still shuddered at the memory of the grimy, sticky tiles in the entrance halls, and the dingy carpets on the stairs that had been so dirty no one was even sure what colour they were supposed to be. She remembered fluorescent lighting and grimy bathrooms, and kitchens with two-ringed electric cookers and even, in one room she'd inhabited, a bed that was propped up on bricks as two of its legs were missing.

This building was nothing like that thank goodness. Someone was clearly in charge of keeping the communal areas immaculate, as the paintwork was spotless, the tiled flooring sparkling, and the carpet on the stairs was thick and clean. There were even paintings on the walls, and a large Yucca tree in the corner of the hallway. She should have known really. Someone like Jackson would never tolerate grubbiness.

She began the climb up the stairs, feeling she may as well have been mounting an expedition up Everest. She used the mahogany handrail to her left to help haul herself up the endless steps, feeling herself start to flag as she reached the landing of the first floor.

'You're bang on time.'

Abbie looked up, startled to see Jackson standing outside a wooden door which bore a brass plate with the number three engraved on it. He was wearing a navy-blue shirt and jeans and she crumbled at the sight of him. Lord, he was handsome.

'I thought you'd be on the second floor,' she admitted. 'I was gearing myself up for another climb.'

He smiled. 'There's a basement flat. That's Flat One. You look shattered. You'd better come in and sit down before you fall down.'

'I'm a bit out of shape it seems,' she said, feeling embarrassed. She'd hoped to compose herself before knocking on his door. Now he'd know just how badly out of shape she really was. Well, almost.

He held open the door and she ducked beneath his arm, entering his domain, and bracing herself for the worst. As she looked around, she winced inside at the comparison between this impressive space and the undeniable mess he'd walked into during that first visit to The Gables.

'I'll show you round in a few minutes,' he offered. 'First though, I think you should sit down and get your breath back while I put the kettle on.'

'That would be great,' she admitted, sniffing the air appreciatively. Whatever he was cooking it smelt delicious.

'Tea, coffee?'

He already knew she didn't touch alcohol. She felt a tingle of pleasure at that tiny detail and inwardly laughed at herself. Anyone would think she was a silly teenager.

'Tea please. No sugar and just a bit of milk.'

'Coming right up. Please, take a seat.'

He waved in the general direction of what Abbie supposed was a living room, and she opened the door, finding herself in what could easily have been a furniture showroom. It was immaculate. There wasn't a single thing out of place anywhere, not a crumb on the carpet, not a speck of dust on the television, nothing.

Abbie groaned inwardly. No wonder he'd looked so shocked at the sight of The Gables. Her home must have looked as if it needed condemning to his eyes.

She sank into one of the large, squashy, black leather sofas and thought how much easier it would be to keep them clean than the fabric sofas she had at home. Spilt drinks from the children and endless hairs from moulting dogs meant they never looked as pristine as they had when she'd bought them, no matter how many times she scrubbed and vacuumed them. These would just need a quick wipe over really. Why hadn't she thought of that?

They were wasted here she thought. How much mess could one man on his own make anyway? She imagined bringing the dogs and the children here and went cold at the thought. Glancing around the living room, she couldn't imagine that any child had ever crossed the threshold. This place had invisible "Keep Out" signs all over it.

White walls! Who had white walls? No one with sticky-fingered toddlers or muddy-coated dogs, that was for sure. Abbie conceded that the white walls, grey carpet, black furniture, and glossy black and white photographs dotted around the room looked stylish and clean, but they weren't exactly homely. The place was desperately in need of splashes of colour and texture.

'Here you go. Tea, no sugar, and a drop of milk.'

Jackson handed her a mug and sat down on the opposite sofa. They faced each other across a glass coffee table that held a couple of large hardback books on music and a stack of leather coasters. He pushed one of the coasters towards her and she placed her mug on it, praying that she wouldn't knock the table and spill her tea. Any sort of spillage in this place would be a capital offence. She thought of The Gables and felt a pang of fondness for her messy but comfortable home.

'Well,' Jackson said.

Abbie stared at him, waiting for him to finish the sentence, but he seemed to have nothing else to say. Clearly, nerves were biting at him too. She took a sip of her drink for something to do, wishing she had the courage to tell him that, although she'd asked for little milk, she would at least have liked enough to change the colour of the tea.

'Something smells good,' she said at last, thinking it wasn't just the food. When he'd handed her the tea she'd breathed in the clean, male scent of him, and her stomach had lurched most disturbingly.

'It's not my best recipe,' he replied. 'I wasn't sure how you felt about seafood, so I played it safe with lemon chicken. Is that okay?'

'Perfect.' She put the mug down again and tried to keep her voice steady. 'For future reference, I love seafood.'

He smiled. 'I like that.'

'What? That I love seafood? Yes, I've always—'

'The future reference bit.'

She blushed. 'Mm. This is a very, er, stylish flat.'

'Yes, I suppose it is. But it isn't you is it?' He held up his hands to ward off her protests. 'It's okay, you're right. It isn't.'

'I can see why my house horrified you,' she admitted.

'Your house didn't horrify me,' he said. 'I just thought you needed a bit of help to make the most of it, that's all. You always said it could be lovely and you were right. It is.'

'Thanks to you.'

'It was your vision and your money,' he pointed out.

'But you did all the work,' she argued. 'Without you, it would still just be a vision. You made it reality. I can never thank you enough.'

'Abbie, please can we get past all this gratitude?' He reached out and took hold of her hand. 'Whatever it is you think I've done for you I can assure you that you've done far more for me. I don't need you to keep telling me how appreciative you are, okay?' He squeezed her fingers gently. 'Let's just say we made a great team.'

She squeezed back. 'We still do.'

His lips curved upwards in a full-beam smile and Abbie stared at him in fascination, thinking how much a smile changed his face and how utterly and divinely handsome he was, and why on earth had it taken her so long to notice?

It was a moment before she realised the smile had dropped and so had his hand. He ran a finger along his upper lip, a sure sign that he was thinking about something, then stood abruptly.

'I'll see to that chicken,' he said and left the room.

Abbie blinked, wondering what on earth that was about. Maybe, she thought, he'd been like her—in danger of losing all sense of reason and forgetting about the chicken entirely. She had to admit, if it wasn't for that one thing she'd be tempted to tell him to switch off the oven and take her to bed. Part of her longed to throw all her inhibitions aside and do as Rachel had said—make the most of every moment. But the obstacle that loomed between them was insurmountable. Unless she mustered every ounce of courage and told him the truth, that was. Well she would. Of course she would.

Just not tonight.

Tonight, she decided, they were going to relax, eat (hopefully) good food, cuddle up together on the sofa, talk and get to know each other a bit better. Then she'd go home and tomorrow—

She couldn't go as far as tomorrow. Tonight was enough to deal with for now.

Jackson, it turned out, could make a mean lemon chicken. He served it with sautéed potatoes and broccoli and Abbie enjoyed every delicious mouthful, despite being all too aware of the gleaming kitchen diner they sat in to eat. How, she wondered, had he managed to cook a complete dinner and not make a mess? It was beyond her. When she cooked, the kitchen ended up looking as if a paintball derby had just taken place there.

They talked briefly about the children: Jackson enquired if she'd heard from them, and she confirmed that she had and that they were having a fabulous time but were missing her.

'Missing the dogs more like,' she said, laughing. 'I've missed them though. I can't wait to have them home.'

'I don't blame you. It must feel so quiet and empty for you now. I know when I get home after working at The Gables and I close the door behind me and it's just me, well…' He shook his head. 'I never noticed before but being around your kids has made me see how quiet my life is.'

'Sorry,' she said ruefully.

'No, it's a good thing,' he said quickly. 'I mean, you don't notice do you? What's so obvious to others about your own life. How small it is—how much your world has shrunk without you even realising.'

There was such sadness in his voice that she'd paused, fork halfway to her mouth, and stared at him in surprise. Was he saying he *liked* being around her kids? That they *didn't* drive him crazy, as she'd suspected they must?

'We're getting too serious,' he announced, switching on a smile. 'Let's talk about something else.'

The conversation switched to light-hearted topics: their favourite foods, programmes, and films they'd seen recently, amusing incidents at work.

Before she realised, Abbie had cleared her plate and she leaned back in her chair, deciding she'd never eat another thing. He said there was a choice of ice cream or cheese and biscuits to follow but he, apparently, was as full as she was. Jackson stacked the dishwasher and Abbie helped, even though he tried to stop her.

Eventually they returned to the living room, cups of fresh coffee in their hands, and after a brief argument about who was the funniest comedian they'd ever seen—he said Billy Connolly and she said Michael McIntyre—they settled down to watch a DVD of Laurel and Hardy's *The Music Box* because in the end they both agreed it was a work of genius.

As it finally finished Abbie wiped her eyes and announced that, with all due respect, Stan and Ollie beat both Billy and Michael hands down, and Jackson conceded she was right.

'Talking of music boxes,' she said, 'I expect you'll be glad to get back to school next week so you can play the piano. You must miss it.'

'I do,' he admitted. 'There's something incredibly soothing about making music. When my fingers touch that keyboard it's as if all my problems and worries just float away, like notes on the air.'

'I'd love to hear you play some time,' she murmured.
'I'd love to play for you.'

They gazed at each other, and Abbie found herself drowning in Jackson's deep brown eyes and all her inhibitions and fears seemed to dissolve. Maybe she could do this after all? Maybe it wasn't such a hopeless cause?

He kissed her gently and stroked her hair and she responded eagerly, wanting him to kiss her longer and deeper. They would talk. She would explain. He would understand. Surely, he would understand?

His hand nestled in the small of her back and she relaxed into his hold, her arms around his neck.

His hand moved upwards, he stroked her neck, her throat, and she quivered at his touch. She was lost and she knew it. She wanted him as badly as he wanted her.

He stopped kissing her and gazed at her, his lips flushed, the desire evident in his eyes. He waited, clearly asking her if it was okay. 'Abbie?'

Oh god, this is really happening.

Abbie pushed him away, gripped by a sudden panic. 'Don't!'

Jackson pulled away, clearly shocked. 'I'm sorry. I—'

'It's—it's not your fault. It's me. I'm just not ready. I'm sorry.'

He looked bewildered. 'Abbie, there's no need to apologise. If I overstepped the mark it's me who should apologise. I thought—well obviously I was wrong.'

'Yes. I mean—no. Look, we just got swept away didn't we? I can't—I'm sorry, I really can't do this.'

She leapt to her feet and reached for her bag, not able to look at him. She couldn't bear to see the hurt and confusion in his eyes. He hadn't done anything she hadn't wanted him to. Or at least, she'd thought she hadn't. Turned out she wasn't ready after all, but that wasn't his fault, and he'd backed off instantly. Now he looked full of guilt, as if he'd done something wrong, and he really hadn't.

'It's not your fault,' she repeated, wanting to cry. 'I think—I think maybe this was a mistake.'

He traced the line of his upper lip with his finger, watching her in obvious confusion. 'What was a mistake? This kiss? All the kisses? Us?'

She gave a nervous laugh. 'Us? Well, it's not really *us*, is it? I mean, it was just a few kisses, that's all.'

'Right. I see.'

'It's just, you know, we've been working together for so long, we were bound to get carried away at some point. But really, it would be a mistake wouldn't it? I mean, we're so different, and this would never work. Let's just say we had a pleasant evening and things got a bit silly and put it behind us. What do you say?'

Jackson didn't reply for what felt like forever. He continued to stare at her for a long, long moment, and Abbie felt her heart thudding in her chest. Tears were pricking her eyes and she just wanted him to accept her statement and let her go before she did something really stupid and told him the truth.

Eventually he held up his hands and shrugged. 'Fine. Whatever you say.'

He led her to the front door and unlocked it for her,

holding it wide open. 'Goodnight, Abbie.'

She wanted to turn around and tell him she was sorry and that she hadn't meant a word she said—that she was just afraid and didn't know how to deal with her fears, and could he please, please help her?

But she didn't. Instead, she headed downstairs and into the street to the safety of her car, murmuring tearfully, 'Goodbye, Jackson.'

Chapter 18

'Great you're on time!' Tyler's welcoming smile died, and Jackson realised he must look as miserable as he felt as his brother reared back and said, 'Whoa! What's the matter with you?'

Behind him, Jeannie appeared behind her husband, her face wreathed in smiles until she too clearly realised something was wrong. Her expression became one of concern and she practically pulled Jackson into the hallway, shutting the door behind him.

'What is it? Where's Abbie?'

Jackson didn't even know where to begin. His carefully constructed excuses evaporated from his mind as he stared at them both. All that planning and rehearsing. All the going-over of Abbie's fictional reasons for not attending the dinner that he'd practised endlessly on the drive over to Moreton Cross—gone, just like that.

'Where are the boys?' It was all he could think of to say.

Jeannie blinked. 'Sleeping over at a friend's. It's all been arranged so we could really get to know Abbie.' Her disappointment was evident in her tone. 'She's not coming is she?'

Jackson opened his mouth to speak but his mind was a blank. All he could do was shrug.

Tyler sighed and put his arm around his shoulders. 'Come on. Let's go into the living room. Looks like you could use a brandy.'

'I'm driving,' he protested but his brother was having none of it.

'You can stay over tonight,' he said. 'You can take Joshua's room. Don't argue. I'm not letting you go home in this state.'

'What state?' Jackson tried to clear his head. 'I'm fine.'

'You don't look fine,' Jeannie said. 'And why isn't Abbie here?'

He'd known of course that they would want to know the whole, unvarnished truth. They always did. He just wasn't sure how he could explain when he wasn't sure what had happened himself.

Settling in the living room, in one of the deep, plush armchairs, Jackson sipped a brandy and pulled a face. 'Ugh. I don't even like brandy.'

'It's medicinal,' Jeannie assured him.

'So's Gaviscon. You wouldn't offer me a glass of that would you?'

She rolled her eyes. 'It's for shock.'

'Who says I'm in shock?'

'Well, if you're not I am. Your face is enough to terrify anyone.'

'Wow,' he breathed, 'you're all heart.'

'So,' Tyler said, watching him steadily, 'are we to take it that the budding romance is off?'

Jackson took a large gulp of the brandy then shuddered. It really was vile. But easier to drink that than answer Tyler's questions.

'I guess it is,' he said eventually. 'Not that it ever got started. Well, not really.'

'But it sort of did?' Jeannie's voice was eager. 'It's just that, when Tyler went over to fit the bathroom, he said that you were just friends. Did it move on?'

Jackson realised he'd well and truly fallen into the trap. He could have bluffed his way out of this awkward dinner after all. Made up some reasonable excuse why Abbie hadn't been able to attend that evening. Instead, he'd revealed far too much, and he'd never be able to get away with fobbing them off now. Then again, did he even have the energy to try?

It had been a long and tortuous day. Jackson had gone over and over what had happened the previous night and tormented himself with all the things he'd done wrong. Despite knowing that she wouldn't contact him, he hadn't been able to stop himself from checking his phone every five minutes, the pain of the blank screen stabbing through him every time.

When the message finally pinged into his inbox mid-afternoon he'd felt a rush of hope, but his heart had sunk when he read the text. She'd simply stated that she wasn't feeling up to dinner with Tyler and his wife after all and could he please send them her apologies.

He hadn't expected her to go to Tyler's with him. Not really. But it still felt like another rejection when it came.

He had no reason now to ever go to The Gables

again he realised. The work was completed. Everything he'd said he'd do he'd done. Bertie was no longer in his class so he couldn't even use that as an excuse. How, he wondered, had it gone so badly wrong?

'Well?' Tyler said gently. 'Did it?'

Jackson blinked, suddenly remembering that Jeannie had asked him a question.

'Yes,' he admitted. 'It had moved on.' He ran a hand through his hair and stared at them both, bewildered. 'I just don't know what I did,' he burst out. 'At least, I don't *think* I did anything wrong. I mean, she seemed to—' He broke off, glancing awkwardly at Jeannie.

Jeannie looked at Tyler. 'I think I'll go and check on dinner,' she said. 'I'll leave you two to it.'

Tyler nodded and Jeannie left the room, leaving the two brothers facing each other.

'Another brandy?'

It was on the tip of Jackson's tongue to refuse, but suddenly another brandy seemed like an excellent idea.

Tyler poured the drink and replaced the bottle in the cabinet, then sat down again. 'So come on,' he said gently. 'What happened?'

Briefly, not looking at him, Jackson gave him the gist of what had happened the previous evening.

Tyler listened, not saying much, nodding sympathetically now and then, widening his eyes, then narrowing them again. 'Hmm.'

'Is that it? Is that your brotherly wisdom?' Jackson drained his glass. 'Wow, I'm so glad I poured my heart out to you in exchange for such sound advice.'

Tyler grinned. 'Still got your sense of humour I see.'

'It's pretty much all I *have* got left.'

'Don't be daft. Seems to me you have plenty left, not least your self-esteem.'

Jackson gaped at him. 'My self-esteem? Are you kidding me? I have none left. Zero. I've never felt so worthless in all my life.'

'I don't see why,' Tyler said calmly. 'If what you said is true—and I have no reason to doubt it—then you behaved like a perfect gentleman. You should be proud of yourself.'

'Did you not listen? She rejected me. She couldn't—' Jackson took a deep breath, the pain tearing at his insides, 'she couldn't get away from me fast enough.'

'But she clearly wanted you at first,' Tyler persisted. 'Something stopped her, but I doubt very much that it's got anything to do with you or anything you did.'

'You didn't see her.' Jackson hung his head, misery overwhelming him. 'The way she looked at me, Tyler. It was like…'

'Like what?'

Jackson shrugged. 'It's not the first time she's looked at me like that. It's happened a couple of times now. Hell, it even happened earlier that night.'

'Jackson, for the love of God, will you please explain what you're talking about.'

'This!' His finger traced the outline of his scar and he stared at Tyler in dumb despair.

'Oh no, not again.' Tyler threw himself back in the armchair and groaned. 'You're not serious?'

'She was staring at it, I'm telling you. I didn't imagine it.'

'Jackson, you really do have to get over this. It's barely noticeable and it's certainly not enough to put a woman off kissing you, for goodness' sake! Whatever Abbie's reasons, that scar is not one of them, I'll guarantee it.'

'Then what?' Jackson said helplessly. 'What did I do wrong?'

'I don't think you did anything wrong,' Tyler said, his eyes warm with sympathy. 'Whatever drove Abbie away, it's one of her demons, not yours.'

'Maybe it was the flat.'

Tyler spluttered with laughter. 'The flat? You mean your beautiful, neat, clean flat? Yeah, that will be it.'

'But that's just it, don't you see? That flat is like the showroom of all my issues. Abbie will have looked at it and thought what a mess I clearly am inside. She knows what I'm like and—'

'You just said it,' Tyler pointed out. 'She knows what you're like. I'll bet the flat was exactly what she was expecting, so why would she be startled into leaving? I'm telling you, Jackson, this isn't about you. Whatever made Abbie change her mind and say those things to you, it's about her, not you. You must believe that.'

'You think it's her ex-husband?'

Tyler blinked. 'I never mentioned her ex-husband. Why, do you?'

'I don't know.' Jackson shrugged, at a loss. 'They're still good friends.' He frowned. 'He seemed very concerned about her. Protective. Over-protective even. Do you think, maybe, they're still in love?'

'But if they are why did she get involved with you in

the first place?' Tyler shook his head. 'I doubt very much that he'd have taken a job in the States if he were still in love with her. Think again.'

'Then what? I just don't understand it.'

'There's only one way to find out,' Tyler said, 'and I don't have to tell you what that is, do I?'

Jackson felt the colour drain from his face. 'I can't. I just can't. What if she rejects me again?'

'And what if she doesn't? If you don't try, you'll never know. Sometimes, bro, you've just got to suck it up and deal with things you'd rather not face. I think, maybe, this is your moment. You've pushed cruel truths away all your life, but you've finally found something—or someone—that you care enough about to be brave for. Haven't you?'

And that, Jackson realised, was the question. How brave could he be? And how much did Abbie really mean to him?

Chapter 19

At least Rachel sounded pleased to hear from Abbie when she called her that evening.

'You're sure you're not busy? I haven't disturbed you?'

'Don't be daft, Abbie. We were just watching television, that's all.'

'Oh. If you want to watch—'

'I don't! Xander and Sam are glued to some boring programme about robots and—don't give me that look, Xander. It's true! It's boring as anything—and anyway, as I was saying, I'm just sitting here feeling my behind go numb along with my brain. Mum's out with Merlyn so, to be honest, I'm glad you rang. Hang on, I'll just take the phone into the kitchen.'

There were a few muffled noises and the sound of a door shutting, then Rachel said, 'You still there?'

'I'm still here,' Abbie assured her. *Where else would I be?*

'I'll just get comfy. Hang on. Good job I had a fresh cup of tea to hand. Right, that's me on the sofa. Oops, Darwin's just given me a filthy look. It's not your sofa, kitty. Sorry, but you'll have to share.'

Abbie laughed. 'Bless him. Is the entire menagerie

there with you?'

'Not tonight. Duke's upstairs on Sam's bed.' She hesitated then added, 'I don't think he's got much longer to be honest with you. He's asleep most of the time now and Merlyn examined him the other day and said to prepare Sam for the worst.'

Abbie thought about the old, gentle Border collie cross, and her heart went out to Rachel. 'I'm so sorry.'

'Yeah, it's sad. But you know, he's had a really good year with us that he wasn't supposed to have, and he knows he's loved very much. I cried buckets when Merlyn told me, but Xander said we must accept these things if we want to give all these animals a home. Death is a part of life after all.'

Abbie shivered, feeling nauseated. 'I suppose.'

'Folly's in the living room with Sam. They're inseparable,' Rachel continued, totally oblivious to the fact that Abbie was desperately squeezing back the tears and praying that she wouldn't have to speak for a moment or two. She needed time to regain her composure.

Rachel went quiet and Abbie racked her brains for something to say. She rather wished she hadn't called her friend after all. Maybe it was a bad idea. She really wasn't in the mood for conversation.

'So, what are you calling for? Not that I'm not delighted to hear from you but…'

Abbie swallowed. 'Just for a chat.'

'A chat? Hmm. Great job.'

Abbie rubbed her eyes and tried hard to think of something to talk about. The truth was, she'd just wanted to hear a friendly voice. She hadn't got as far as thinking up a conversation topic.

'Oh to hell with it. I may as well tell you. I was going to ring you tomorrow,' Rachel said suddenly. 'I've got some news for you.'

Abbie took a deep breath and forced herself to sound intrigued. 'Ooh, really? And what's that?'

'We've booked the wedding!'

'Rachel!' For a moment, Abbie forgot her own worries in the excitement of Rachel's announcement. 'That's fantastic. When? Where?'

'It's in December. We've had a heck of a job trying to find somewhere, I'll tell you. We wanted somewhere private and not too far from here, but places do get booked up so quickly. We've really struggled and thought we might have to put it off until next year, but then one of Xander's friends came up trumps.'

'Really? So?'

'So, we're getting married at a local stately home. You'll probably have heard of it. Kearton Hall?'

Abbie mentally nodded, picturing the large Elizabethan house that lay on the outskirts of Kearton Bay. 'Of course I've heard of it. I remember now. I read that they'd just started doing weddings. Surprised they had a vacancy this year though.'

'Strictly speaking they didn't. But Xander's friend Joe knows the owners and pulled a few strings and, hey presto. So, make sure you keep December 23rd free, okay?'

'Isn't that a Monday?'

'Yes, but don't worry. I've already had a word with

Connor. He says they'll get a couple of locums in for the afternoon, and I'll just make sure no appointments are booked for me that day. The service isn't until four o'clock in the afternoon, so you'll be able to work the morning.'

'It sounds wonderful.'

'I think it will be. I'm going to ask Sam to be the ring bearer, and I want Holly, Anna, Izzy, and Nell to be my bridesmaids.'

'Lovely.'

'But I want you to be my matron of honour, Abbie. Would you?'

'Oh, Rachel, I'd love to. Thank you so much.' Abbie hoped Rachel didn't hear her gulp.

'Aw, I'm so glad. Thank *you* for saying yes.'

There was an awkward lull in the conversation.

Rachel tutted. 'And now we're back to the silence.' The sound of a loud sigh came through the earpiece. 'Right, now that I've got my news out of the way, are you going to tell me what's wrong?'

Hurriedly wiping away a rogue tear, Abbie said, 'Who says anything's wrong?'

'Well, you rang me up at half past eight at night for no apparent reason, had nothing to say to me, which forced me to gabble like a lunatic about my wedding, and your voice gives the impression that you've just had a gas bill through that's going to swallow your entire year's earnings, so I'd say there's *something* bugging you. Am I right or am I right?'

Abbie wrinkled her nose. Was she really that obvious? 'You're right,' she admitted with a sigh. 'I screwed up, Rachel. Big time.'

'I highly doubt that,' Rachel said, and Abbie could almost hear the smile on her friend's face. 'Since when did you develop this gift for the dramatic? You're beginning to sound like Holly.'

Despite her misery Abbie spluttered with laughter. 'Thanks a lot.'

'You're welcome. So, is this anything to do with the handsome Mr Wade?'

'Could be.'

'So it is then. Okay, I'm intrigued. Are we going to play guessing games for the next hour or are you going to tell me what's happened? Only, that awful robot programme won't last forever, even though it felt like it already had when I was watching it, and I guarantee that as soon as it finishes I'll have two hungry males in here demanding supper, even though it will be Sam's bedtime and Xander's supposed to be watching his weight. Not to hurry you of course, but…'

Abbie sniffed again and said, 'I suppose I'd better get on with it then.'

'That's the spirit. Tell Nurse Rachel all about it.'

Half reluctantly, half relieved, Abbie obeyed, and Rachel listened patiently without interrupting once, although Abbie could swear that she heard the occasional sharp intake of breath and one or two impatient clicks of the tongue.

'See?' she finished at last. 'I've screwed up haven't I?'

Rachel seemed to take forever to answer, which didn't make Abbie feel any better. 'Not exactly screwed up, no. But I can understand why Jackson looked confused. I'm pretty confused myself. You said you really wanted him, so why did you push him away?'

'Like I said, I just had a change of heart. I panicked.'

'But what about? What stopped you? I mean, don't get me wrong, any woman has the right to change her mind, but I'm a bit baffled since you say you wanted him just as much as he clearly wanted you, and you obviously regret not going through with it. So, why didn't you?'

Abbie bit her lip. This was the question she'd dreaded, and one she simply didn't have the ability to answer. 'It's a long story,' she hedged in the end.

'I'm listening,' Rachel replied.

When Abbie didn't respond she sighed and said, 'Okay, just tell me one thing. Is this anything to do with your ex?'

'Nick?' Abbie pulled a face. 'Of course not. Why would it be?'

'Just wondered if, maybe, you were still carrying a torch for him.'

'God, no! I mean, don't get me wrong, I really love Nick. I always will. He's the father of my kids and he's a good man. We're friends, but that's all we are. Anything else died a long time ago.'

'Right, well that's something. And I take it you like Jackson?'

'I just said so didn't I?'

'Actually no. You said you wanted him. There's a difference. Maybe, deep down, you know he's wrong for you and that lust isn't a good enough reason to sleep with someone.'

Abbie considered the matter. 'Nooo,' she drew out eventually, 'it's not that. I mean, to be honest he might well be wrong for me. Or at least, I might be wrong for him. We're complete opposites in so many ways. But—I don't know—there's more to it than just fancying him. Although—' she sucked in her cheeks and clutched the phone a little tighter, '—I really do fancy him rotten. I really *like* him, Rachel. He's kind and generous and caring and hard-working and intelligent and—'

'Stop, stop!' Rachel laughed. 'At this rate I'll be dragging Jackson Wade down the aisle instead of Xander. You've sold him to me, okay? So that begs the question, what's holding you back?'

What *was* holding her back? Fear. The fear that if she revealed the truth about herself to him he would run. Could she take the chance and risk losing him forever? But if she didn't, she'd lose him anyway. She shivered, knowing she had no choice.

'I think I've figured it out, Rachel,' she said, her throat full as she contemplated facing Jackson and telling him everything.

'Great! And can you do something about it?'

Abbie cleared her throat and nodded, even though her friend couldn't see her. 'I can. It's going to be really hard, but I don't think I have a choice.'

Rachel's tone softened. 'Whatever it is, I can hear from your voice that it's a big deal. I hope it all goes well, Abbie. I'll keep everything crossed for you.'

'Thank you. And, Rachel, congratulations again. I really am so pleased for you, and for Xander. You're a great couple.'

'Thanks, Abbie. I think you and Jackson can be too. Let me know what happens, okay?'

'Will do.'

Abbie ended the call and sat for a moment, her heart thudding. Easy to say she knew what to do and how to put things right, but when it came to it, she wasn't sure she had the courage.

She stayed curled up in the armchair, nibbling her nails and trying to pluck up the courage to do what she must. Albus and Willow lay on the rug in front of the fire, eyeing her curiously. They must sense something was wrong because normally they'd be trying to get on her knee by now. She'd even managed to confuse her dogs with her weird behaviour.

Eventually, sick of battling the maelstrom of emotions in her mind, she decided to act.

Her bedroom wasn't the prettiest room she thought, glancing round in dismay and comparing it most unfavourably with the children's rooms in all their newly painted, freshly carpeted glory. Jackson—if he ever got as far as crossing this threshold—would no doubt be itching to start redecorating it immediately. Though perhaps he'd have other things on his mind…

Carefully, she peeled off her shirt and unfastened her bra, dropping them to the floor.

She realised her hand was trembling as she pulled open the wardrobe door. She kept her eyes fixed on the rail of clothes, as she always did, and stared at the array of blouses, trousers, skirts, and dresses that hung before her. There was a swirling sensation in her stomach, like a balloon that had burst and was flipping around in the air before coming to land on the floor, deflated and useless. For a moment she closed her eyes and turned slightly, her hands groping at the wardrobe door.

'One... two... three.' Abbie forced herself to open her eyes and stared at the sight that confronted her in the full-length mirror on the door. The image that she'd refused to allow into her thoughts for so long swam into focus through her tears, and she swallowed hard, refusing to give in to her urge to look away.

One whole, rounded, reasonably pert breast. One misshapen, puckered, and scarred breast; the battle-weary survivor of a war that had waged since the days after Poppy's birth. Like that balloon: deflated, withered, useless. Yet somehow still in place. Not pretty. Not pert. But *there*.

Bit like me.

She was exhausted, wounded, and scared.

But I'm here.

The bedroom door was nudged open and Albus and Willow padded in, uncharacteristically solemn, their eyes warm with sympathy and understanding.

'How did you know?'

She sank onto the floor and let them comfort her as the tears flowed freely, and the sobs tore at her throat. Dogs never cared what you looked like. They didn't mind the lack of symmetry, or the misplaced nipple, or the scars. They just loved you anyway.

But how understanding would a man be? A man who liked everything just so, who sought perfection in all things.

A man like Jackson Wade.

Chapter 20

The message, when it pinged onto his phone at six-thirty the following morning, set Jackson's heart thumping. It wouldn't have woken him up if he'd been asleep, but sleep had deserted him a couple of hours prior to that and he'd given up trying to recapture it, settling instead for an early morning cup of coffee and a session of lesson planning at the kitchen table.

That quiet, insignificant notification was enough to make him pause, pen in hand, as a thousand thoughts and anxieties flitted through his exhausted brain.

✉ FROM ABBIE

Would you be able to come to The Gables? I have something to discuss with you and I need to do it in person. It's important. Please, Jackson.

He didn't even stop to think about it. If he'd had even a fleeting thought of staying away those two little words at the end of the message would have been enough to sway him. With some effort, he eventually tapped out a message, his hands shaking and clumsy.

✉ FROM JACKSON

Of course. Just tell me when.

He waited, finger outlining his upper lip as he stared impatiently at the screen, willing her to answer. A minute went by, two minutes. Jackson picked up his cup, put it back down, grabbed it again, stomach churning.

'Answer, for God's sake!'

He almost spilt the cold remains of his coffee as the phone pinged.

✉ FROM ABBIE

I'm at work at nine but I have an hour or so around lunchtime after visits, if you can make it then? Unless you're free before work of course.

✉ FROM JACKSON

I'm on my way.

As he drove towards Bramblewick, Jackson could almost hear Ash and Tyler telling him to play it cool. Don't appear too eager, they'd say. She was the one who rejected you, remember? Let her do the work.

Too late for that he thought. The indecent speed with which he'd answered her text must have shown her how desperate he was for some answers.

Whether he would like the answers she gave him

was another matter.

Her car was on the drive at The Gables. Jackson carefully opened the new gates then drove in, pulling up behind it.

She seemed to take forever to answer the door, even though she was expecting him, but when she did finally appear he forgot all about his own anxieties and focused all his attention on her because, good grief, she looked so fragile.

If Jackson hadn't had much sleep, Abbie appeared not to have had any at all. She was deathly pale, with dark shadows under her eyes, and—he stared hard at her but there was no mistaking it—she'd been crying. Her eyelids were swollen and red-rimmed. Jackson felt all his anger and fear and confusion melt away, replaced by only one emotion: concern.

'What's happened? Are you all right?'

Stupid question. She was obviously far from all right.

'You'd better come in.'

Her hands gripped the door as she pulled it wide open, and as he stepped into the hallway he noticed the skin stretched tight and shiny over her knuckles.

'You're really worrying me,' he told her softly as they stood in the hall, barely registering Albus and Willow as they trotted up to him, faces eager. Absently he fondled their ears and patted their backs, all the while his gaze fixed on Abbie.

She hurriedly shut the dogs in the kitchen, which seemed out of character, then told him to follow her. He did so, his eyes widening in surprise when she headed up the staircase.

Outside her bedroom door she turned to face him. 'This isn't easy for me…'

'Abbie, what are you doing? What are we doing here?' His mind groped for some sort of explanation, but her behaviour wasn't making sense. 'You don't have to do anything you don't want to,' he said hurriedly, in case she was in danger of making some rash gesture.

'I have to do this,' she said quietly. 'I owe you—'

'You don't owe me anything!' God, what did she think he was? Horrified, he grasped her hand. 'Let's go back downstairs. We can talk in the kitchen.'

She wrenched free and shook her head, her chin tilted firmly, her eyes showing resolve. Yet he thought he detected a flicker of fear too and felt sick with shame.

'I don't want anything from you, Abbie,' he told her. 'I don't know what you think—'

'Jackson, we must do this. I need you to listen to me and I don't want you to say anything. Not yet. There's something I have to do, something I must show you. You must know this if—if we're to have any chance of a future together.'

So, there *was* a chance? He wanted to hug her words to him, but her behaviour was alarming him. Bewildered, he followed her into the bedroom and, at her bidding, perched uncomfortably on the edge of the bed, staring at her in confusion.

'I know. Bit of a tip isn't it?' She gave a mirthless laugh and he blinked, wondering what she meant. Then he realised she was talking about her bedroom. He gave it a cursory glance and shrugged.

'It can be fixed in no time.'

She smiled. 'That's what I love about you, Jackson. Everything can be fixed. Except some wounds can't be fixed, and some scars never heal.'

Involuntarily, his hand flew to his mouth, and he stroked the line of his own scar. 'You mean, like this one?'

Better to get it out in the open. They'd danced around it for long enough.

She looked puzzled. 'What?'

'This scar.' He tapped his upper lip, mentally challenging her to deny having noticed it.

She shook her head. 'Oh, that. Huh! No, I was talking about much bigger scars than that, Jackson.'

He frowned. Were they discussing physical or emotional scars here? He was lost.

'This doesn't bother you?'

She looked vaguely irritated. 'What?' she repeated.

'This scar on my lip.' He had to know. Had to be sure. 'I was born with a cleft lip as I'm sure you've noticed. I had surgery when I was a young child, but it left its mark. I know it's ugly. That's why I grew a beard to be honest, but I get that it's still very noticeable.'

Her eyes seemed huge as she fixed her gaze on him, her mouth slightly open. 'Are you serious?'

Her dismissal of his anxieties wounded him.

'Don't do that,' he said quietly. 'Please. Not you of all people.'

She blinked, seeming to come out of a trance, and hurried over to sit beside him on the bed.

'Jackson, I'm sorry. I didn't mean to do that, really I didn't. God, I wouldn't, not ever. I just didn't realise it bothered you so much. Honestly, I've hardly noticed, but if it hurts you then it's not trivial and I didn't mean to just wave it away as if it didn't matter.'

She reached out a hand and gently stroked the scar.

'It really doesn't bother you?'

She smiled and her eyes, he realised, were shimmering with unshed tears. 'It really doesn't.' She took a deep breath. 'However, if we're talking about scars…'

Jackson frowned. 'What's all this about, Abbie?'

'There's no easy way to say this,' she told him, 'so I guess it's better if I just show you.'

To his astonishment, she began to unbutton her blouse.

'What are you doing?'

She shook her head and a tear rolled down her cheek and dropped onto her chest. She wiped it away and then stood, turning away from him. He watched her fumble with the last few buttons then she stood still, and he saw her take a deep breath.

'Abbie?'

She turned to face him, her hands holding her shirt wide open. She didn't have a bra on, and Jackson's immediate thought was to cover her up, turn away. She didn't have to—

He gasped and regretted it immediately as she flinched, and her lip trembled.

'What—I mean, I—'

'I wanted you to see it for yourself, so you

understand why I couldn't just go to bed with you without some sort of warning.' She laughed, making light of something that was clearly agonising to her. 'Imagine the shock if you'd discovered this during a moment of passion. You see? It had to be in the cold light of day didn't it? Forewarned is forearmed as they say.'

Her fake smile and the anxiety in her eyes broke his heart. She followed his gaze and glanced down at her left breast.

'I'm quite lucky really. I only had to have a lumpectomy. Well, I say *only*...' She shrugged slightly. 'It was an awful mess at first. I mean, you think this is bad? You should have seen me after the surgery!'

There was that mirthless laugh again and Jackson could only stare at her, wondering how she got to be so brave, and why she hadn't told him before, and what on earth could he say to someone who'd been through so much, and how pathetic she must think he was, worrying about a tiny insignificant scar on his upper lip.

'I looked like a lump of meat, and there was all the bruising too. But hey, look on the bright side. After three kids my boobs were kind of heading south, and at least this one is a bit perkier now. It's got a lovely tuck, see? Should get the other one lifted to match really...' She gulped and he grabbed her hand.

'Abbie, I had no idea.'

'Well, why would you?'

'When did this happen?'

She sat down on the bed beside him, pulled her blouse over her breasts and began to fasten the buttons with trembling fingers. 'It was just before I had Poppy that I found it. I ignored it at first. Pregnancy does strange things to breasts so I thought it would go away. Except it didn't. I was having problems breastfeeding her and a midwife was trying to help her latch on, and she noticed the lump. I told her it had been there before I had Poppy and, well, that was the beginning of it all.'

She fastened the last button and her shoulders sagged. 'That was one of the worst things about it. I lost all that precious time with Poppy because life became all about hospitals and tests and surgery. After I'd had the lumpectomy I couldn't pick her up for ages and then the exhaustion was just too much. Nick pretty much looked after her single-handedly.'

Jackson didn't know what to say. Anything he thought of seemed so trite. He imagined the days after Poppy's birth: all that exhilaration giving way to terror and pain. It must have been a nightmare for them all.

'How bad was it? I mean, I know it's all bad but—'

'Like I say, I was lucky. I've treated patients far less fortunate than I was. I had a 3mm tumour and it was confirmed as stage 2. I had fifteen fractions of radiotherapy on the full breast, followed by five fractions of intense radiotherapy at the base of where the tumour was, and they put me on medication for five years initially. I have annual check-ups of course, including a mammogram.'

She spoke almost in a monotone, as if she were reciting something. She was obviously doing her best to disconnect her words from her emotions.

'So you're on medication now?'

She nodded. 'And I'm afraid that—as grateful as I am for it, and believe me, I *am* grateful—it does have its side effects, not least the terrible hot flushes which come at the most inconvenient times. Sometimes,' she managed a wry smile, 'I have to lie and say I have a cold.'

He remembered that day at the school when she'd been red-faced and frantically mopping her face. 'Oh, Abbie.'

'It's okay. I cope with them. And, anyway, they say it's a good sign, so... Oh, and I don't sleep very well. I spend all my days battling exhaustion. And to put the tin hat on it I can't drink alcohol either. I discovered that when I had a couple of glasses of wine and got very dizzy and lightheaded, then had the worst hot flush ever. It doesn't affect everyone in that way. Most people are fine, others not so much. I'm in the latter camp.'

'Hence the lemonade.'

She nodded. 'Hence the lemonade.'

'But—' He wanted to ask her if she was going to be all right. He needed her to tell him she was—how could he put it? Cured, he supposed. Back to normal. But what if she said no? How could he ask her?

She watched him, her eyes narrowed, and he knew she was waiting for him to finish the sentence. He opened his mouth to speak but no words came out and he looked down at his lap, too ashamed to meet her gaze.

'You want to know if I'm going to die don't you?'

'Abbie!' Horrified he turned back to face her. 'Don't say that!'

'But it's what you're thinking.'

'It wasn't what I was thinking!' Well, not really. 'That is, I was wondering...I mean, when do you know?'

She bit her lip, watching him carefully. 'Five years is the usual benchmark. I'm a couple of years off that yet.'

He felt his stomach plummet and swallowed down the sudden nausea that attacked him. His heart was thumping, and he had a sudden urge to rush from the room, away from all this fear. Except he knew the fear would follow him.

It always did.

'There are no guarantees, Jackson,' she said gently. 'I can't sit here and promise you that I'm definitely out of the woods, but it's looking good so far. Really good. My oncologist is pleased and, like I said, I was lucky. The lymph nodes were clear, so the cancer hadn't spread. I have good reason to be optimistic. Put it this way, if this were me talking about one of my patients, I'd be feeling pretty positive about their chances.'

He nodded, trying to process what she was telling him.

'It's been hard,' she admitted. 'I was so scared for so long. I didn't want to talk about it all. Crazy. In my job I discuss other people's diagnoses with them all the time. I talk about treatment options and have difficult conversations about their prognosis. Sometimes I refer them for palliative care. Yet this is the first time I've really gone over what happened *to me*. Somehow, I managed to compartmentalise my own disease. For my own sanity, I mostly pretend it never happened.' She paused, reflecting on what she'd just said. 'You know, that's probably why I took the job at Bramblewick in the first place. We'd been happy in Hull, but I wanted a clean page. I needed to feel like I was leaving all the bad stuff behind me.'

'And Nick?' Jackson felt a sudden anger towards her ex-husband. How could he have left her when she was going through all this?

'Nick was great, truly. The fact is, he and I were drifting apart long before we got divorced. We were shocked when we found out Poppy was on the way, but we stuck together and did our best to rebuild our marriage. But when all this happened, well, it was too much for us to deal with. Don't get me wrong,' she added hastily, obviously seeing the contempt he was feeling reflected in his face, 'it wasn't Nick's fault. Believe me, he was a rock through it all. He took care of the kids, dealt with a newborn baby, looked after me, drove me to all my appointments and sat with me, holding my hand, when it was all too much. Honestly, I couldn't have asked for more.'

'Yet you still divorced?'

She sighed. 'When I started to recover, when I was able to go back to work and start to feel normal again, I realised that our relationship was no better deep down than it had been before we had Poppy. And the one thing I've learned about life is, it really is too short to waste on things that don't enrich it. So I sat Nick down and we discussed how we felt. He was hesitant of course. Didn't want to hurt me, put me through any more stress. But once I'd reassured him that I just needed the truth, he admitted he felt the same way. We agreed to separate, and I don't think either of us have ever regretted that decision. Especially when the job offer came through from New York. If we'd still been together, he might have felt he couldn't accept. And I wanted a fresh start too, so, it all worked out for the best.'

Jackson frowned. 'But what about the kids? How did they deal with all this? Was it the best for them?'

Abbie's brow creased and he realised he may have sounded more judgmental than he'd meant to.

'We did everything we could to ease things for them. I think knowing that Nick and I still loved each other and were friends helped a lot. Put it this way, if we'd stayed together that love and friendship may have died, and that wouldn't have been easy for them to watch. This way, it survived intact.' She nudged him. 'Like me.'

How could she joke about it? About everything she'd been through, about what the children had suffered? Her whole world—their whole world—must have been tipped upside down. He couldn't begin to imagine the turmoil, the distress, the sheer terror of it all.

Abbie put her hand in his. 'I understand this is a lot to take in,' she murmured. 'And I wouldn't blame you for walking away. I know what it's like for you, how anxious you get. Honestly, I would understand if you felt this was all too much. That's why I wanted you to know it all before we got more involved. Before things went too far.'

Jackson nodded, fighting down the panic.

'And, about your scar,' she continued. 'I really wasn't dismissing how you felt about it you know. I know it may be small compared with the two I have, but I understand how something can grow in your mind until it seems like the biggest obstacle in the world.'

Jackson closed his eyes momentarily then stood. 'This is—this is—'

'Huge?'

Huh! 'That's one word for it.'

She was quiet for a moment, then she gently let go of his hand. 'Jackson, I think I'd like you to go now.'

Was it wrong that he felt relief at those words, even as he protested that he was going nowhere, that she needed him?

'What I *need* is for you to go home and think about all this. I can't be around someone who drags me down, do you see? I've spent the last three years doing my absolute best to be positive, and if you're going to be permanently terrified that I'm about to keel over, it will undermine everything I've worked to achieve.'

'Abbie, that's not fair.'

'Maybe not to you, but to me and my kids… Look, Jackson, we've had a long time to get used to this and we're still dealing with it. It's raw for you. You need time to think so I don't want you to make rash promises right now. You need to take some time to really consider if you still want to be with me. If this is something you can deal with in your life. Right?'

His heart thumped and he wanted desperately to tell her that he didn't need any time at all. He already knew that he wanted to be with her, and he would cope with anything, just so long as he could be by her side. But the words wouldn't come.

'Okay,' he murmured. 'If that's what you want.'

She didn't reply.

Resisting the urge to run he headed out of the bedroom and down the stairs, desperate to get home and despising himself more with every step he took. Abbie had clearly sensed that he wasn't up to the job, that she deserved better. And she was right. She was a brave and mighty lioness, and he was nothing but a cowardly lion.

The truth was, he was no use to her at all.

Chapter 21

The Gables was finally quiet after an afternoon of chaos.

The children had returned home just after lunchtime, and after hugs and a massively overexcited exchange of information, they had dashed upstairs to inspect their bedrooms. Even Poppy could be heard whooping in delight.

Nick grinned. 'Guess they're a hit.'

Abbie smiled back. 'Do you know, you're beginning to sound a bit American.'

He rolled his eyes. 'That's what the kids kept saying. Isla has been teasing me mercilessly because I made the mistake of saying sidewalk instead of pavement, and cookie instead of biscuit. My work colleagues, on the other hand, think I sound like some English toff. They're always taking the mickey. Ruby's nicknamed me Hugh Grant, can you believe? I told her, I'm not that posh honestly.'

'Ruby, eh?'

Nick flushed. 'She's just one of my workmates.'

'You've mentioned her several times though,' she pointed out gently.

'Have I?' He rubbed his chin. 'Hell, I didn't realise

that. Sorry.'

'It's all right, Nick, honestly it is.' Abbie patted his hand. 'If there was something between you I'd be happy for you.'

He looked sheepish. 'Well, we're not exactly dating, but…'

'But maybe one day?'

He nodded. 'Yeah. Hopefully. Are you sure that's okay?'

'More than okay,' she assured him. 'I'd be delighted.'

Of course, the children wanted to show their father their bedrooms and he and Abbie headed upstairs to join in the general excitement.

'It's exactly what I wanted,' Isla told her, her eyes shining. 'Thank you so much, Mum.' She threw her arms around Abbie's waist and hugged her.

'Your room's okay but mine's the best,' Bertie announced. 'It's so cool with all the flags and the bunk beds. Thanks, Mum.'

'Jackson did most of the work,' Abbie admitted. 'And to be absolutely straight with you, it was all his idea. He wanted to do something nice for when you got home.'

'Jackson's ace,' Bertie said.

'Where's Jackson?' Poppy demanded, looking up at her mother with large, blue eyes.

Abbie scooped her up and buried her head in Poppy's fair curls, mainly to hide her face from the others. She needed a moment to compose herself.

'At home I expect,' she managed eventually. 'He does have other things to do besides run around after us, you know. Now, shall we go downstairs, and you can tell me more about this fascinating trip to—where was it —Gulliver's Gate?'

'I liked the Seaglass Carousel better,' Bertie announced.

'The Staten Island Ferry was the best,' Isla argued.

'All right, all right, let's go downstairs and you can tell me more about all those things,' Abbie said, keen to talk about anything other than Jackson.

It wasn't long after dinner that the children began to flag, which wasn't surprising, given their long journey home. Poppy had eaten early and was already tucked up in bed, clutching her new *I Heart NY* teddy bear in her arms. However much Bertie and Isla protested, Abbie could tell they were exhausted.

As she stacked the last of the dishes in the dishwasher, she informed them that, whatever they said to the contrary, it was clearly time for bed.

'But Dad—'

'Will still be here in the morning,' he assured them. 'I'm sleeping on your mom's sofa tonight and I'm not heading back to Berkshire to say goodbye to your grandparents until tomorrow afternoon, so we'll have the whole morning together, okay?'

Reassured, the two of them finally agreed to go to bed, encouraged no doubt by the thought of sleeping in their beautiful new bedrooms. Hugs and kisses took far longer than usual, and Nick had to swear that he would be there when they got up the following morning, which he did with great solemnity.

Eventually peace reigned, and Abbie and Nick

collapsed, cup of tea in Abbie's hand and a glass of whisky in Nick's.

'Boy, I'm going to miss them when I go home.' Nick leaned back in his chair and sighed heavily, swirling the whisky round in his glass.

'It must be hard for you,' Abbie sympathised. 'I missed them terribly when they were with you. I don't know how you cope.'

'You think they'll be okay when I leave?'

'They'll be upset, of course they will, but they'll settle down. They know you'll be calling them in a few days, and they have Christmas to look forward to after all.'

'You still okay with that? Me having them for the Christmas holidays I mean?'

'I had them last Christmas,' she reminded him. 'It's only fair. Besides, they loved New York in December so they'll be ecstatic to be there for the big day itself.'

'I'll make sure they're home for New Year's Eve,' he promised. He took a mouthful of whisky and smacked his lips together in appreciation. 'That hit the spot.' He gave her a faint smile. 'Not easy is it? This joint custody thing.'

'Not when you're on separate continents, no,' she agreed. 'But we make it work better than most.'

'I guess we do.' He paused a moment, watching her through narrowed eyes. 'Is something wrong, Abbie? You don't seem as bright as usual.' He leaned towards her, his tone suddenly gentle. 'Everything's okay, isn't it? No—no unexpected news while we were away?'

She shook her head. 'I'm fine, Nick. Stop worrying.'

'Well, if it's not that…' He hesitated then said, 'Is

this to do with that Jackson fellow?'

Abbie's face burned, and she knew it wasn't down to a hot flush. 'Why would it be?'

'Hey, if I've mentioned Ruby a few times, you should hear how many times the kids mentioned Jackson while they were at my place. It was all Jackson this and Jackson that. A father could get quite paranoid.'

'Sorry.'

'I'm only kidding. Hell, I'm not stupid. I guessed there had to be something between you when I came to pick the kids up.'

'But there wasn't!' She protested. 'Not then anyway.'

'So, something happened while we were in New York?' He nodded. 'I'm not surprised. I could see in his face that he idolised you. Besides, what guy offers to do so much unpaid work for someone if there's nothing between them? It didn't add up.'

Abbie realised Nick was becoming blurry and blinked the tears away furiously. 'But that's just it. He did. There was nothing in it for him at all, except the pleasure of helping me out. He's like that you see. Kind and generous to a fault.'

'Sounds like the perfect guy.'

'He's not perfect. No one is.'

'Abbie, did he do something to hurt you? Because if he did—'

'He didn't. Can we please change the subject?'

'Are you sure?'

When she didn't reply, merely nodded, he drained his glass and leaned back again. 'Okay. Well, if you don't want to talk about Jackson, there's something I want to talk to you about.'

'Oh?'

'Don't take this the wrong way okay? I really think we should talk about Isla.'

'Isla?' It came out louder than she'd intended, and she clapped her hand over her mouth, casting a nervous look at the living room door, as if Isla would burst through it at any moment, demanding to know why they were discussing her. 'What about Isla?' she finished, her tone gentler.

Nick looked suddenly edgy she realised and felt a pang of anxiety.

'Did something happen to her in New York?'

'No, no, nothing like that. Don't worry. No, the thing is, Abbie, I'm worried about her. I've been worried about her for a long time to be honest. This isn't meant as an attack on you, not by any means, but she's struggling. She's been struggling for ages.'

'Struggling?' Abbie blinked, puzzled. 'With what?'

Nick cast his gaze to the ceiling, as if the answer was written above him. 'With you. With what happened to you.'

'You mean…' She shook her head. Despite being a doctor, she still found the word hard to say. Funny, because she'd had no problem before it had affected her personally. 'You mean the cancer,' she managed eventually.

'She's found it hard to deal with and needed someone to talk to. That's why I got her the mobile phone. I know you said she was too young, and I've no doubt you were pretty angry when I got her one for her birthday, but the thing is, you're always around when they video call me, and she really wanted to tell me things in private, without you hearing.'

Abbie tried hard to dismiss the hurt she felt at his statement.

'Anyway, she wrote to me and told me how she was feeling, so I got her the phone and she's been calling and texting me regularly.'

'Glad you're paying her phone bill,' Abbie said, making a feeble attempt at humour in a bid to quell her anxiety which was growing rapidly. 'So what has she been telling you? Is this about the state of the house, because if it is I've been addressing that, as you can see.'

'She was worried about you taking on the house, true,' Nick admitted. 'Partly because she missed her old home and school and her friends, but mainly because she was worried that you'd taken on too much and wouldn't be able to cope.'

'Well, that's sorted now,' Abbie said, feeling uncomfortable. 'She doesn't have to worry anymore.'

'Thanks to Jackson.'

She gritted her teeth. 'Yeah. Thanks to Jackson.'

'Okay, Abbie, why don't you just tell me what's happened? I can hear in your voice that something has, and it's obviously got something to do with him. Hey, I won't judge, promise. I'm your friend, aren't I? I still care. Please, if something's hurting I want to help.'

'You can't help, Nick. Not with this. This is too big.'

'Try me.'

His tone was so gentle and kind that Abbie found

her resolve crumbling. Bit by bit, she told him what had happened between herself and Jackson over the last couple of weeks. How they'd seen each other in a whole new light, had faltered, both afraid to pursue their feelings. How they'd somehow found the courage to open up to each other. How happy she'd been when she'd realised he loved her, just as much as she loved him.

Then, slowly, painfully, she recounted what had happened in the bedroom. How Jackson had clearly been so shocked, so repulsed, that she'd sent him away, hoping against hope that he'd refuse to go.

'But he walked away from me without a backward glance,' she finished, wiping away the tears. 'Guess it's over before it even began. And who can blame him?'

'You really think your body repulsed him?' Nick blew out his cheeks. 'Are you sure?'

'Of course I'm sure,' she murmured. 'Did you not hear what I said? He walked out on me. What does that tell you?'

She jumped, startled, as the door was pushed open and Isla rushed in.

'What are you doing up? I thought you were asleep.'

Isla had clearly been crying and Abbie held out her arms to her as she sat beside her on the sofa and buried her head in Abbie's hair.

'Isla, what is it?'

'I couldn't sleep, 'cos Dad promised he'd talk to you tonight about what was going on with me and I was nervous. I sneaked downstairs so I could hear what he was saying, and I heard it all. Everything about you and

Jackson. And I'm sorry, Mum, honest I am, but you're wrong. You've got it all wrong again.'

'What do you mean, got it all wrong *again*?'

Abbie lifted her head and gazed across at Nick, her brow knitted in confusion.

He put down his empty glass and reached over, taking her hand. 'Isla's had a hard time dealing with all this, Abbie. Hard enough to know her mum's had breast cancer; hard enough to watch her go through all that treatment, worrying whether or not the treatment will work, worrying whether the cancer will return. But what's made it so much harder for her is that you won't let her talk about it. You won't let her ask questions. You shut her down, Abbie. Simple as that.'

Abbie's mouth fell open. 'I—I what?'

'I'm not having a go at you, Mum, honestly I'm not,' Isla managed between sobs. She lifted her face and Abbie's heart contracted at the tears that streaked her daughter's cheeks. Tenderly she wiped them away, feeling tears tracking a similar path down her own face.

'I know, sweetheart,' she soothed. 'I know.'

'It's just that, there were so many things I didn't understand. So many questions I wanted answers to, and I couldn't ask you anything because you wouldn't let me talk about it. It was like, I don't know, it was a forbidden subject or something. And I was bursting to talk to someone, but Dad went away and then we left school, and I couldn't talk to Mrs Hapton any longer and—'

Nick looked enquiringly at Abbie.

'One of her teachers in Hull,' she murmured

through the lump in her throat.

'There was no one,' Isla sobbed. 'And I just kept getting angrier and angrier, and more and more scared. And I'm sorry I'm horrible to you sometimes, but I just don't know where to put all these feelings, and sometimes they have to come out and you cop the lot, but I don't know how to stop it.'

'I know. It's okay,' Abbie soothed. 'I understand.'

'But you don't, do you? Because if you did, you'd talk about it. But you act as if it never happened. We all have to pretend that the cancer never existed.'

'I—I don't think—'

'But you do, Abbie,' Nick said, his eyes kind and his voice sympathetic. 'I understand why you do it, really I do, but I'm not sure it's entirely healthy, and as a doctor you must realise that deep down. Once you went back to work it was as if the entire experience had been a nightmare that you'd woken up from and you dismissed it from your mind. I know that was your way of coping, but the trouble is you expected us to do the same. Now, Poppy had no inkling of any of this, and Bertie was young enough to be sheltered from most of it, but Isla! Isla was ten years old. She understood enough to be scared witless. Do you know she's been terrified this whole time that you were going to die? Every time she tries to talk to you, you change the subject. She daren't even ask you what happens at your check-ups, and you never tell her how they go.'

'Oh, God. Oh, Isla, I'm so sorry.' Abbie was openly crying now as she held her daughter to her. 'I just didn't want to think about it. I wanted it to go away, and I thought if I didn't give it any attention it would. And the last thing I wanted was for you to worry. I thought I was doing the right thing, that I was protecting you. I've made such a mess of things haven't I?'

'Mum, are you going to be okay?' Isla whispered.

Abbie's throat was so full of tears she could hardly speak. She didn't want Isla to worry any longer, but she had to stop pushing her daughter away and start telling her the truth.

'Every year I have check-ups,' she told her, 'and so far everything's clear. I can't say I'm cured yet, Isla, but the doctors are very optimistic. I promise you I will tell you what happens at my next check-up, and if you have any questions, or if you just want to talk to me about anything, I'll be here, listening. I'm so sorry. I got this so wrong.'

'You may have got it wrong,' Nick said, 'but you did what you did for all the right reasons, and Isla knows that, don't you, sweetheart?'

Isla nodded and wiped her nose with the back of her hand. 'But, Mum, what about Jackson?'

Abbie straightened. 'What about him?'

'Don't you see? You're jumping to conclusions about him already, but you can't do that. You can't make decisions about other people like that. When I found out you had cancer I was so shocked I didn't know what to do. I'll bet that's just how Jackson feels.'

'I have no doubt about that,' Nick said with feeling.

'You know how kind he is,' Isla continued. 'But you know how anxious he gets too. I mean, he's lovely and everything, but he's got issues hasn't he? If dog hair freaks him out, imagine what your scars did to him.'

She managed a smile and Abbie spluttered through her tears. 'Yes, well, that's one way of putting it.'

'But he was just doing what you told him to do. It's like what you did to me. You don't give us the chance to say what we think, and you don't give us time to take everything in. You dropped all that stuff on him and then, just 'cos he didn't react the way you wanted you sent him packing. But people react differently to things, and some people need more time than others.'

'Wow, Isla.' Nick shook his head. 'When did you figure all this stuff out?'

'The thing is,' Isla said, 'you must really love Jackson a lot, so you need to give him another chance.'

'Really?' Abbie managed a smile. 'I must love him a lot, must I?'

'Yes,' Isla's expression was earnest. 'You told him about the thing-we-must-never-mention. Doesn't that prove it?'

Nick reached over and ruffled his daughter's hair. 'I don't know about you, Abbie, but I reckon our daughter is one smart cookie.'

Isla pulled a face. 'Biscuit.'

Nick laughed. 'No one says smart biscuit,' he told her. 'Nice try.'

Abbie looked from one to the other of them, dazed.

Nick left the armchair and sat down beside her, so she was suddenly being comforted on either side by two of the people she loved most in the world. The tears welled up again as they held her tightly.

'Go and see Jackson,' Nick urged. 'Give him the

benefit of the doubt, okay?'

As she nodded blindly, Isla added, 'But, Mum, you must be honest with him, right? If he has questions, let him ask them. Don't push him again. Give him a chance, yeah?'

'You did a brave thing, telling him,' Nick said. 'It's the first step to healing properly if you ask me. Your physical scars may be much better than they were, but mentally you need to let those wounds see the light of day so the fresh air can heal them. You've told Jackson what happened, you've let Isla talk to you about it, now you need to keep that going.'

'What if he can't deal with it?' she whispered. 'What if it's too much for him?'

'You'll never know unless you try,' Isla said. 'But whatever happens, you'll always have us. Right, Dad?'

Nick planted a kiss on her forehead, then one on Abbie's. 'Always,' he promised.

Wherever her relationship with Jackson was heading, Abbie realised she was already one of the lucky ones. She had a family who loved her, despite her selfish and short-sighted behaviour. She had already been through the worst that life could throw at her; and if Jackson Wade couldn't deal with it, she still had much to be thankful for.

She could cope with the loss of one man. However much she loved him.

Chapter 22

'It's a complete disaster,' Izzy moaned. 'I can't believe that all the suitable wedding venues around here are booked up already. The way it's going it will be next summer before we can get married, at the earliest.'

She was sitting in the garden of The Ducklings, enjoying the last rays of the early evening September sunshine, along with Abbie, Nell, Anna, Holly, and Rachel.

Connor and Riley were at Chestnut House, taking care of Gracie, Eloise, and Aiden. Meanwhile, at Folly Farm, Janie and Xander had kindly offered to look after Isla, Bertie, and Poppy, along with Sam.

It was a Friday evening in mid-September and, after a frantic start to the new term for Izzy and a return to the surgery for Anna, they'd both decided that a get-together with their friends was called for. Since Nell always offered to cook—she was strange like that they all agreed—it seemed easiest to meet at The Ducklings, Nell and Riley's house, which looked out over Bramblewick Beck. With the men childminding the women were looking forward to a few hours without work, babies, or children to fret over.

Of course, Abbie thought, with two weddings in the

offing it wasn't surprising that the conversation had quickly turned to preparations for the events. It seemed, however, that Izzy's and Ash's wedding might not be happening as quickly as expected after all.

'What about The Bay Horse?' Holly queried. 'You can't actually get married there, but you can have a nice ceremony at Whitby Registry Office and then back there for the reception. I know it's not very big, but you did say it was going to be a fairly small wedding, and I'm sure Ernie and Sandra would pull out all the stops for you.'

Izzy wrinkled her nose. 'I know, but it's—you know—The Bay Horse. I mean, it's a lovely little pub, don't get me wrong, but we go in there all the time. We want our wedding day to be something different. Something special.'

'I know what you mean,' Rachel said. 'We were very lucky to get Kearton Hall. We looked at a few venues, but it was important to us that we found somewhere private. The wedding planner's lovely. She really seems to get what it is we want, and it's all gone very smoothly so far.' She tapped the wooden table they were sitting around. 'Touch wood,' she added.

'Lucky you.' Izzy sighed. 'I just said to Jackson, he can cheer up 'cos it looks as if he won't have to do his best man's speech after all. I know he's dreading it.'

Abbie felt her stomach lurch in shock. 'Jackson's at your house?'

Izzy sipped her wine and eyed her cautiously. 'Yes, he is. Ash invited him round since he's been a bit in the doldrums lately.'

Holly—who'd been back to her old self since her evidently successful holiday with Jonathan—widened her eyes as she turned to Abbie. 'Ooh, what's going on? I thought you and Jackson were—'

'Whatever it is,' Rachel interrupted quickly, 'I'm sure it's none of our business. Now, Izzy, how far afield were you willing to go for this wedding of yours? Because there's a lovely little hotel in Freydale that was advertising the other day. That might be suitable.'

'Hmm. I suppose that's not too far.' Izzy considered. 'Might have to Google it.'

As the group gathered round the table, scanning mobile phones, and drinking wine, Abbie found her mind wandering. Impossible to concentrate on wedding plans when Jackson was sitting just a few minutes' walk away in Rose Cottage. And Izzy said he was *in the doldrums*. What did that mean? Of course, she was far too nice to hope that his misery was down to what had happened between the two of them. On the other hand she was only human. She couldn't help but hope that he was still thinking about her, perhaps even missing her.

'More lemonade?' Rachel said suddenly.

Abbie blinked. 'Sorry?'

'Your glass is empty.' Rachel said, giving her a hard stare and nodding towards the house. 'Fancy a top-up? I know I do.'

'Oh, oh yes. Lovely.' Abbie stood, glass in hand, and glanced around at the others. 'Anyone else want a drink while I'm going inside?'

There were a few vague murmurs as their friends

gestured to the wine bottles on the table and their half-full glasses before turning back to Izzy's mobile phone.

Rachel grinned at her, and they headed into the kitchen of Chestnut House, where Abbie braced herself for *the talk*.

Sure enough Rachel wasted no time. 'Are you mad?'

'What do you mean?'

'Abbie, did you not hear what Izzy said? Jackson is at Rose Cottage right now, and he's in the doldrums! Now, I don't know what went on between you, but I do know you've been an absolute misery for the last couple of weeks. It sounds as if he's just as low. So why don't you go there and sort it out?'

'To Rose Cottage?'

'Yes.'

'With Ash there too?'

'Ask Jackson to step outside. Ash won't be nosy. He's not like that.'

'But they might be having a good time, watching a film or something.'

Rachel raised an eyebrow. 'You think that would be more important to him than fixing things with you?'

Abbie folded her arms. 'But he knows I'm here,' she pointed out. 'Izzy told him. There's nothing to stop him coming to Chestnut House to see me, but he hasn't has he?'

Rachel gave her an incredulous look. 'This is Jackson we're talking about! You know how antisocial he is.'

'He's not antisocial,' Abbie protested. 'He's just a bit—shy.'

Rachel grinned. 'Sorry. Didn't mean to offend you. Okay, so he's a bit shy. There are six of us here. Can you imagine him having the nerve to turn up on the doorstep and ask to see you? I mean, it's just beyond belief isn't it? Whereas you've only got Ash to deal with, and a lot more confidence than Jackson has.'

'That's all you know,' Abbie muttered. 'Sorry but it's out of the question.' She twisted a strand of her hair between her fingers, wishing she could be braver as Rachel stared at her, fingers tapping impatiently on the Blakes' granite worktop.

She felt a momentary relief when her phone rang, and she fished in her pocket for it. At least it was a distraction, although she had a moment of panic that it might be Janie calling to tell her something was wrong with one of the children.

She frowned, realising she didn't recognise the number that flashed up on the screen.

'Hello?'

'Dr—Abbie?'

'Speaking.' She was almost certain she knew that voice. Deep, posh, and rather sexy. 'Is that Lewis?'

'Hey, you remembered me! Great. Right, am I okay to come to yours tomorrow to start making plans? Only I've got a new full-time job starting in a few weeks, so the sooner I get on with your garden the better really.'

Abbie glanced up at Rachel who was watching her steadily.

'Everything okay?' Rachel mouthed.

Abbie shrugged, baffled by the conversation. 'Sorry, Lewis, what exactly are you talking about? What plans do you mean?'

There was a momentary silence then he said slowly, as if explaining to a child, 'The plans for your garden, what else? Jackson did tell you, right?'

Jackson! Abbie gripped the phone a little tighter. 'What's Jackson got to do with this?'

'Ah, right.' There was a sigh. 'He's booked me to landscape the garden for you. Said I'm to do whatever it is you want, and he'll pay for it. Look, this is okay isn't it? Only I cancelled another job to fit you in as a favour to you both and I'll be right in it, cashflow wise, if this falls through.'

Abbie's lips tightened with anger. Now she was in an impossible situation. She didn't want any help from Jackson Wade, but she could hardly let Lewis down could she?

Forcing herself to sound pleased she said, 'That's fine, Lewis. About ten o'clock tomorrow morning?'

She heard the relief in his voice. 'Phew! Had me worried there, Abbie. Great, see you tomorrow. Bye.'

'What on earth was that about?' Rachel demanded. 'You've got a face like thunder as my dad used to say.'

Shaking with nerves and anger Abbie relayed the conversation to her.

'Wow!' Rachel blew out her cheeks and then burst out laughing. 'You've got to hand it to Jackson. He's got class. Not many men give a landscape gardener as an apology.'

'I can't accept it,' Abbie said. 'I mean him. I can't accept him—Lewis. His work. Oh, hell.'

'Take a deep breath,' Rachel advised, 'and just think

about this.'

'There's nothing to think about,' Abbie said. 'Now I've got to find the money to pay for the blasted garden because I won't take a penny from Jackson.'

And how was she going to do that? She'd still got plans for the house, but it looked as if they were going to be put on hold.

Well, at least this had made her mind up and given her the courage to confront the situation head on. 'I'm going to Rose Cottage right now to give him a piece of my mind. I want nothing from Jackson Wade.'

'Hmm. If you say so.'

At least, Abbie thought, the uncertainty would be over. She couldn't go on living much longer with this stomach-churning, soul-destroying doubt, so she might as well find out one way or the other what was going on in his head. If they were over for good it was better to know now.

'Right,' she said. 'Wish me luck.'

'Luck,' Rachel said, grinning. She waved her crossed fingers at Abbie. 'But you won't need it. I have a funny feeling about this.'

Abbie wished she shared her friend's optimism. Throat tight, mouth dry, butterflies flapping frantically in her tummy, she headed to the front door and wrenched it open.

A fist almost hit her in the face, and she reared back, terrified.

'Oh, God! I'm so sorry! I was just about to knock.' Jackson held up his hands, a mortified expression on his face.

'Well, thank goodness I wasn't a second later,' Abbie managed. She took a moment to regain her composure then looked Jackson in the eye. 'What do you want?'

He hesitated and his brow furrowed as he met her gaze. She saw the tension in his mouth and the anxiety in his eyes and, despite everything, her heart melted along with her anger.

'Jackson?'

'You, Abbie,' he murmured at last. 'I want you.'

***

They found a quiet bench overlooking the beck and sat together in silence, watching the ducks on the water, and listening to the distant bleating of sheep in the fields.

Jackson thought that perhaps Abbie was gathering herself together just as he was, in that moment of tranquillity. His heart was still thumping, and he tried desperately to quell his nerves by concentrating hard on the little ripples on the water left by the ducks as they swam past, totally oblivious to the two human beings in turmoil just feet away from them.

'I can't believe you came to Chestnut House for me,' Abbie said at last. Evidently, she'd recovered from the shock more rapidly than he had.

'What else was I supposed to do?' he said, not looking at her. 'I've waited for you to make some sort of contact with me but… I had to do something, and tonight just seemed like the right moment.'

'*You* walked away from *me*,' she reminded him. 'Why

would I come looking for you?'

'You sent me away!'

'Because you wanted to go!'

He couldn't deny it. He realised his finger was circling his scar again and hastily dropped his hand. 'I didn't *want* to leave you,' he murmured.

'Well, it sure as hell felt like that,' she replied.

He risked a glance at her and saw the hurt in her eyes. How could he possibly repair the damage he'd done to her?

'I'm so sorry,' he told her. 'You must hate me.'

She shook her head. 'Of course I don't hate you. If I hated you it wouldn't hurt so much, would it?' She paused then burst out, 'I was coming to find you. Izzy told me you were at Rose Cottage, you see and—'

'You were?' He felt a vague fluttering of hope. Maybe he hadn't broken this beyond repair?

'What do you think you're playing at, hiring Lewis to do my garden for me?'

His hope stopped fluttering and cowered in the pit of his stomach. 'Oh, I see. I thought it would be a nice gesture. I knew how much you wanted the garden landscaping, and that money was tight, so I thought—'

'You thought you'd step in and be the hero again. It's your default mode isn't it? Tell me, Jackson, do you rescue everyone you come across or am I a special case?'

He winced. 'That's not fair, Abbie. I just wanted to do something nice for you because—because yes, of course you're a special case.'

When she didn't reply, he took hold of her hand,

hope resurging when she didn't wrench it away. 'I know what you're thinking,' he said, 'and I understand why, but you're wrong. You're so wrong.'

She tutted. 'Huh! And what am I so wrong about, Mr Wade?'

'You're wrong about the reason I left. You think I couldn't cope with the scar don't you? But it's not that at all.'

Her hand trembled in his and he squeezed it tightly.

'Really? So I show you the ugly truth and you can't get out of the house fast enough, but that's just a coincidence?'

'No, not at all. Look, I know how you feel about your scars, honestly I do. I've been paranoid about this,' he said, gesturing to his lip, 'for as long as I can remember. And I know that, compared with what you've been through it's nothing, but it was a huge deal to me. But the truth is, your scarring didn't shock me or repulse me at all. It's not as bad as you think it is. It's like when people always tell me that they haven't noticed mine, but in my head it's practically a flashing neon sign. Well, I'm sure that in your mind your scarring is much, much worse than it actually is.'

'Right,' she said. 'So, I'm imagining how lopsided my breasts are am I?'

Jackson puffed out his cheeks, thinking. 'Well, they're a bit wonky,' he said finally. 'But so what? No one's perfect, right?'

'A bit wonky!' She glared at him.

'Have I said the wrong thing again? I didn't mean to insult you. I was just—'

'I know what you were doing,' she snapped. 'You were trivialising a major life event, that's what. Have you any idea what I went through? What I'm still going through?'

'But that's it,' he said, feeling helpless to articulate what he was feeling. 'That's why I left when you asked me to. It wasn't because of the scars. It was because I was scared that I wouldn't be able to cope with what you're going through. The last thing I want is to let you down, don't you know that?'

She frowned. 'I don't understand you, Jackson.'

He sighed. 'You know my issues, Abbie. You know my anxieties. I like everything just so: neat, ordered, safe. Maybe if you'd said to me that this was five years ago and your tests were clear I could have coped with it much better. I could have put a tick against it and put it away in a filing cabinet in my mind. But this is an open case, and I don't deal with insecurity and uncertainty very well.'

'You think I do?' she said angrily. 'I'm terrified every single time my check-up looms. I hold my breath every day in the shower, checking for lumps. I've just had to comfort my thirteen-year-old daughter because, it turns out, she's bloody petrified I'm going to die on her, and I had no idea. You think it's tough for you, Jackson? Try being in my head, in Isla's head. But it's okay because you can walk away from all this. Leave us to it. It's not your problem to worry about after all.' Her words ended on a sob, and she got to her feet.

Jackson grabbed her hand and pulled her back onto the bench. 'Abbie, please, don't cry.' He put his arms around her, and she pushed him away angrily.

He tried again. 'Abbie, I'm not walking away again. Not ever, no matter what you say. That's what I'm trying to explain in my usual clumsy fashion. I can't walk away because I love you. I love you so much. And whatever it is you're going through I'm going to be right beside you.'

She stopped struggling and stared at him, her face tear streaked. 'But you can't, can you? It's too much for you. It's like you said. You don't do uncertainty.'

'Then it's time I dealt with it,' he said. He wiped away her tears and took her hand in his again. 'So I've found a counsellor. I'm going to get help, Abbie. My brother's been nagging me about this for years, but I always resisted. I guess I just never wanted to deal with my issues before now, but I know it's time. I must sort myself out so that I can be the rock and the support that you need and deserve. I must face my own demons.'

Her expression consoled him a little. It was clear that she understood that this was a big deal to him, although he doubted she knew exactly how big. He had, after all, rejected all pleas by Tyler to undertake therapy. It was a measure of how much Abbie meant to him that he'd finally acted, and it was when he picked up the phone and rang the counsellor to make his first appointment that it had dawned on him how deeply he must love her.

He knew therapy was going to hurt, but he was willing to face the past at last so that he could build a future with the woman he adored. She needed him. Her children needed him. He wasn't going to let them down.

Abbie sat quietly, watching the ducks heading downstream, her hand still in his. Jackson said nothing. She needed a little time to absorb what he'd just said. He could only hope that it would make a difference. That she would give him another chance.

'What are *your* demons, Jackson?'

Her question, asked so calmly and reasonably, shattered his thought processes, and unnerved him.

'Sorry?'

'You said it was time to face your demons. What demons? What made you so anxious in the first place? Surely it can't all be about your scar?'

His eyes widened. Now that the moment was upon him, he had no idea how to begin.

She held his hand between both of hers and stroked it gently with her thumb. 'I told you about *my* demons,' she reminded him softly. 'I showed you something very few people have ever seen. Don't you think it's time you shared your secret with me?'

She was right. She'd been pale and trembling that morning when she'd finally revealed the truth to him, but there'd been an almost defiant look in her eyes as she'd waited for him to react. She'd reminded him of a lioness, he remembered. If she could be that courageous for him, he could do the same for her.

'It goes back a long way,' he warned her.

'Once upon a time?'

He managed a smile. 'It was no fairy tale though. You asked me once about my parents, and I told you they were away travelling.'

She nodded. 'I remember. Although you were a bit vague about it. You didn't mention where they were travelling.'

'No, well, that's because I haven't a clue. The truth is, Tyler and I have no idea where they are. We haven't seen them since I was eleven years old.'

She gasped. 'Eleven? But why? What happened?'

He circled his upper lip with his finger, even while his other hand gripped hers tightly.

'They went to jail,' he said simply. 'They went to jail for neglect and cruelty. That's what they were you see. Neglectful and cruel. I don't know what would have happened to us if it had carried on much longer.'

Abbie's mouth was open, and he could see the shock in her eyes. 'They—they—oh no! No, Jackson!' She turned away but not before he'd caught the gleam of tears. Her hand remained holding his, and he felt the pressure increase as she processed the information. 'What did they do to you?'

Her voice was so faint he barely heard her.

He shrugged, suddenly feeling calmer. Now that he'd said the words it all seemed so much easier to talk about somehow.

'I suppose it was textbook. The sort of thing you see on the news all too often sadly. They didn't care about us, that's the truth. They spent most of their days stoned. Never worked a day in their lives that I ever knew. It just got steadily worse as the years passed. Once they decided I was old enough to look after Tyler—I think I was about six or seven at the time—

they were rarely at home. They'd hang out with their mates all day, coming back in the early hours of the morning, if at all.'

He felt Abbie's tremor and pulled his hand free, suddenly feeling a need to protect himself. He folded his arms, tucked his chin into his chest, and shivered as the ghosts of the past settled beside him.

'There was very little food in the house. We were always hungry. I remember Tyler crying one afternoon and I looked everywhere for something to give him to eat. All the cupboards were empty, not enough in the fridge to feed a mouse. I ended up trawling their bedroom. Found half a bag of crisps and a Mars Bar in Dad's drawer. It wasn't much but it stopped Tyler crying for a while.'

Abbie's hand flew to her mouth. 'Oh, Jackson.'

'The neighbours didn't see anything untoward, or if they did they didn't care.' He forced himself to speak calmly, battling the bitter memories. 'To be honest, they steered well clear of my parents. Dad could be a bit aggressive, even when he hadn't taken anything, and Mum was almost as bad. But we had to go to school because our parents didn't want social services coming around, and the teachers spotted it.'

'Did—did your parents hurt you?' she whispered.

'If you mean, did they hit us, then not much. Only when they we nagged them for food or needed money for school. We learned, early on, not to ask for anything, so there were few marks or bruises or anything obvious like that. The teachers picked up on everything else though. I saw the papers, after the court case, and apparently it was our physical appearance that alerted them. We were dirty, scruffy, smelly. And we were clearly hungry. We got free school dinners during term time, which saved us, but we were still always starving because that was pretty much all we ate. One of the teachers found Tyler rummaging in a waste bin one day. He'd found a half-eaten apple and had eaten it before the teacher could stop him.'

He heard Abbie's stifled sob and turned to her. 'I'm not telling you all this for sympathy. It's just so you understand where it all came from: the need to have food in the cupboards, the desire for order and neatness, the obsession with hygiene.'

'I know,' she assured him. 'I see that.'

'When social services couldn't get in they returned with a police officer.' He fell silent, reliving that moment when fear had turned to relief. 'He cried. The police officer. Not noisy sobs or anything like that, but I saw the tears and I thought, *he's going to help us. We're going to get out of here.* It said in the papers that we were living in squalid conditions, and that's how I remember it. The dirt. The smell. And it was so cold, Abbie. It was so cold.'

He shivered, back in that bedroom momentarily, cuddling Tyler in a desperate bid to keep his little brother warm as the worn, dirty blankets failed to keep the chill from their bones. 'I don't know what would have happened to us if they hadn't investigated. When I got older all I wanted was to be a teacher like ours, so I could keep an eye on other people's children. Make sure they were okay, that they were safe.'

'And spot anything untoward, like homework diaries not getting signed, hair not brushed, mud and dog hairs on trousers,' Abbie said. 'I get it now. No wonder you turned up at The Gables. You wanted to make sure I wasn't neglecting my children.'

'It was nothing personal,' he said anxiously. 'I didn't know you then, Abbie. I just had to be sure…'

'Of course you did,' she reassured him, reaching over to stroke his face. 'The world needs people like you, Jackson. Never apologise for caring.'

He hesitated then cautiously reached out an arm. Abbie smiled and shuffled along the bench, leaning into his embrace.

'What happened after that?' she enquired. 'I'm guessing a court case and jail for your parents, but what happened to you and Tyler?'

'We were lucky. After a couple of short-term placements we found long-term foster parents who were quite happy to take us both. I stayed with them until I left for university. They were an elderly couple, but they were wonderful to us, and we were always welcome back at their home whenever we wished. Long after they'd discharged their foster caring duties they still treated us like sons, and we spent most of our holidays at their house in Lincolnshire.'

'Do you still see them?'

'Like I said, they were elderly even then. They died, within a few months of each other, around ten years ago. I'll never forget them though.' He smiled, a warm and genuine smile. 'Terry and Dorothy Wade. Our real parents.'

'Wade? So—'

'We took their name as soon as we turned eighteen. Deed poll. The name we were born with is buried. Forgotten. It's not who we are, not anymore.'

'And your real parents—sorry, I mean your birth parents?'

He shrugged. 'Served their time, which wasn't very long considering. When they got out, they didn't want anything to do with us, thank God. They had a battered old camper van and, from what I can gather, they decided to travel the world in it. Remembering the state of it I'd be amazed if they got as far as Dover, but who knows? I certainly don't and I care even less.'

'And Tyler feels the same, I assume?'

'He does. He doesn't remember it all quite as well as I do, but some things will stay with him forever. He tells me he can still feel that awful, gnawing hunger sometimes. Probably why he's such a foodie now,' he added with a rueful smile. 'He always says I saved him, which I didn't. But he worries about me too much. He's spent years begging me to get counselling and I always refused. I just didn't want to go over it all again. I thought it was better buried and forgotten. Like our old name.'

'I understand that,' she said with obvious feeling. 'I thought the same. I've spent so long pretending the cancer never happened that I almost believed it. But I wasn't doing myself any favours. Wounds must be aired if they're to heal. I've learned that much. You're doing the right thing, Jackson, really you are.'

'I know.' He hugged her a little tighter then said,

'Wow, that was quite a conversation, wasn't it? So, what happens now, Abbie? Between you and me I mean.'

He held his breath as she clearly hesitated. Had he scared her off? She'd got enough to deal with without all his issues and hang-ups. Maybe it was too much. He couldn't blame her if she decided to call it a day. Not really.

Abbie moved away from him a little and for a moment he thought she was going to leave, but she turned to face him, her expression earnest.

'What you need to accept, Jackson, is that I can't sit here and promise you that I'm in the clear. Don't misunderstand me: things are looking very positive, and I have no reason to disbelieve the consultant who seems very optimistic that they caught the cancer in time. Nevertheless, I can't tell you it's definitely going to be all right.'

'I know that. But like I told *you*, I'm getting help to deal with my issues. The fact is no one knows what's in store for them. We don't come with guarantees, and I want—I need—to learn to live with uncertainty. That's what the counselling will help me to do. All I want is for us to be together.'

'I don't think you could live at The Gables,' she cautioned. 'Not yet anyway. All those children and dogs and mess would be too much for you to cope with just now.'

He wanted to protest, but when he thought about it he realised she was right. He was much, much better than he'd been at the start of the summer and had even grown quite fond of both Albus and Willow, tolerating their moulting and slobber rather well. He no longer flinched when Poppy put things in her mouth, even though it might be something as awful as a beetle or dog food, and he'd grown more relaxed about the toys and games left lying around the rooms. But even acknowledging the improvement, he had to concede that if he lived at the cottage permanently it wouldn't be so easy. Right now he could escape to his flat if it all got too much. Living with Abbie and her children would mean any bolthole was out of the question, and he needed that bolthole, as he grudgingly admitted to her.

'But that's okay,' she soothed. 'You're getting there, and one day…'

'You really think we can make a go of this, Abbie? You and me, living together?'

She grinned. 'After everything we've been through, living together should be a walk in the park don't you think? Besides…'

He raised an eyebrow. 'Besides what?'

'Well, what's the point of me putting a piano in that spare room and turning it into a music room if you're not going to be there to play?'

'A piano? You'd do that for me?'

His heart contracted as she cupped his face in her hands.

'I'd do anything for you, Jackson.' Her eyes twinkled and she nudged him. 'I suppose it's the least I can do since you hired Lewis. Anyway, I couldn't think what else to do with that room, and you need a piano but have nowhere to put one. Seems like the perfect solution to me. Of course,' she added hastily, 'I'll put a lock on the door, so the kids only go in there when you're around to keep an eye on them.'

'You mean, *I'll* put a lock on the door?' he teased.

'All right, Mr Handyman. *You'll* put a lock on the door. What do you think?'

'I think,' he said, his smile widening, 'that would be perfect. Thank you.'

'We really do have to stop thanking each other,' she told him. 'At least verbally. If you want to show your appreciation I can think of better ways.'

So could Jackson. Forgetting all about the scar that had blighted his life for so long, he pulled her into his arms and kissed her.

It was a tender kiss that spoke not only of mutual appreciation, but their longing and desire for one another, their relief at finding each other, and their hope for the future.

A kiss that fired the starting gun on their road to recovery.

He knew they were right at the beginning of that difficult journey. Both he and Abbie had a long way to go, and there were no guarantees. But they had each taken that first step and, hand in hand, they would face each day as it came.

Good times and bad, through sunshine and storms, they would deal with it all in the only way that mattered: the only way they could.

Together.

To find out more about Sharon Booth and her books visit her website

www.sharonbooth.com

where you can also sign up for her monthly newsletter to get her latest news, cover reveals, release dates, giveaways and more.

Next in the Bramblewick Series

Christmas at Cuckoo Nest Cottage

Holly knows something's not right about her life, but she can't figure out what it is. Where did it all go wrong? She has a job she enjoys in Bramblewick's surgery, friends she's known and loved for years, a surrogate grandmother in her next-door neighbour, Lulu, and a boyfriend she adores.

Yet Holly's become increasingly unhappy and confused. So much about her life no longer makes sense, and she's uncertain who she can trust. Are her friends really on her side? Is she still capable of carrying out her job to satisfactory standards? Why does she keep messing things up with Jonathan, the boyfriend who puts up with more than anyone else ever would?

With two weddings to attend and Christmas rapidly approaching, all Holly wants is peace, calm, and an end to the confusion; instead she finds herself facing an impossible choice that makes her worries about being the only fat bridesmaid seem irrelevant. How can she decide between the two people she loves most in the world?

Then there's Lewis … Newly arrived in the village, calm, easy-going and straightforward, his only vice appears to be his addiction to pear drops. Through him, Holly realises she's been losing a war she had no idea she was fighting. Can she muster the strength for one final battle?

Maybe all she needs is a little help from her friends …